By DONALD E. WESTLAKE

Once Against the Law
(*anthology edited with William Tenn*)
The Mercenaries
Killing Time
361
Killy
Pity Him Afterwards
The Fugitive Pigeon
The Busy Body
The Spy in the Ointment
God Save the Mark
The Curious Facts Preceding My Execution and Other Fictions
Who Stole Sassi Manoon?
Up Your Banners
Somebody Owes Me Money
The Hot Rock
Adios, Scheherezade
I Gave at the Office

I GAVE AT THE OFFICE

BY

Donald E. Westlake

SIMON AND SCHUSTER · NEW YORK

MIDDLEBURY COLLEGE
LIBRARY

PS
3573
E9 I2

5-1971
Gen'l

ALL RIGHTS RESERVED
INCLUDING THE RIGHT OF REPRODUCTION
IN WHOLE OR IN PART IN ANY FORM
COPYRIGHT © 1971 BY DONALD E. WESTLAKE
PUBLISHED BY SIMON AND SCHUSTER
ROCKEFELLER CENTER, 630 FIFTH AVENUE
NEW YORK, NEW YORK 10020

FIRST PRINTING

SBN 671-20839-X
LIBRARY OF CONGRESS CATALOG CARD NUMBER: 71-139666
DESIGNED BY EVE METZ
MANUFACTURED IN THE UNITED STATES OF AMERICA
PRINTED BY MAHONY & ROESE INC. NEW YORK
BOUND BY H. WOLFF INC. NEW YORK

To Lee Johnson, who rekindled my faith in the American businessman, I fondly dedicate the following doorstop.

Although certain rumors, news reports, past television specials and a great deal of hearsay went into the germination of this book in its author's mind, no incident herein is intended to portray any incident occurring in reality, nor is any character or institution herein intended to portray or suggest any specific person or institution from real life. This is merely a novel, yet another. They do keep coming along, don't they, despite McLuhan?

We are waiting for the long-promised invasion. So are the fishes.
—WINSTON CHURCHILL, *October 21, 1940*

TAPE ONE, SIDE ONE

WELL, now, let's see. I have my documents about me, the tape is running, I'm ready to report. This is in response to the letter from the legal department asking me to give a detailed summation of my part in the Ilha Pombo Affair. I know the request was for a written summary, but I tried writing it all down twice and I just couldn't do it. I'm a radio man—I'm a Network man—and I'm much more comfortable with a microphone in my hand. And since I know that certain people are prepared to blame me for the whole situation and the current mess the Network is in, I think I'd better be sure I get my own side of it down as accurately and completely as I can. Therefore, this tape. The legal department can borrow a cassette from an engineer in the news department, if necessary, and play this report through the speaker in one of the elevators at The Hub.

First of all, let me say here and now that I am behind the Network on this, and I do mean totally. I have been a Network man for twelve years, and I would never purposefully do anything to harm the Network or stain its name. Its initials; stain its initials.

I'm not even going to use its initials. We know who we're talking about. You, whoever you are from the legal department, listening to this report, you know what Network you're in the legal department of; you know in what building you are riding up and down in the elevator listening to this report. Why should I tell you things we both already know, when there's so much to tell you that you don't know and should know if we're going to get the Network off the hook on this thing.

I know that some people say, "Jay Fisher's been acting funny ever since the divorce." You'll hear that; you've probably already heard it. Well, it isn't true. Marlene and I, frankly, have a better relationship now that we're divorced than we ever did when we tried to live in the same state. Now she's happy in Wilton and I'm happy in New York. And even if it were true that the divorce had an emotional effect on me, and I'm not saying it had no emotional effect at all—I mean, my God, you don't just get divorced without feeling *something*, even if it's only a twinge at the expense—but even if I did have an emotional reaction in my personal life, I never for one second allowed it to interfere with my duty to the Network. Which I suppose in a way was what the divorce was all about, Marlene claiming I cared more about the Network than I did about her. I tried to explain that although my loyalties were similar, and probably equal, they were not at all conflicting, but there was no reasoning with her.

Well, that's neither here nor there, and has nothing to do with Ilha Pombo Island. It's just that canards are in the air, and I thought I ought to put up some flak of my own, in a manner of speaking.

In fact, before I get directly to Ilha Pombo, let me put on the record a few facts about myself. Jay Fisher. Thirty-seven. Graduated Northwestern University at twenty-one. Did radio and television in college, got an announcing job on a local station—AM, FM, TV—in Peoria, had a few other radio and television jobs around the Midwest, then got picked up by the Network for their St. Louis AM outlet twelve years ago. Three years there, two years in Chicago, and the last seven years here in New York. I was proud to be chosen by the Network twelve years ago, and I've been proud to be associated with the Network ever since, and I am still proud to be a Network man today.

I differentiate, by the way, between the Network, which I respect and feel loyalty toward, and certain executives within the Network who are prepared to shoot down every loyal employee in The Hub to save their own skins.

Anyway, the Network has had me do various things since bringing me to New York seven years ago. I emceed an afternoon game show for a while, until my hairline began to recede. I did promo voice-overs for the new TV shows one fall, I did a stint of radio news—I was the Middle East expert, since I was neither a Jew nor an Arab—and for the last fourteen months I've done the Townley Loomis lunchtime interviews.

Now, there's another canard going around about my attitude toward the Townley Loomis lunchtime interviews, so let me say right now, state unequivocally, that *I did not mind them.* I liked them, in fact. I got to meet a lot of famous or almost-famous people, I ate a lot of great lunches—gained twenty-two pounds the first year, most of which I have since lost again, the only good result of the Ilha Pombo Affair—and all in all I believe I stockpiled a lot of worthwhile experience doing those interviews. Why should I have had any objection?

Now, I don't know who in the legal department is going to be listening to this report, but I have noticed in the last few weeks an astonishing ignorance about the Network among the personnel in there, to the point of practically never watching any Network programing, not even the top-rated shows, so maybe I'd better explain my connection with the Townley Loomis lunchtime interviews.

Townley—we've been on a first-name basis for almost a year now—is one of our top announcers. He does special reports on television, does frequent in-depth reporting for the evening news, and is noted especially for his penetrating interviews, both on television and on his own show on radio. Now, a man like Townley can't be everywhere at once, so he concentrates mostly on his television work and merely dubs in the questions on his lunchtime interview radio show, and somebody else goes to lunch at The Three Mafiosi and feeds the questions to the interviewee.

For fourteen months I was the somebody else. I'd report to my office on the eleventh floor of The Hub at about ten-thirty in the morning, and on my desk would be the material for the day's interview. The list of questions I was to ask, a summary of the guest's *shtick,* and a copy of the book if the guest had written one, which most guests had. It's fantastic how many people still write books in this day and age.

Anyway, I would look over the questions and the summary and

skim the book if there was a book, and then at noon the engineer and the sound man and the director and I would all leave The Hub and walk south two blocks to the General Texachron Building and go up to The Three Mafiosi, their fabulous restaurant on the twenty-first floor, from which, by the way, you can get a fantastic view of The Hub.

So. We'd meet the guest and shake hands all around and sit down at our usual table, between the windows and the closet where our equipment was kept between interviews. Then the engineer and the sound man and the director would fuss around with the equipment while the guest and I got to know each other and I explained about Townley being unable to be present, and so on. Then we'd sit down and have a drink to warm the guest up, and then I'd read the questions and the guest would make up his own answers and the engineer would look at his dials and the director would look at his watch and the sound man would clink silverware against a plate for the proper restaurant background effect on the tape. Then, when we were done, the sound man and the engineer and the director would pack everything up and leave, and I'd stay to have lunch with the guest. Originally, we would all leave after the interview, but one of the guests complained to somebody that it was embarrassing to wind up eating alone at an important midtown luncheon restaurant like The Three Mafiosi, and also there was some suspicion that a couple of guests had snuck friends in after the Network people had left and the friends' tabs had wound up on the Network bill, so a policy memo came down to tell me to stick around after the interview and have lunch with the guest, make him feel at home, and see to it he didn't bring in any free-loading friends.

It was odd, by the way, how many guests had a bad reaction to Townley not showing up. I suppose a lot of them were disappointed at not getting to meet a famous man like him after all, but some of the guests who objected the most strenuously were just as famous as Townley, in their own fields, or almost so. And the one who walked out in a huff, an Englishman, was so famous even the legal department would know the name. He said one or two very funny things before he left. Nasty, but funny. I had to laugh myself.

The one time it was really strange, though, was the interview with Senator Dunbar. We all got to the restaurant, and a man I'd never seen before was sitting at our table. Everybody knows what Senator Earl Dunbar looks like, and this man wasn't him. I called the headwaiter over and said, "Luigi, what's the story with this guy?"

The story was, he was Senator Dunbar's press secretary. We'd had to submit questions in advance for his approval, of course, the senator's approval, and since the senator had a conflict of appointments today he'd sent his press secretary along with a written-down set of his answers, so that after that a copy of the tape could be sent to the Senator and he'd dub in his own voice. So the press secretary and I sat there and read our papers to each other, and the engineer watched his dials and the director watched his watch and the sound man clinked silverware against a plate, and afterward the press secretary didn't have time to stick around and have lunch, so I didn't either, which meant nobody had lunch there that day, which was a substantial savings to the Network right there.

I'd like to point out that I could just as well have called a friend or two to come over and have lunch with me that day on the Network's tab and nobody the wiser, and I didn't do it, and so much for another canard that's been circling around The Hub, about me not being a true Network man. I am a true Network man, and the people saying I'm not are exactly the same people who found fault with Gary Francis Powers for not killing himself when his U-2 was shot down. Exactly the same.

Anyway, I was always surprised at how often guests thought there was something peculiar in me asking the questions and Townley dubbing them in later. I'd explain that it was standard practice throughout the industry, not just with Townley and not even just with our Network. After all, the idea is that we're selling a product, right? The guest is doing the interview because he has something to peddle—usually a book, or maybe a re-election as in Senator Dunbar's case, or whatever it is he wants the public to buy—and the Network is selling entertainment. So many of these people seemed to think the point was *them* having *lunch* with *Townley Loomis.* Who the hell in New York can afford to have a lunch that doesn't mean anything?

The point I'm trying to make is that even though many of the guests didn't understand what my job was really all about, and even though some of our own executives—and some people in the legal department, too, apparently—don't seem to understand what my job was really all about, I *did*. The only people who could think that I found it demeaning or self-emasculating or any of these other paperback psychology terms that are being bandied about the halls of The Hub are people who so totally fail to understand what being a Network man is all about that I can only think they themselves aren't really Network men but just people collecting a salary every week.

A Network man enjoys the jobs the Network gives him. It's as simple as that.

So. What I'm trying to do is demonstrate that I did not wangle the Florida assignment in order to get away from the trauma of the divorce, and I did not wangle the Florida assignment in order to get away from the Townley Loomis lunchtime interviews. The fact of the matter is, I didn't wangle the Florida assignment at all.

Here's what happened. The interviewee one day was a fellow named Bob Grantham, who'd written a book about pot smoking. Marijuana, you know. It seems marijuana was legal in the United States until 1935, and it was just a sort of low-intensity fact in American culture. Like Cab Calloway had a hit song in the early thirties called "Reefer Man," about a pot-smoking bass player. (One of the most rewarding parts of the Townley Loomis lunchtime interviews for me was all the interesting things I learned about in the course of those fourteen months, things I never would have known otherwise. Another proof that I didn't dislike the job.)

Anyway, Bob Grantham had done this book about pot smoking back when it was legal. References to marijuana in popular culture—like "Reefer Man"—the economics of the weed when it wasn't a crime to possess it or sell it, photographs of pot smokers, historical connections, one of these grab-bag pastepot books they come out with by the millions every year around Christmastime. So we had him on the show, and the questions were all about the medical evidence for or against bad effects from pot smoking and whether or not the stuff should be made legal again, and Bob Grantham fearlessly answered *maybe* to all questions—he was one of the good guests, one of the ones who understood we were selling a product and not championing a cause on our program—and after the interview the two of us got to talking about this and that, and it turned out he went to Northwestern, too; he was a freshman the year I was a senior, and so on. This was just about a month or two after the divorce, I was still new to the apartment in the city, and frankly I tended to get a little lonely from time to time, so when he asked me for my phone number—maybe we could get together sometime—I gave it to him. And that was that.

Until about three weeks later, when the phone rang about ten o'clock in the evening—I was watching the first re-run of the "Industry Struggles to Conquer Water Pollution" special—and it was Bob Grantham. "I'm in Wednesday's with a pal of mine," he said, "and I think you might be interested in him. Or your Network might be. You free right now?"

This was before I met Linda, of course, and except for the special, which I'd already seen on its first airing, I was completely free. So I said, "Come on over," and a while later they came on over.

It has been said that people look like who they are, and generally speaking I've found this to be true. Bob Grantham, for instance, with his pipe and his neat little beard and his leather elbow patches and his brown shoes with blue-gray slacks, looked exactly like a writer. And Arnold Kuklyn, the fellow he brought over with him, looked like the kind of guy who might sell you a hot TV set. And of course that's what he was, as it turned out.

At the time, though, all I knew was that Bob was introducing me to a guy named Arnold Kuklyn, whose suitcoat collar was turned up indoors, who looked over his shoulder before he shook hands with me, and who was five feet three inches tall and looked very bitter about it.

Nobody ever called this fellow Arnie or any other nickname, by the way, nothing but Arnold. In fact, most people called him Kuklyn.

Bob called him Arnold. He said, "I know you're in the Network news department, Jay, and Arnold's got something that ought to be right up your alley. We thought at first there might be a book in it—we'd collaborate on it, Arnold and me—but really where this belongs is television."

"Like the Berlin tunnel," Arnold said. He had a nasal voice, but he spoke very low all the time, as though he wasn't entirely sure he wanted anybody to hear what he was saying. Throughout my association with Arnold Kuklyn, I always wanted somehow to turn up the gain whenever he said anything.

I said, "Like what Berlin tunnel?"

Bob was the one who answered me. "The one that was turned into a television special a couple of years ago. Where the camera crew went right in with them when they dug the tunnel and when they brought the refugees through."

"Yeah, I remember that," I said. "Very powerful special."

"This could be the same kind of thing," Bob said. "Tell him, Arnold."

"Guns," Arnold said. And then he just looked at me.

"Tell him the whole thing, Arnold," Bob said. I'd poured out Scotch on the rocks all around, and Bob's was empty already. He said, "Mind if I build myself another?"

"Go right ahead," I said. Mine was still half full, and Arnold had barely sipped at his. I said to Arnold, "What do you mean, guns?"

"Smuggling guns," he said. Then he leaned forward—he and Bob were sitting on the sofa, and I was in the chair facing them, except that Bob was now on his way to the kitchen for another drink—and he said, "Running guns out of the country." He looked at my left wall, and then at my right wall, as though he were going to cross the street, and lowered his voice even more and said, "Into the Caribbean."

I didn't have the slightest idea what he was talking about. I said, "You mean somebody's dumping guns in the ocean?"

"No no," he said. He leaned even farther forward—I was afraid he'd topple over and smash his chin into my coffee table—and then he had to lean back while Bob went past him to sit down again, all in a confusion of knees.

"Excuse me," Bob said, and sat down and drank his glass half-empty at one gulp.

Arnold leaned forward again. "I got a contact," he said. "He's selling guns to these people in Florida, and they're shipping them out to the revolutionaries on Ilha Pombo."

Now I had it. "Like Cuba," I said. "Smuggling guns to the revolutionaries."

"That's right. Only these revolutionaries are good revolutionaries. Pro-American."

"That's good," I said. "I didn't know we had any revolutionaries on our side."

Arnold glanced at Bob, whose glass was empty again, and studied him for a second as though wondering who he was and whether or not he could be trusted. Then he looked at me again and murmured, "You want to film them?"

"The revolutionaries?"

"No, the guns."

Bob said, "See, the idea is, you get a camera crew, you follow the guns every step of the way from the warehouse they start in till they get on the boat off the Florida coast."

"Hmmm," I said, because I saw possibilities in it. "A special on the traffic in guns. I see possibilities in that."

"I thought it was right up your alley," Bob said. "Mind if I build myself another?"

"Go right ahead," I said. I waited while Bob and his knees got past Arnold and his knees, and then I said to Arnold, "You're sure we can get these people to cooperate?"

Arnold extended his right hand and rubbed his thumb back and forth along the side of his first finger—the old sign language for cash on the barrelhead.

I said, "I see. The Network would have to pay a little money."

He winked. Nothing sly or cute or coy about it, just a simple wink, the rest of his face remaining perfectly expressionless. I'd never seen anybody do anything like that before—a wink is usually a humorous thing—and I lost my train of thought for a second while I looked at him. Then I put myself back together and said, "But aren't these people taking a risk?"

"No risk," he said. He sipped at his drink, which made two sips so far.

I said, "But if we photograph them, the police will be able to identify them."

"Nobody's breaking the law," he said. "You see what I mean?"

"No," I said.

He said, "The only thing illegal is taking the guns out of the country. I sell you guns, that's legal. You sell Bob the same guns, that's still legal. He sells them to the guy next door, that's still legal. The guy next door puts them on a boat and ships them out of the country, now you got something for the cops."

"Well, what about that, then?" I asked him. "What about the last man in the chain, the guy who puts them on the boat?"

He shrugged; it wasn't a problem. "No faces," he said.

"Excuse me," Bob said, and struggled his knees past Arnold's knees again and sat down.

I said, "You mean, the camera crew should keep from shooting the faces of the people at the end of the chain, because they're the ones breaking the law."

"Good," Arnold said.

I thought about it, and I could see it. I could see the drama in it, I could even hear the narration: "Forced to work in darkness and anonymity, these links in the chain would permit filming only if . . ." etc, etc. "That's interesting," I said.

"I thought you'd like it," Bob said. Damned if half his drink wasn't gone again.

"I'll suggest it tomorrow," I said, and I did, to Mr. Walter J. Clarebridge, Vice President, Special Projects, News & Current Affairs Department.

Mr. Clarebridge said, "How much do they want?"

"I don't know," I said.

"Well, find out," he said. And that is all he said at that time, and I'll say so under oath. He didn't give me any warnings, he didn't say the Network would not want to involve itself in foreign adventures, he didn't say *any* of those things I've lately heard he claims he said at the first meeting in his office when I initially suggested the idea to him. He didn't say anything at that time, and he didn't say anything at any other time, not until well after the fit had hit the shan, at which time he prefaced a lot of comment with "I told you," etc. But he hadn't told me. He said what I've just said he said, and that's *all* he said.

I just want to get the record straight on this.

Anyway, I went back to my office and called Bob at home and woke him up. This was about three-thirty in the afternoon, and he came on with a voice like the M-G-M lion. And probably a breath to match. He and Arnold had hung around the night before until my Scotch and bourbon were both all gone, and I only had two drinks, and Arnold never did finish his first—Bob did—and both bottles had been about three quarters full to begin with.

Which you'll notice I never charged the Network for.

Anyway, Bob and I talked for a while until we established what time it was and whether or not he thought he would live, and then he had me hold on for a second—I heard a clink of glass against glass, far away—and when he came back his voice and optimism were both higher. "What's up, Jay?"

"I presented the idea to the people here," I said. "They want to know how much."

"How much what?"

"Money. Arnold said last night it would take some—"

"Oh, yeah, right! Christ, Jay, I don't know. That's Arnold's department. He'd talk to these people, you know? Find out what the story is, how much they figure it's worth to them, what with the risk and all."

"But they're not breaking the law," I reminded him. "Arnold said just the last people."

"Well, it's still kind of a shady business, you know, moving all these guns around. Listen, I tell you what. You say you talked to somebody there?"

"Mr. Walter J. Clarebridge. He's Vice President, Special Projects."

"That sounds like the man we want. Listen, why don't I round up Arnold, and we'll come on over and talk to this guy?"

"Well, I don't know," I said. Mr. Clarebridge is a very fastidious type—a couple years ago he led the unsuccessful attempt to ban miniskirts in the steno pool—and I wasn't quite sure how he'd take to a couple of guys like Bob Grantham and Arnold Kuklyn.

"Leave it to us," Bob said. "You presented the idea, now let us sell it. No reason you should have to do all the work."

"Well— I tell you what, can you hold on a second?"

"Sure."

I put him on hold and called Mr. Clarebridge and told him the situation and Bob's suggestion, and he said, "Can he be here by four-thirty?" Once again, that is absolutely all he said.

"I'll find out," I said, and put Mr. Clarebridge on hold and got Bob back. "Can you be here by four-thirty?"

"What time is it?"

This was what we'd talked about for the first two minutes of the conversation. "Twenty-three minutes to four," I said.

"Can do," he said.

"Fine. Just come up to the eleventh floor and ask for me and I'll take you in to see him."

"Great. You're a pal, Jay."

"Sure thing," I said, and disconnected from him and tried to get Mr. Clarebridge back and couldn't find him. I remember that distinctly, this sudden feeling of panic: I've lost Mr. Clarebridge! Like he was fallen away in the wiring somewhere.

See, what happens, I have all these different lines on my phone, with plastic buttons to switch from one to the next. And there's a light that goes on inside the plastic button if that line is in use. But the plastic button lights on my phone have some sort of loose connection or something, and they keep going off. Then they'll come back on, and then they'll go off again. The only time I'm positive they'll work is when I call the phone company to send the man around again. He comes around and picks up the receiver, and the pushed-down button for the line in use goes right on. "Seems to be working all right now," he says, and looks at me.

So it was out again. The light in the plastic button. Without which there was no way to know on which line I'd left Mr. Clarebridge. Except to start pushing buttons and saying hello to each line, which is what I did:

"Hello? Hello? Hello?"

"Hello?"

"Mr. Clarebridge?"

"That's odd. I was dialing Mr. Fisher."

"This is Mr. Fisher."

"Well, this is Donnelly in Accounting, and we have a question here about dependents. Now, since your divorce you—"

"Listen, let me call you back, will you, Donnelly? I left Mr. Clarebridge on another line."

"Well— You guys always say you'll call back, but you never do."

"I really will. I promise."

"And then *we* get hell from the IRS. It's a simple matter, it won't take a minute to clear up. See, to qualify as a dependent—"

"I've really got to go, Donnelly, I'll call you back." I pushed the next button and said, "Hello?"

"Fisher?"

"Mr. Clarebridge?"

"You may not realize it, Fisher, but up here on twelve we are frequently very busy."

"Yes, sir, I'm sorry."

"Do you know just how long you've had me sitting here holding this phone?"

"I'm sorry, sir, I had a little trouble here."

"Well, are these people coming at four-thirty or aren't they? Do I cancel my sauna or don't I?"

"You cancel, sir. I mean, they're coming. Four-thirty. I'm having them come here, and then I'll bring them up."

"Fine," he said. He didn't say anything about being reluctant, about seeing these people as a favor to me. He didn't say anything but "Fine." Period.

So for the next forty-five minutes I went on answering fan mail—at that time I did some of Townley's fan mail too, the northeast quadrant of the United States and the eastern half of Canada—and at twenty-five minutes to five the phone rang. But of course the plastic button didn't light up to tell me which line it was, so I went through my push-hello routine until I got the receptionist's weird voice—she'd learned her British accent at the same time she was losing her Bronx accent, and the two had wound up entwined together in a sort of private Esperanto—and she told me two "gintlemun" were here to see me.

Bob looked like hell, but of course I'd expected he would, and with writers it's all right. People in the communications industry have come to accept the fact that writers have only a sporadic understanding of the conventional world, and whenever an individual dressed like a bum or a gypsy queen or a Bolivian admiral or whatever-you-want enters a receptionist's office anywhere in television or publishing or anywhere else in the media, the receptionist always finds out first whether this visitor is a writer before calling for assistance to chuck him out. And more often than not he's a writer. The rest of the time he's usually a messenger; the messenger services hire very unusual people, particularly in the winter. But I suppose triple-A people don't apply for the job very often.

Anyway, that was Bob. Arnold looked as though he'd come to cop a typewriter. He had a cigarette *stuck to the corner of his lower lip*. He had to squint one eye all the time, and the cigarette bobbed when he talked. It was incredible. It was something out of science fiction; I almost looked around for his time machine.

So I reassured the receptionist that the gintlemun were all right, that Bob was a writer and so forth—I more or less gave her the impression that Arnold was an exhibit—and then we took the winding staircase up to the executive floor, one flight up. I dealt with the receptionist at this level, and soon Mr. Clarebridge's secretary came out—no one had ever learned if she had knees, but at her age and with that face no one much cared—and she led us through the labyrinth to Mr. Clarebridge's office. He didn't have a corner, but he did have two windows and a rug and walls that went all the way to the ceiling and a brass hat rack and permission to hang a personally owned painting on the wall. His wife had done it; it showed a crying clown in close-up, with a sort of vague but sparkly background; she'd sprayed sequins on it while the paint was still wet.

So we went in, and I introduced Bob and Arnold to Mr. Clarebridge, and he said, with that frosty smile of his, "Well, Jay, I know you're in a hurry to get caught up on the day's work." He called me Jay when other people were around, and Fisher over the phone or when we were alone.

"Yes, sir," I said. I called him sir exclusively. I left and went back downstairs to my own small cubicle and finished a letter from Townley Loomis to a woman in Bangor, Maine, telling her that while it was certainly true that sex education proponents did sometimes tend to push their theories to extremes, it did not necessarily follow that they were all Communists, nor that sex education carefully supervised by parents and clergy could not be beneficial and not inevitably sap the physical strength and moral fibers of American youth and lay them open to Communist enslavement. Though on the other hand . . .

That night around eight-thirty I was watching something on television—I don't remember exactly what—and the doorbell rang downstairs. Now, I had a button to push to let people in and a lever to pull to talk to them through the mouthpiece, and for months I went on doing it wrong. I'd push the button and shout, "Hello!" into the mouthpiece and nobody would answer, and I'd give up and go back to my TV or my TV dinner or whatever I was doing, and in two or three minutes the upstairs doorbell would ring, and I'd go over, and whoever it was coming to see me was standing outside the door, and I'd say, "How'd you get up here?" and they'd say, "You buzzed."

Which is what happened this time. I suppose I probably would have let Bob and Arnold in anyway, but I would have preferred a chance to think about it. And to hide the replacement bottles of Scotch and bourbon, which I hadn't even opened yet and which were standing in plain sight on the drainboard in the kitchen.

Bob came in expansive and beaming, rubbing his hands together and shouting salutations at me. Arnold came in the same as ever, casing the joint for pockets to pick.

"Well, thanks to you we've got a gig!" Bob said, and slapped me on the shoulder and insisted on shaking hands.

I said, "It worked out, eh?"

"This calls for a celebration!"

I was afraid it might. I went away and broke the federal seal on the Scotch bottle and put ice cubes in three glasses and poured Scotch on the ice cubes and brought the three glasses back to the living room.

Bob was pacing the floor, happy, exuberant, rubbing his hands together. Arnold was loitering on the sofa; everywhere he went became a bus depot.

I handed out the glasses, and Bob held his up in the air and declaimed, "To Jay Fisher, a true friend!" Arnold touched his lips to his drink, I took a swallow, and Bob knocked down the whole thing at a gulp. He looked at the glass, looked at me.

"Go ahead," I said. "Build yourself another."

"Thanks, Jay."

I didn't want another evening of knees, so while Bob was in the kitchen I sat down myself on the sofa next to Arnold, leaving the armchair for Bob to sit in. 'Well," I said to Arnold, "it worked out, did it?"

"Yeah," he said. Not very enthusiastic.

Bob came back with the bottle. "The way we drink," he said, "why not just leave the bottle right here?" And he put it down on the coffee table.

"That's a good idea," I said.

Bob dropped into the armchair and raised his glass again. "Old college friends," he said.

I said, "Well, tell me about it. What did Mr. Clarebridge decide?"

Bob, building himself another, said, "He went for it. Thinks it's a great idea. Wants me to write the narration." He winked at me; his winks were the usual kind—humorous, not like Arnold's. "We'll get you to narrate," he said. "What do you say to that?"

"I wouldn't mind at all," I said. And I'd like to point out that this was the first suggestion anybody made that I narrate the program or have anything to do with it at all, and the suggestion did *not* come from me. I'd just like to point that out.

Having built himself another, he sat back in his seat and grinned at me. "Wanna come to Oklahoma with us?"

"Oklahoma? Why Oklahoma?"

"First step in the chain of freedom," Bob said airily. "It's where the guns start from." He demolished another glass and leaned forward toward the coffee table. "Build you another?"

"No, thanks, I'm still okay. When are you leaving for Oklahoma?" Meaning, When can I buy some more booze?

"Tomorrow. Right, Arnold?"

"Got to call first." Arnold was as wordy as ever.

"That's right," Bob said. "Arnold has to call his contact in Oklahoma, a little later tonight. But we don't anticipate any trouble, do we, Arnold?"

"Depends," Arnold said.

Bob smiled happily. "See? No problems. And tomorrow we take off. What we're going to do, we're going to follow the route of the guns, talk to the people along the way, set everything up. Then we'll come back, get together with a camera crew, and go down there again and film a shipment from start to finish."

"Sounds great," I said. "I'm glad it worked out for you."

"And it's all thanks to you," he said.

"Oh, not really," I said. And I go on saying it, too. And nothing will stop me from going on saying it. I'm not going to be the one holding the baby.

Anyway, we talked about general things after that, the three of us, for several hours. The two of us, I mean; Arnold dropped an occasional word in, like the triangle player at the Philharmonic, but I wouldn't have called him a full-time member of the conversation. Bob and I traded anecdotes about our overlapping worlds in the media, and it turned out he'd done two other books in addition to *Pot Pourri*, one called *The Enthusiast's Pictorial Guide to Sports Cars Through the Ages* and the other called *An Illustrated History of Ragtime*. He'd also been on the staff of several magazines at one time or another—*Argosy*, I think, and maybe *Time*, and some others—and for a few months one year had sold textbooks school to school for Prentice-Hall or McGraw-Hill or somebody. He had been a charming raconteur at our first meeting, the Townley Loomis lunchtime interview, and away from a microphone he was just as charming and quite a bit dirtier. I wouldn't have thought people could fit half the things into their behinds that Bob claimed personal knowledge of.

A little after midnight Arnold said, "Use your phone?"

"Sure," I said. "Use the extension in the bedroom."

"Thanks." He stood up and worked his knees past my knees and left the room, and Bob said, "Of course, the funniest thing about that girl Nancy was—" And so on.

Arnold came back about five minutes later and said, "We ought to get going."

"Right you are," Bob said. He knocked off the current glassful and reached for the bourbon bottle, saying the inevitable: "Guess I'll just build myself one for the road." The Scotch bottle was long since empty, of course. Of the bourbon, oddly enough, there was over half left, even after Bob had built himself one for the road.

I seem to be running out of tape. I'm ready to take a break anyway and go on with this after lunch. I'm starving, I don't know why. I don't see how I can eat at all, the pressures I'm under, but the bodily functions go on and on, come what may.

Well, I'll keep going till I reach the end of the tape. Where was I? The night of the day I'd presented Bob and Arnold to Mr. Clarebridge, who had gone for their idea. Bob had built himself one for the road, following which he shook my hand at great length, telling me over and over what a pal I was and how he appreciated me helping him put the idea over like this, and then he and Arnold left and I went into the bedroom to see if everything was there that had been there before Arnold had entered unchaperoned. I counted cuff links, and there was the same number as ever—seventeen; I don't know where the *hell* that other Emmy-shaped cuff link went—and it wasn't until about six weeks later when I got my phone bill that I discovered Arnold had used my phone to call Oklahoma.

And I didn't charge the Network for *that* either. So much for all talk of—

Woops. End of ta

TAPE ONE, SIDE TWO

FOOD JUST DOESN'T SIT WELL on my stomach these days. I don't know if any of the rumbling and grumbling can be picked up by this mike or not, but in case it can, you from the legal department, there's nothing wrong with the elevator. It's my stomach, and I apologize.

I wonder if there's such a thing as an overdose of Alka-Seltzer. It doesn't say anything on the bottle. I think I'll ask around the shop, next time I go in for one of these conferences we've all been having, where we pass the buck swiftly from hand to hand until the music stops. We've run enough of their goddam commercials; somebody at The Hub ought to know something about them.

I've become a hard-core Alka-Seltzer drinker by now. Back in the beginning I took the stuff like anybody else—on the rocks, slice of lemon, swizzle stick. Lately, it's been water from the tap in a jelly glass and chug-a-lug.

Enough of the present. Let's harken back to the days of yesteryear again and my part in the Ilha Pombo Affair, which began innocently, as I have described on the other side of this tape—and if you're listening to this side first, you from the legal department, stop at once and turn the tape over—and in the course of which I never wanted anything but what was best for the Network. I had no selfish motives, I did not then or later ask for or receive from any of the other participants any of the money the Network paid out in the course of the Ilha Pombo Affair, and at no time did anyone offer to pay me to use my influence to get the Network interested in the matter. In fact, in the conversation I've just described on the other side of this tape, Bob Grantham didn't even *tell* me about the fifteen hundred dollars Mr. Clarebridge had given him that afternoon for his expenses on the exploratory field trip. And if he had told me, I wouldn't have expected him to give me any of it.

In further fact, I didn't know about that particular fifteen hundred dollars until long after the fit had hit the shan, when one of those *papier-mâché* people from the FBI was questioning me and asked me how much of it had been my cut. And if Bob Grantham really did tell anybody that he'd given me five hundred dollars of that money, I don't know why he did, but he's wrong. Mistaken, probably, and possibly even, for reasons of his own, a liar.

Well. The events I described on the other side of this tape took place in late November of last year, and I heard no more about it till February. Though maybe I ought to mention the December incident and clear *that* up while I'm taking care of everything else.

It is perfectly true that I behaved badly in Wilton in the latter part of December, that the police were called in, that I did struggle somewhat with a policeman and break his false teeth, that I did shout Black Panther and New Left and other radical slogans all night in my cell, and that I was found guilty of drunk and disorderly the next morning and fined one hundred and fifty dollars. But to try to find a connection between this incident and the Ilha Pombo Affair is absurd on the face of it. I was not establishing mental imbalance to be later used in my defense should prosecution arise from Ilha Pombo. I was not attempting to recruit a revolutionary army in the Wilton, Connecticut, drunk tank. I was not doing any of the fantastic things it has been suggested I was doing. The December incident in Wilton was strictly a matter in my personal life, and though I am sorry about the besmirchment of the Network initials in the headline of the one-paragraph item in the *Times*, I insist that the incident had no direct connection with the Network and no connection in any way with the Ilha Pombo Affair.

Look. The date alone will tell you: December 27. The terms of the divorce gave me December 26 with the kids—I have two girls, eight-year-old Jackie and five-year-old Angela—but I had a conflict; I had to go to Chicago to do a Townley Loomis interview with a guy in the death house there—not a lunchtime interview, just a regular radio interview—and Marlene wouldn't let me switch to the next day. She said she'd already arranged all sorts of things for the holidays, and the divorce was supposed to have freed her from having me louse up her schedules and I could have the kids on December 26 or not at all.

Well, I didn't think it was such a hot idea to take two little girls to the death house in Chicago the day after Christmas, so I passed, and just phoned them from the Windy City after the interview—that fellow's still in the death house, by the way, and will probably die of old age there—and got home to my apartment in New York around three o'clock the next morning, and to be perfectly honest about it I was lonely and unhappy and I started to drink. I'd slept on the plane coming back, not enough to be rested but enough to keep me from going back to sleep once I hit the apartment, and I drank on through the rest of the night and fell asleep around noon the next day and didn't wake up until the wrong-number phone call a little after six. I had the day off, by the way, because of having had the assignment to do the remote in Chicago.

I think it was the wrong number that broke the camel's back. I'm in the apartment fifteen consecutive hours, and the only person out of the four billion people in this world who calls me is somebody who was trying to call somebody else. That left me with a feeling of disgust and rage and frustration and loneliness and all the rest of it, and I sat around and brooded a while longer, and drank some more, and ultimately took the ten-seventeen out of Grand Central to Wilton and found this fellow Bricker in my house. Wilbur Bricker. An *insurance* man, for God's sake! That slender black leather case with its zip-zip-zipper is attached permanently to his left arm, I swear it is. He wears a dark gray tie five eighths of an inch wide at its widest point, and every ten or fifteen years he's in style again. Talk about the one fixed point in a changing age, this guy *is* the Rock of Gibraltar!

This is the guy that sold me the life insurance policies I've been living on lately. And the major medical I'm continuing to pay for

Marlene and the kids. And this is the guy I find in my living room in Wilton, Connecticut, two days after Christmas, with his suitcoat unbuttoned. And may I ask whose Jade East after-shave is that on the coffee table in front of him, in close proximity to some recently crumpled Christmas wrapping paper? And why is Marlene nervously tucking her blouse into the top of her stretch pants? And why is that Mantovani album—which was *our* album, way back in the springtime of our love when we didn't think it was tacky to make love to tacky music—playing on the stereo, the first time I've heard the damn record in maybe six years?

I know at this point that I'm very drunk, and naturally my first thought is my own dignity, and I do my damnedest to stop lurching and back-pedaling around the living room, while Marlene is yapping away in the south forty of my perception, and Bricker is advancing on me, professional smile in place, hand outstretched, voice saying, "Well, hello there, Jay. Haven't seen you for a while."

His shoes are off! Little black-socked feet coming at me, left—right, left—right. I look at him, at that round neat head with those round neat glasses and round neat smile, and I know for an absolute fact that if I take a swing at him I will miss him and I will fall down. My balance is lousy as it is, and I know I will fall down. I will miss him, simply because there's no chance on earth that I could aim at him and connect, and if I miss him I will fall down.

So I stamp on his foot.

Now we've got something! Now *everybody* is making noise. Marlene is shrieking at me that I'm a criminal and a madman and I will never stop ruining her life, and Bricker is hopping around on one foot and holding the other and yipping like a goddam terrier, and I'm falling over pieces of furniture and throwing the Jade East at the wall and yelling that Marlene is a whore *etcetera,* and afterward, thinking about it, I realized that was what I needed that night, a little human contact. Voices, movement, action, response. Something to show me I was still alive.

At any rate, I now announce to Marlene, over Bricker's fading yips, that I will not permit my daughters to stay under the same roof with a harlot, exposed to this sort of degenerate influence and so on; no court on earth would argue my right and duty to rescue my children from an environment so sordid as to defy all description, and so on and so on, and I head upstairs to wake the kids and carry them off to the apartment in New York.

Marlene follows me at first, screaming and yelling, but when I go into the kids' room she simply announces she's going to call the police, and she leaves me.

I think at that point I knew I was making a mistake, but I was well along on my path and could see no hope of turning back, so I simply bulled forward, with no expectation of really getting anywhere, and hoped for the best. Like a lineman in football who intercepts a lateral and at once rumbles his three hundred pounds toward the far-off goal line even though he knows there are at least ten opponents on the field who could catch him with their ankles tied together. I was that lineman; there was no sane reason at all why I should have the ball, but I did, so there was nothing left to do but run with it.

So I woke Jackie, the eight-year-old, and asked her how she'd like to take a nice train ride with Daddy, and she said, "You smell terrible." I managed to smile, and convince myself that I really didn't want to fling my own daughter at the wall, and said, "Well, you just get dressed, because we're *going* for a nice train ride."

And in comes Bricker, limping but no longer yipping, back to the smooth, bland, *unruffled* impersonality that is the man's quintessence, and he starts saying things like, "Why don't we talk this over, Jay?" Just exactly the same way he used to say, in the old days, "Why don't we take a look at your protection package, Jay?"

So I swung at him, naturally. And I missed, and I fell down. Lying there on my daughters' pink rug, with Jackie sitting up in the bed to my right and Angela sound asleep in the bed to my left, I felt a great sort of patient despair about myself, as though I had all the time in the world to plumb the depths of my inanity, and it simply put the last nail in the lid when I heard Jackie say, with a sort of easy long-lived-with contempt, "Daddy's drunk, you know." I turned my face on the tickly pink rug and looked up at her, but she was looking up and past me at Bricker, and I'd never realized before how totally she looked like her mother. Same disgusting expression on her face and everything.

"You go back to sleep, Jackie," Bricker said, and the tone of that toneless speech told me without any doubt and permanently and forever that he was living here now. Which meant that I was not, I was really and truly no longer living here, not even *in absentia*. I had been replaced.

The bastard helped me to my feet. I would have pushed him roughly away if there'd been any chance of my standing up without his help. As it was, my brain made a lightning calculation, weighing the relative humiliations involved in being helped to my feet by Wilbur Bricker or having to leave my daughters' room on all fours, and I chose to exit like a man—on my feet, leaning on an insurance salesman.

Rage had heretofore kept me from behaving quite as falling-down drunk as I really was, but now rage had washed away and my legs were rubber bands, and Bricker had to help me all the way down the stairs to the first floor. Where Marlene put the steel in my backbone once again by running up and screaming at me that I had to leave the house at once, she'd called the police, and I had ruined her life for the last time. So when the cops arrived I had a full head of steam up once more, and from there on it was one disaster after another.

The cops, of course, were an impossibility for me to deal with, considering the fact that I was drunk and Marlene was the local citizen. Also, when they wouldn't listen to my loudly slurred demands that they arrest Marlene and Bricker as adulterers, I shifted gears and began a long vague harangue about Connecticut blue laws, of which Connecticut has more than its share. At one and the same time, I sneered at these cops for being cops in a state that had such laws on the books, and then vilified them for not enforcing the one on adultery by arresting Marlene and Bricker.

This was my first more or less professional contact with officers of the law. Unfortunately, due to the Ilha Pombo Affair, it was not to be my last. Since then I have learned that all police everywhere, whether municipal, state, or federal, have one thing in common: They are elbow freaks. You can be a reporter and interview them and you will never know this, but meet one in the course of his duty, when his duty is *you*, and I'll bet you a dollar before the meeting is over he will have grabbed your elbow. Not even to take you anywhere, but simply because that's what they do. Cops grab elbows.

These days I know about that, and when a cop grabs my elbow I don't pay any more attention to it than he does, but at that time I wasn't used to it—like the first time you're at lunch with an Arab and right after the meal he belches loud enough to rattle windows

—and I was in a bad mood anyway, and I was drunk, and I was unhappy, and when the cop grabbed my elbow I hit him in the mouth and broke his false teeth. So the other one rammed me in the stomach with the point of his nightstick—as though I were a high school girl at a demonstration—and I threw up on him.

I don't think I want to describe any more of this. If the legal department is interested, for any weird reasons of its own, the rest of the story can be found encapsulated in that one-paragraph item in *The New York Times* for December 28, last year, that I already mentioned.

About the only thing left to say about the whole incident, actually, is that it cleared the air for all time between Marlene and me and ended whatever emotional problems I might have been walking around with as a result of the divorce. What I mean is, when I called her from New York two days later to apologize—an apology I was heartfeltfully sincere about, by the way—she also apologized to me, for her previous hard-nosed attitude about me seeing the kids, and said she understood at last that I did have emotional ties to the children and so on, and in the future she was sure I would find her much more understanding about working out arrangements for me to see them. And so it has been. We've gotten along fine all this year, and in fact just two weeks ago I got an invitation to the wedding, which will take place in about ten days from now, of Marlene and Wilbur Bricker.

It's comforting to know, really, that if anything happens to me, the insurance man is there to take care of my family.

Well, so much for that. I know you're probably getting bored in that elevator by now, so please excuse this side trip, the only point of which was to demonstrate that it *was* a side trip, that the incident in December had absolutely nothing to do with Ilha Pombo, that it was strictly involved with personal problems of my own, and that in fact it was the crisis point of those personal problems, following which there was a rapid recovery which made any allegations about my emotional state as a contributory factor to the Network's current quandary obviously false and more than likely malicious.

So. After the holidays, my life ran along in its ordinary way from the beginning of the year till the middle of February, when the doorbell rang one evening while I was watching one of our midseason replacement shows, a program there's no need to mention by name since it's no longer on the air. I went over and pressed the button that unlocked the downstairs door and shouted, "Hello? Hello?" into the grille, and naturally got no answer. I grumbled and muttered—I always blamed neighborhood children for ringing the bell, and I was always wrong—and went back to the television set, and a couple of minutes later the doorbell up here rang, and once again I realized what I'd done.

(The fact is, I didn't have that many visitors in those days. If people had been coming around to the apartment all the time, I would very quickly have sorted out the button-lever business. But there'd be long periods of time between the doorbell rings, and in the course of those empty spaces I'd manage to forget all over again. Recently, of course, the bell has been ringing quite a bit, and I have finally learned. I more or less had to, considering.)

Anyway, it was Bob Grantham, naturally, who appeared at my door on that evening in mid-February. Without Arnold. I invited him in and turned off the TV and brought out the Scotch and glasses and ice, and he sat on the sofa and drained off the first drink I gave him and said, "Boy, I hated to come back up here. You can't believe how sunny and warm it is down there."

"In Oklahoma?"

"No, in the Caribbean. And Florida. All around down there. Mind if I build myself another?"

"Go ahead," I said. That was what I'd left the bottle and the ice bucket on the coffee table for. He built himself another, and I said, "Where's Arnold? Still down there?"

"*En route,*" he said. "Cheers."

"Cheers. *En route* here?"

"No, to Florida." He grinned sort of loosely at me and said, "How'd you like a little sunshine in your life, Jay?"

"I wouldn't mind it," I said. You remember last winter, of course; it was lousy.

"Well, you've got some coming," he said, and winked at me, and finished his drink.

I frowned at him and watched him build himself another, and wondered what the hell he was talking about. You may think this is hindsight, but I always did feel a little uncomfortable around Bob, a little bit as though I didn't really know entirely what he was up to, as though he was maybe less reliable than, say, Wilbur Bricker.

Anyway, he toasted me again and then leaned forward and said, "What would you say if I told you you were going to Florida the end of this week?"

"I'd say this is the first I heard of it," I said. And I now repeat: "I'd say this is the first I heard of it," I said. A little instant replay there, while we all notice that that *was* the first I'd heard of it. No wangling by me, no angling by me, nothing by me at all. The whole thing was Bob Grantham's idea, and to those who suggest that Bob Grantham was going to an awful lot of trouble for somebody he didn't really know all that well, all I can say is, You're absolutely right, and as it turned out I wish he hadn't. But he did, for whatever reasons of his own he might have had in his head—I've heard it suggested he wanted me around because he thought I wasn't very bright, a theory that doesn't make me happy but which at least shows there's *some* possible method in Bob's madness—and whatever his reasons were, my reasons for going along with him were simple: The Network told me to go.

As Bob, on this evening I'm describing, said would happen. "Tomorrow," he said, "Wally Clarebridge is going to have a talk with you. And you know what he's going to tell you?"

I shook my head, a bit dazed, mostly by hearing anybody call Mr. Clarebridge Wally. Before this, I'd never even heard anybody call him Walter.

"He's going to tell you," Bob said, "that you are going to go to Florida tomorrow."

"He is?"

"With me. And a camera crew. They're going to film some guns, and you're going to interview some of the undercover people."

"I am?"

"You are," he said, and I did.

I must say at this point that Bob had already been drinking somewhere else before he arrived at my place that evening, and the result was that the coherent part of his conversation came to an end very shortly after the part I've already recorded. He started to tell me about the people I would meet and interview in Florida—Ramon, he said, and told me I'd "better watch out for" Luis, but didn't then tell me why—but very shortly he switched over to a description of a girl named Isabella that he would introduce me to down there, a description that was very physical and very favorable, and shortly after that he lapsed into total incoherence, and sometime after that he fell asleep.

Which is the *only* reason he spent the night at my place, then or any other time. He got drunk and passed out, and I didn't feel like dragging him out into the hall. It does *not* indicate collusion between us, and it *certainly* doesn't indicate any of the other things that have been whispered up and down the halls at The Hub.

Anyway, Bob was still asleep the next morning when I left for The Hub, so I wrote him a little note suggesting he make himself at home and leave fairly soon, and when I got to my office there was a note on my desk that Mr. Clarebridge wanted to see me, so I went straight upstairs and his secretary announced me and ushered me in.

Wally. I looked at him then and tried to think of anybody calling him Wally, either to his face or behind his back, and it was just impossible. I have continued to think about it from time to time, and I have actually heard Bob *call* him Wally in direct speech between the two of them, and I still can't imagine it. It's like seeing a desk fly; even if you *saw* one fly, you wouldn't believe it.

Now, Mr. Clarebridge these days is doing his best to downplay his connection with the Ilha Pombo Affair, which is certainly understandable, and I don't want to be thought of as the kind of guy who goes around telling tales on his bosses, and I think if you check around with people who know me at The Hub they'll tell you I've never had that kind of reputation, but what I'm dealing with here is the facts, for my own good as well as the good of the Network, and it is a fact and I'll swear to it that ever since last February, Bob Grantham has called Mr. Clarebridge Wally *to his face*.

Anyway, Mr. Clarebridge said to me, "We have a special assignment for you. You're going to take a crew to Florida."

"Yes, sir," I said.

"While there," he said, "you'll be under the supervision of"—and he then paused and pretended to check a piece of paper on his desk "—a man named Robert Grantham. It's his project."

"Yes, sir," I said. And I wondered two things, even that early in the game. I wondered why Mr. Clarebridge pretended he didn't know Bob well enough to remember his name. And I wondered how he'd managed to forget that I was the one who'd introduced him to Bob in the first place.

While I wondered these things, Mr. Clarebridge went on to explain the assignment to me, as though I'd never had any connection with it before. I can only assume, by the way, that at that time he was under the impression there would be credit and rewards coming to all concerned with the gun-running special and was therefore shouldering me away from the trough ahead of time. Since Mr. Clarebridge was well rumored around The Hub as one of the executives who taped all private conversations in his office, it seems as though an energetic investigator from the legal department should certainly be able to find the tape of this conversation and verify what I'm saying here. And thereby notice the total shift Mr. Clarebridge has taken since—from aceing me out of credit for the origination of the idea to trying to shift the whole origination onto my shoulders.

Back in February, though, we were pretending the special—then called "A Sea of Guns"—was a brand-new subject to me, and Mr. Clarebridge told me all about it. Naturally I considered telling him I already knew what was going on, but one doesn't do that with one's boss. One goes along; I went along.

To Florida, with Bob Grantham and a crew of eight.

Our affiliate in Miami handled most of the housekeeping details for us, of course. They arranged our hotel accommodations, put camera and sound equipment at our disposal, rented cars for us, and gave us interpreters to send out for coffee.

The first three days in Miami, we did nothing at all. That is, I swam in the pool—I hate swimming in the ocean, though I wound up in it before the whole thing was over—and overate at Network expense, and sat in from time to time at the crew's perpetual poker game, and watched Bob build himself another, and watched Bob on the phone to The Hub telling "Wally" that everything was going great, and watched Bob on the phone locally trying to get me dates, and watched Bob drive off in the rented red Mustang on mysterious missions preceded by a wink.

About Bob and me and dates, by the way. There's been a lot of talk about Bob and me being party types, with orgies in the lush tropics at Network expense and all that, and to be perfectly honest I was far enough from the divorce by then to be *ready* for an orgy in the lush tropics—even at my own expense, if necessary—but it never happened. What Bob's sex life on his own was like I have no idea, happily, but when it came to organizing a group including me he never did come through.

The pattern was established even before we left New York. The day Mr. Clarebridge told me I was going to Florida, I went home after work to find that Bob was still there, that he'd taken the make-yourself-at-home part of my note to heart while completely ignoring the and-leave-fairly-soon part. And he had made himself at home to the extent of bringing up a friend. Anita, her name was, and she looked like a World War II pinup, only with black hair. What I mean by that, well, this might be difficult to explain. I don't know if you people in the legal department ever look at girls or not, but if you do you may have noticed that girls today are three inches narrower and three inches taller than girls during World War II. By which I don't mean that girls back then were fatter or girls today skinnier. I'm talking about body outline, silhouette. If you were to take a girl from a forties movie—Ann Sheridan, say, or Priscilla Lane—and stand her next to a girl from a current movie—Jane Fonda, say, or Faye Dunaway—and turn the lights out in front of them and leave the lights on behind them so you only had a silhouette to look at, and they were both facing you directly, you would notice that today's girl is three inches narrower and three inches taller.

How did I get to that? I don't know; the point is, this girl Anita that I found lounging around my apartment when I got home from work that day was a throwback to 1943; three inches shorter and three inches wider. Also, she chewed gum. In fact, if I remember clearly, she *snapped* gum. When was the last time you heard anybody snap gum?

The girl belonged with Arnold, really, but it was Bob she was with. And from the look of Bob, when he listed out of the kitchen to welcome me home, he'd been building himself one after another for quite a while already today. How had he done it? He'd finished off most of the available booze in the apartment last night.

He explained how without my having to ask, after the salutations and introductions were through: "We ran out of hooch. I ordered up some more."

At last, I thought, he's buying a bottle or two. "Good," I said.

"Paid for it out of your coin jar," he said. "The one on your dresser."

"My—" I just stood there.

He peered at me, somewhat blearily. "Something wrong?"

"No no," I said. "Everything's fine." Because how could I tell him what he'd done? Even if I'd explained it to him he wouldn't have understood.

In the first few months after President Johnson debased our silver coinage in 1965, there was still some of the earlier coinage around, quarters and dimes without that suspiciously brown smear around the edges. During the time that Gresham's Law was weeding the old coins out, I collected as many of them as I could, on the assumption that someday they would be very valuable. Whenever I got one, I put it in a jar I kept on my dresser at home in Wilton, and at the time of the divorce it was one of the few tangible assets I took away with me to New York. My coin jar, full of coins that would appreciate fantastically in value in the years to come; perhaps my one chance—aside from Wilbur Bricker's insurance, of course—to lay down the basis for a family fortune. I could see my great-grandchildren drifting through the Mediterranean on one of their yachts, toasting my memory in champagne.

And now those hoarded coins had gone for hooch. I just stood there and felt the disaster drape itself over my head and shoulders, like an awning that has just fallen off a building, and I discovered again—as I had discovered at the time of the divorce and at various other times in my life—that my reaction to disaster is to become immobile. I just stand there, and possibility washes away from me like the tide going out.

I did it then too. I thought of dashing out to the liquor store and demanding the return of my coins. I visualized myself tracing down every customer the liquor store had serviced all afternoon, getting back my dimes and quarters one at a time, rebuilding the family lodestone from scratch. I imagined the scenes in my head, but I didn't act them out. Instead, I excused myself and went into the bedroom to change out of my suit, and found at the bottom of my coin jar three quarters and a dime.

Even if they become one hundred times more valuable than they were to begin with, that's still only eighty-five bucks. I think my great-grandchildren, if they do make the Mediterranean, will probably be serving canapés to the Onassis kids.

When I went back to the living room, Anita was on the phone, and Bob explained that she was lining me up a date for tonight. "It's off to sunny climes tomorrow," he said. "Tonight we celebrate."

I went along with that idea, not so much because I felt I had anything I wanted to celebrate as because I felt I had things I wanted to forget. So I said, "Good idea." And seeing him veer kitchenward again, I called, "Build me one while you're at it." It seemed a hell of a good idea to get drunk. Have congress with some brunette Betty Grable, forget unclad coinage with unclad wolf-bait, drink myself stinko, and sky sunward—as *Variety* would say—in the morning.

Only part of which came true. Anita called and called, the message units piled up like stacks of coins—everything was coins, for a while there—and she found me nobody. Bob ultimately took over, dialed and dialed and dailed, and the closest he came to scoring for me was one of the wrong numbers he reached; but that one's husband came home unexpectedly just as Bob was about to hand the phone over to me.

"There's a couple places they might be," Bob told me finally, lurching to his feet. "You wait here; we'll take a look and give you a call when we find one."

"Why don't I come along?"

"Not cool," Bob said. "Three people, it looks like the extra guy's hungry. This way, we find a girl, we're doing *her* a favor."

"Good thinking," I said. Bob was always very good at figuring out things like that. The fact they very seldom worked merely shows, it seems to me, that human nature is more complex than any scheme that tries to encompass it, but when it comes to developing the schemes I never found anybody who could work out more complex ones than Bob.

Anyway, they left, Bob and Anita, and I sat by the phone and watched television and built myself one after another and fell asleep during the eleven o'clock news—our local sportscaster has a voice that will put me to sleep even when I'm not drinking—and the phone never did ring, and I didn't see Bob again until the next day, at Kennedy for the charter flight to Miami. He was much more hung over than I, and I wasn't feeling all that great either, and neither of us mentioned the night before, then or ever.

Nevertheless, the pattern had been established. Anita didn't return into my life—or into Bob's, so far as I know—but a stream of other girls did, and day after day I sat in hotel rooms in various cities of the Western Hemisphere and watched these girls—and Bob—make phone call after phone call trying to find me a date, and none of them ever did. I very soon became more than faintly embarrassed about this recurring daymare, but Bob always treated it in full, as though it were the first time and had no chance of failing, and of course for each of the girls it *was* the first time, so there never seemed to be anything for me to do but sit there each and every time and wait through it, which is what I did.

I did it through the first three days in Florida, during those spare moments when I was neither swimming in the pool nor losing my shirt to the crew at poker, and between Bob's undercover jouneys away from the hotel in the rented red Mustang. And then, on the fourth day, I dove yet again from the low board into the pool, made my underwater parabola, surfaced through blue water into hot sunlight, shook my head to get water and hair out of my eyes, blinked, looked toward the hotel, and there was a rip in the picture. The hotel, against the bright blue backdrop of sky, was a white wedding cake, a photograph of itself blown up for a calendar, and in the middle of all those pastels there was a jagged tear, small and thin and somewhat crooked, as though a cat had ripped a claw through the canvas. And the rip in the picture was Arnold, standing at the opposite end of the pool in the same black suit as ever, collar turned up, hands in pockets, cigarette stuck to the corner of his lower lip. Bob was beside him, big and hearty by comparison, looking like a tennis player gone to seed, and at the same time they both gestured to me; Arnold did a minute movement of the head to indicate that I should join them, and Bob waved both arms in the air and yelled, "Hey, Jay! Come over here!"

I went over there and stood dripping in front of them. "Hello, Arnold," I said, and Arnold dipped his head slightly.

Bob said, "You want to get your people together, Jay? We're going out to the site at two o'clock."

"The site?"

Bob gave me a meaningful look. "*You* know."

"Oh!" Then a doppelganger of the other part of his sentence reached me, and I said, "Two o'clock? What time is it?"

Bob looked at his watch. Arnold looked at it, too. "Ten-thirty."

"Christ, Bob, that isn't much notice."

"Well, that's the way these things are, Jay."

So I rushed into the hotel to dress and call the crew and get everything arranged, and incredibly enough we made it. At two o'clock our convoy left the hotel in three rented cars, a red Mustang, a yellow Dodge Dart, and a green Nova. We stopped off at our affiliate's offices to pick up two remote trucks and some more crew, and then we headed south out of Miami along the coast, and after a while turned inland, the driver of the lead car following Arnold's mumbled directions.

In our car, the lead car, were four people; the driver, who was one of the technicians from the local affiliate, Arnold sitting beside him, and Bob and me in the back seat. As we rode, I asked Bob questions and he filled me in on what was going on.

"This is the last stage," he said. "The guns start out in Oklahoma and go to different places, and then they come here, and from here they go to a place on the coast and then onto the boat."

"Why don't they come straight here from Oklahoma?"

He said, "Well, there's government restrictions on the sale and movement of guns, you know. Grahame can't just send out a shipment of rifles straight to a boat off the Florida coast; he'd lose his license."

"Grahame?"

"Jack Grahame. He's the licensed gun-dealer they're using. He's sympathetic to the cause of freedom everywhere, a true anti-Communist."

"Jack Grahame," I repeated.

"Jaekel," he said, and spelled it. "Jaekel Grahame. But everybody calls him Jack; he's a regular guy. You'll like him."

"He's going to be here today?"

"No, of course not, he's back in Oklahoma. You'll get to meet him, don't worry."

"Well, who's going to be here today?"

"The people I told you about. Ramon and Luis and a few others. Cuban Freedom Fighters."

"But these guns aren't for Cuba, are they?"

"No, they're going to Ilha Pombo Island. Ramon and Luis and the others are simply fighters in the cause of world freedom, and while waiting for the day when they can rescue their enslaved homeland they do what they can to help other freedom fighters." He beamed and punched my leg and said, "It's goddam like Hemingway, isn't it? This small scattered army of brave men, speaking different languages, coming from different homelands, but united by the same call to liberty burning inside the breast of every one of them."

I remembered at that point that Bob was the writer on this

project, and it certainly sounded as though he had the tone down pat. I said, "Will there be anyone here from Ilha Pombo?"

"No. Too dangerous. Mungu's spies are everywhere."

I wasn't sure I'd heard him right. "Mungu?"

"He's the dictator of Ilha Pombo Island."

"The one they're going to overthrow."

"That's right."

In the meantime, Arnold had directed us off the blacktop road onto a dirt road, and we were traveling through land that was half scrub and half swamp. The air shimmered in the distance, the sun beat down everywhere, and our passage frightened largish birds, which flapped off in slow-motion panic, beating the air with heavy wings. In our air-conditioned car, it was like looking out at a wraparound movie; the reality was in the car, and all that out there was fake.

The dirt road grew more and more tentative and more and more bumpy. We jounced along, and when I looked out the rear window I could see the mobile units rocking dangerously from side to side. I said, "How much farther?"

Bob relayed the question to Arnold, who nodded at the windshield and said, "Over there."

I looked, and ahead of us I could make out some low buildings that seemed half sunk in the reedy swamp. I said, "What place is that?"

"Headquarters," Bob said, "of the Ilha Pombo Island Expeditionary Force."

"The buildings look old."

"They are old. They were used around the turn of the century by flamingo rustlers."

I looked at him. "By what?"

"You never heard of the flamingo wars they had down here?"

"Never. Flamingo wars?" So far as I'd seen, he hadn't brought a flask with him.

"Back around the turn of the century," he said, "it was a big fashion for women to have flamingo feathers in their hats. So the flamingos around here almost got wiped out, and then some laws were passed to protect them, so they wouldn't become extinct."

"This is on the level?"

"I swear and vow," he said, and held up three fingers in the Boy Scout salute. "There were gangs down here for a while that went after the flamingos in defiance of the law. This was one of their camps."

We were very close to the flamingo rustlers' camp now, and I could see that the buildings were very old indeed; maybe a dozen of them all told, only four or five with their roofs still up. They were low wooden shacks built on stilts to raise them about six inches off the wet ground, and half of them had sagged off their stilts and were rotting from the ground up at the same time that they were crumbling from the roof down.

There was a dry open space in the middle of the cluster of buildings, and that was where our cluster of cars and trucks came to a stop. We opened the doors and stepped out, and the soggy heat hit us like the atmosphere of another planet; Venus, maybe. It didn't seem possible that human beings could breathe this stuff, which was so cottony and dense I was surprised I could see through it.

But I could. And what I saw was half a dozen rough Latin American types in dirty white shirts and dirty white trousers and Salvation Army-reject hats and huge dark sunglasses, and they were walking toward us from one of the few still usable buildings. And behind them, parked on the shady side of the building, were two vehicles—a filthy white Datsun with crumpled fenders, and a rusty old International Harvester pickup truck with one blue door and one red door.

I'm running out of tape again. This is ridiculous, I didn't know it was going to take this long. But there's a lot to describe, really, and I want to be sure I have it all as accurate as I can possibly get it. My future—and the future of the Network—hinges to a great extent on my establishing the limits of my part—and the Network's part—in the Ilha Pombo Affair, and if that means you—you from the legal department—are going to have to ride up and down in that elevator for another tape's worth, I'm sorry, but there it is.

There's still a little tape. What I'm going to do, I'm going to send along a copy of the interviews I did down at Base Camp One, as it later became known, the interviews I did that first day I was there. I think you'll find them interesting. Then I'll get back to the chronological report on tape two. But don't go to tape two yet; listen to the interviews first. The first interview is with Ra

APPENDIX ONE

Jay Fisher Interview with Ramon, Last Name Unknown, Somewhere in Florida, February, Current Year

Q: We set now? Look how I'm sweating; my hands are so wet I can't hold the fucking microphone. You sure you're ready? —I *am* holding it near my mouth. Turn up your gain. —All right. Ramon, you know what this is?

A: A fuckin microphone.

Q: Right. Now, that's the camera over there, but—

A: *I* know that.

Q: Right. Now, when we talk, you look at me, okay? Not at the camera, okay?

A: Why we don't sit in the car? You got air conditionin the car, don't you?

Q: That doesn't give the right feeling, Ramon. You see, when we hunker down together like this, out in the sunlight here, with the swamp in the background, it gives us that Vietnam feeling.

A: This ain't fuckin Vietnam.

Q: I know that, Ramon, but the idea is, people watching on television have to get the feeling of a war going on; that's what our special's all about. A small brush-fire war, and this is one little corner of it. And the way we do that, we give people something familiar to look at. They see two guys hunkered down in sunlight with swamp in the background, and one of them holding a microphone, and right away they understand it's war we're talking about.

A: Why we don't sit in the car? It's son of a bitch hot.

Q: I'm explaining that, Ramon. If we go sit in the car and the camera takes pictures of us in the car with the microphone, the people at home will get all confused. They'll think it's a special about municipal corruption and the giving of bribes, because that's the picture we give them when we're going to talk about municipal corruption and the giving of bribes,—see what I mean? Two guys in a car, talking, with a microphone between them.

A: It's really motherfucker hot out here.

Q: That's another thing, Ramon. When we get down to the real question-answer thing in the interview here, try not to say words like that, okay?

A: You said fuckin microphone.

Q: Yes, I did. But none of this part will go out over the air,—see what I mean? Only the clean parts go out over the air.

A: Jefferson Airplane said motherfucker over the air.

Q: That's a rumor.

A: Bullshit. My other brother seen it.

Q: Well, that's neither here nor there. Let's get to the interview. Now, your name is Ramon, is it not?

A: You been callin me Ramon twenty minutes.

Q: I'm trying to start the interview. Make believe we're just starting to talk.

A: Man, this is endless bullshit.

Q: That could be, but it's my job. Now, let me start it again. Your name is Ramon, is it not?

A: Yeah, Ramon, that's my name.

Q: Ramon what?

A: Smith.

Q: Ramon Smith?

A: You like Jones?

Q: In other words, you prefer to be anonymous, is that it?

A: You got it.

Q: Well, that's understandable. You're Cuban, aren't you, Ramon?

A: That's right, yeah.

Q: And I suppose you still have family back in Cuba.

A: My wife's back there, man.

Q: Ah. It's been years since you've seen your wife, then.
A: You bet.
Q: Yes. Well, naturally, you don't want the Cuban Government to take reprisals on your family.
A: Yeah, sure, that's it.
Q: And I imagine you hope someday to have a part in the eventual freeing of your native land from its Communist overseers?
A: Yeah, we're gonna get em. We're workin at it all the time.
Q: That's right. But in the meantime, you are also volunteering your services—
A: What's that?
Q: What?
A: Volunteerin? What kind of bullshit is this?
Q: Is there something wrong here?
(confused babble of background voices)
A: Yeah, yeah. Just so I get my money, man.
Q: Well, let's leave the money out of it for now. Whether you're getting paid or not, the point is, you are also volunteering your services in the cause of freedom wherever in the hemisphere our pan-American heritage of liberty is endangered.
A: Yeah?
Q: Would you tell us what project you're involved with at the moment?
A: Well, we're gonna get some guns here.
Q: Yes?
A: That's it.
Q: Well, there's more to it than that, isn't there?
A: No, we're just gonna get some guns. They late now, you know that?
Q: Well, tell us about these guns. What they're for, and so on.
A: Oh, yeah. These guns are goin to some people on Ilha Pombo Island.
Q: Tell us about Ilha Pombo Island.
A: Well, it's run by this dictator, Mungu, you know. He's a bad man, you know, he's one sweet son of a bitch.
Q: Uh, without that kind of word, okay?
A: Oh, yeah. Well, Mungu, he's bad. So there's gonna be a revolution and these are the guns they're gonna use.
Q: And what is your own connection with Ilha Pombo Island?
A: Well, you know, we gonna take off from there.
Q: Take off?

A: Yeah. First all these people gonna overthrow Mungu and make a democracy there, and then we gonna go down and build our army there and attack Cuba, you know.
Q: I see. You'll have a staging base in the Caribbean, near Cuba.
A: You got it.
(confused babble of background voices)
Q: What? Oh, all right.
A: Here come them fuckin guns, man. I gotta go now.
Q: Thank you, Ramon.

APPENDIX TWO

Jay Fisher Interview with Luis, Last Name Unknown, Somewhere in Florida, February, Current Year

Q: You are not a native of Ilha Pombo Island, are you?
A: No.
Q: In fact, you're a native of Cuba, is that right?
A: Yes.
Q: One of those forced to flee the current repressive tyranny on that island?
A: Police inspector.
Q: I beg your pardon?
A: Havana police inspector, that's me.
Q: Oh, I see. Under the earlier regime in Cuba, you were on the police force in Havana.
A: Inspector. Vice squad.
Q: Ah. And about these guns that you and your men have just unloaded from the trucks, would you tell us about them?
A: They're guns.
Q: Well, yes. But I mean, further than that. In addition to that.
A: Well, they different kind of guns. All rifles. Some Mausers, eight-millimeter Mausers. Some thirty-oh-six Winchester—
Q: Yes, I see. And could you tell us the purpose of these rifles?
A: They gonna shoot people.
Q: Well, in a larger sense. Could you tell us the purpose of these

rifles in connection with the cause of freedom?

A: They gonna shoot people on Ilha Pombo. The guerrillas there, they gonna take over from Mungu.

Q: And establish a democracy.

A: That's right. The people of Ilha Pombo is oppressed, just like the people of Cuba. That's why we Cuban Freedom Fighters come along to help out. We all brothers together in the war against oppression.

Q: For you, of course, Ilha Pombo Island is simply the stepping stone, is it not?

A: That's right. Once we got a democracy on Ilha Pombo, we can build an army there and go on into Cuba.

Q: And you hope to—

A: No more interview.

Q: Well—I have some more questions here I'm supposed to—

A: No more interview.

Q: Oh. Well . . . uh . . . all right, I—Uh. All right.

TAPE TWO, SIDE ONE

IF YOU STARTED with this tape, don't. I'm going to clearly mark these tapes, but it's possible for things to get mixed up in transit and all that. I'm not accusing you of stupidity or anything, I'm just saying, if you started with this tape, don't. Start with the other tape.

To recap, we are finally at the place that later became known as Base Camp One but that I knew then only as the flamingo rustlers' camp. So. Our vehicles stopped in the cleared dry section in the middle of the building cluster, and we got out to that incredible humidity and heat, and we all stood around inside our sunglasses, drenching our shirts and slacks and socks with sweat, and toward us came half a dozen Latin American types looking exactly like bandidos from a movie about Mexico. On the Network's wholly owned New York City station we sometimes show *Treasure of the Sierra Madre* late at night after the Network programing is done for the day, and this bunch that came out to meet us looked exactly like the bandit gang in that movie, except not so comical. And there were no Federales around to show up at the last second.

It's funny how paranoia can suddenly come out of nowhere and take over your brain, no matter how intelligent and sophisticated you might think you are. I saw this bunch coming toward us, I looked around at the desolation of the area we were in, and for one insane second I thought to myself, *"Ambush!"* Some mad idea about these people murdering us all and selling the mobile units to Mexican TV ran into my brain and immediately back out again.

It's a pity, in a way, that it didn't stay in my brain. Paranoia would have been a good ally at that point, had I only known it.

Anyway, this bunch came up, and their leader, a burly, barrel-chested, fortyish man, came forward smoking one of those crooked little cigarillos that look like a miniature shillelagh, and shook hands with Bob, who introduced us: "Jay Fisher, this is Luis. He heads up this outfit."

Luis took my hand and attempted to grind the bones into meal, all the time giving me a gritted-teeth smile. In my business I run into these machismo-handshake people from time to time, and I've learned over the painful years that the best way to handle it is to squeeze back as hard as possible—not to crush the other guy's hand but to bunch the muscles in your own and lessen the possibility of permanent damage—while at the same time subtly but steadily pushing your arm forward, so that some of his attention and energy has to go into keeping his balance.

Usually, the handshake-as-contest people give up the instant they realize the challenge has been accepted, but Luis was something else entirely. His smile grew more glittery and gritted, he pushed back at me while I was pushing at him, and we might both still be standing there, at *impasse,* if the liaison man from our Miami affiliate hadn't come forward to be introduced in his turn. Luis gave me back my hand, which was wrinkled like a bottom sheet, and turned his tender attentions on the local man, a deeply tanned and deeply worried administrative type named Conford, Richard Conford.

Yes, I know. We'll be hearing more about Richard Conford, but not yet. I want to do everything in chronological order, to be sure I cover all the territory and don't leave anything out. Up to this point in my narrative, Richard Conford is simply the liaison man from the Miami affiliate, along to count the teaspoons and make sure the bunch of interlopers from New York don't go off with any locally owned equipment. (Somebody did take a pair of earphones, by the way, probably inadvertently, and we got a hell of a snotty letter from Conford about a week after we got back to New

York.) And at this specific point in my narrative, Richard Conford is about to shake hands with Luis.

I have seen Conford look surprised and dismayed since that incident,—in fact I've seen him look surprised and/or dismayed more often than not,—but I have never seen him look *as* suprised or *as* dismayed as he looked when Luis took his hand and proceeded to treat it the way the compressing machine at the junkyard treats old automobiles. Beneath the heavy tan, his cheeks and forehead got absolutely white. His mouth dropped open, his eyes started from his head, and his knees actually sagged. I really believe that pain was the only thing that held him up.

Luis contemptuously released Conford's hand and gave me a look of triumph; having conquered one gringo, he'd conquered all gringos.

Bob, meanwhile, was introducing me to Ramon, Luis' second-in-command, a skinny, shifty, bright-eyed little man who made Arnold look like a choirboy. Ramon gave me a suggestive handshake and didn't ask me if I was looking for a girl; I admit I was surprised that he didn't.

The other Cubans weren't introduced and acted as though they hadn't expected to be. They just stood around in the background, slightly awkward and nervous, like spear carriers in a production of local amateur theater.

My sound people and I set ourselves up where we could be filmed without showing any of our vehicles, and Bob produced from his hip pocket a filthy and ragged piece of hotel stationery on which he'd jotted down a few questions he wanted me to be sure to ask in the course of my interviews. I didn't get to ask them all, but a few of them got onto the tape. If you've listened to it, I think you can guess which ones they were.

For the next twenty minutes or so there was a great deal of confusion as the camera crews filmed the buildings and the Cubans and the swamp, and the sound crew and I tried to organize ourselves into a team that was capable of putting legible sound on tape, and then I did the interview with Ramon, in the middle of which the trucks showed up.

Two trucks. Both had Georgia plates, both were moderately old and rattle-trapish, and both were open trucks with slatted wooden sides. The cabs of both had long ago been painted the same red and white pattern, and someone had fairly recently put strips of masking tape over some sort of company name on the doors. It later turned out the red and white pattern matched the pattern used by Gulf Coast Auto Rental, an Atlanta-based outfit that had several trucks similar to these, but nobody has been able to prove that these two particular trucks were owned by Gulf Coast Auto Rental, and the people at GCAR deny the trucks could possibly have been theirs.

Anyway. Big pieces of dirty canvas were thrown over crates in the back of both trucks, about half a dozen crates in each truck. I noticed at the time that the size of the shipment didn't really require two trucks, that the dozen or so crates would all have fitted very easily into just one truck, with room left over, but I assumed the people doing the shipping had some sensible reason in mind, and to be truthful, I thought no more about it. In my own defense I would only point out two things. First, nobody else thought about it, either. Second, I had a number of other things at that time to think about.

The drivers of the two trucks were sullen American Negroes who didn't want to talk to anybody about anything and who vituperatively refused Luis' suggestion that they help with the unloading of the crates. They went over and stood in the shade of one of the mobile units instead and handed a pint bottle of apricot brandy back and forth. The apricot brandy attracted every flying insect for miles around, which added greatly to the joy of the occasion.

In the meantime, the Cubans unloaded the crates. That is, all the Cubans but Luis unloaded the crates; Luis stood to one side and screamed. He screamed in Spanish, a language I don't know—one of the several hundred languages I don't know—and I assume he was screaming instructions to the workers, but for the most part they ignored him and simply went methodically forward, unloading the crates and carrying them over to the nearest usable building and stacking them on the floor inside.

A crate of rifles looks very much like a coffin, except a bit narrower and a bit shorter. It is also, from the expressions on the men carrying them in the heat, very heavy.

While the Cubans carried, our camera crews filmed. We had two of them, and their worst problem was to keep out of each other's picture. The primary reason we had two camera crews was for my interviews. The way we were doing it, the decision hadn't been made yet as to whether or not I would appear in the special, so one camera was showing me from the back and the interviewee over my shoulder while the other camera was bypassing me entirely and simply viewing the interviewee. That gave a wider variety of choice to the editors when the special would finally be put together.

Everything went smoothly almost all the way, and then somebody dropped the next-to-last crate. The Cubans were tired by then, naturally, and their hands were undoubtedly wet with perspiration and therefore slippery, and it happened that a crate being lowered over the tailgate slipped from someone's hands and fell onto the ground. A part of the end of the crate was punched in, but it wasn't really bad, not as though a hole had been made or anything. The crate was still usable.

But Luis carried on as though the whole shipment had just been dropped into quicksand. He ranted and raved and stomped back and forth amid the other Cubans, and they just stood there silently and stared at him, and even from where I was, inside the Mustang—for protection from the bugs as much as for the air conditioning—I could see they were all afraid of him. I mean really *afraid* of him.

Apparently Luis was insistent on finding out which man was responsible for dropping the crate, and the others were all reluctant to tell him. Finally, though, a couple of them did point at a third, and Luis at once became silent. He marched slowly over to the guilty one, who stood there looking terrified, and just stared at him for a minute. Then he said something, fast and low, and all at once punched the man in the face.

You can see this, if you want. We have it on film. We wouldn't have shown it, of course; it just happened that the film crews were still working away at the time it happened.

Well, the man who was punched fell down, and Bob went running out from the shade to make a lot of loud happy noises and pat Luis on the back and cool him down and tell him everything was really okay, just a minor accident, nothing to be upset about, and Luis sulkily but triumphantly allowed himself to be led away. The man he'd punched got to his feet with a bloody nose—blood looks very hot and sticky in the tropics, by the way—and went away to the Datsun wiping his face with his forearm and then rubbing his forearm on his shirt.

The rest of the unloading went on without incident, and afterward I interviewed Luis. Bob came over first, though, and said, "No point saying anything about the little trouble."

"I didn't intend to."

"That's good. You know how it is, the hot Latin American blood."

"Yeah, I saw some of it."

I don't generally feel hostility toward other people, but there was just something about Luis. I kept telling myself I was neutral, I was a reporter, it wasn't up to me to have attitudes about the people I was dealing with, but I just couldn't help it. I didn't like Luis.

And Luis was fond of me, too. I don't know if you can tell from the sound of our voices on the tape or not, but we hated each other roundly. We went through our paces the way we were supposed to, but without joy. And abruptly Luis had had enough, and terminated the interview, and that was that. At first I was prepared to argue the point, but then I saw he was prepared to punch *me* in the nose, so the interview came to an end.

In the meantime, the drivers had gotten back into the trucks, without a word to anybody, and had driven away again, the two trucks jouncing off along the narrow dirt road through the swamp, sunlight reflecting from those few spots that weren't completely eaten by rust, and our crew busily put all its equipment away again. The Cubans produced cans of beer from inside their Datsun, didn't offer us any, and stood in the shade beside the building full of rifles, drinking beer and watching us work.

Bob had been hovering around me the whole time, but Arnold had drifted away shortly after our arrival, and I didn't see him again until we were just about ready to leave. He had taken his suit jacket and shirt off and was walking around in a T-shirt, looking like the guy who gets the sand kicked in his face; I don't believe I've ever seen anybody else that thin and still capable of walking around. Except fashion models, of course, but that's something else. I mean human beings.

The thing that attracted my attention about Arnold, though, wasn't his painful thinness, and it wasn't even that he managed to remain as white as the underbelly of a dead fish no matter how often he was exposed to the sun. No, what attracted my attention was the fact that he had his cigarettes *rolled in the sleeve of his T-shirt!* Shades of the stock car races!

The last ten or fifteen minutes we were there, I sort of walked aimlessly around, feeling as though not enough had happened. We'd taken some film of some crates being unloaded. I'd had two very short and probably useless interviews with people who knew less about what was going on than I did. While I'd been interviewing Luis, Bob had induced a couple of the Cubans to drag one of the crates back out of the building so they could be filmed opening it and inspecting the rifles inside—which the two of them held, by the way, as though they thought they were golf clubs—and that was probably nice, but I still had this vague feeling of incompleteness, as though somehow we should have done more. As though the trip had been a big buildup for damn little. I knew, of course, that this was just one stage in the journey of the rifles and therefore it would only be one small part of the special that would eventually be put together, but I still felt as though we hadn't done enough to justify having come down here.

I mentioned this to Bob on the trip back to Miami, while the air conditioning in the Mustang gradually froze my sopping wet clothes to my sopping wet body, and he said, "Hell, Jay, this isn't all of it. There's the boat too."

"Ah," I said. "The boat. We get to film them loading the guns?"

"Sure," Bob said. "That's what we're down here for."

Arnold turned his head and looked at us in the back seat. "That depends," he said.

I said, "What depends?"

"The boat," he said, and faced front again.

"We'll work that out," Bob told the back of his head.

I said, "What's the problem?"

"No problem," Bob said. "We'll work it out."

And that was the end of that conversation. I know there are those who will fault me on this, and I know it's being said that I was the highest-ranking Network employee present down there in Florida and should therefore have paid more attention to what was going on around me, but I'd just like to point out that "A Sea of Guns" was not my special, not then or later under any other name, but that I had simply been brought along as an interviewer. An interviewer, I might add, who could even be removed entirely before the special was assembled and put on the air. Bob Grantham was the writer, and Mr. Clarebridge had told me specifically that I was under Bob Grantham's orders, which essentially placed Bob Grantham in the role of director-producer. Since the Network, in the person of Mr. Clarebridge, had put its confidence in

Bob Grantham to the extent of making him producer-director-writer of "A Sea of Guns," I had to assume that that confidence was wisely placed.

I grant that I was a regular employee of the Network at that time, on the regular payroll, and that Bob Grantham was at best an irregular employee, but I was *told* that he was in charge. I had to go on the basis of what I was told, and I did.

So much for that.

At any rate, that was the end of the conversation on that subject in the car. As I remember, there was nothing else discussed in the car on the way back that would have any relevance here. Bob told me he was going to get me a date for that night, and so on, but there was no discussion bearing directly on the Ilha Pombo Affair.

Bob didn't get me a date that night, by the way, though he and a girl named Lucinda made one hell of a lot of phone calls.

And it was the next afternoon that I met Linda. I was in the pool again, practicing my dive from the low board as usual, and at one point I surfaced not far from a girl who was clinging to the edge of the pool and waving one arm at me just above the surface of the water. She was a gorgeous creature, wearing one of those bathing caps with imitation curly hair growing out all over it, so that from a distance it doesn't look like a bathing cap at all but real chestnut hair, and when I swam closer to find out what she wanted from me I saw that she had very large and very blue eyes. It was no surprise to me, later on, to discover that the hair under the hairy bathing cap was as blonde as the sun.

Treading water near her, I said, "Did you want me?" She seemed to be looking directly at me, and she'd been gesturing for me to come nearer, but I had trouble believing I was really the one she wanted. I didn't want to play the fool in either direction, not by lunging forward to discover it was someone else she was gesturing to and not by looking over my shoulder and discovering it was me she was gesturing to. So I tread water in her vicinity and said, "Did you want me?"

"Please come closer," she said, and though her voice was no louder than necessary it seemed to me there was a trace of something like panic in the sound of it and in the expression on her face.

So I whisked over to the edge, right beside her, and said, "Is there something I can do?"

Now her expression was one of embarrassment mixed with reluctance. She said, "I'm sorry to ask you, a perfect stranger . . ."

"Not at all," I said. She really had beautiful eyes.

"But you seem like a decent man," she said. "And— This is really very embarrassing."

I didn't know what she wanted, but whatever it was I already knew that if I had it it was hers. "Ask me," I urged. "Anything. Tell me the problem."

"Well, the fact is—" She looked away and bit her lower lip and blushed. Not looking at me, she said, "I lost my top."

I was a bit slow-witted. I looked at her bathing cap first, then realized she hadn't meant that kind of top, and when I looked down through the shifting water I saw that what she'd said was the truth. She'd lost her top. The way the water was sploshing and swirling around it was impossible to see much of anything very clearly, but I could tell at least that much: she'd lost her top.

"It's down on the bottom someplace," she said.

"Your top?" I said. "It's on the bottom?"

"I can't open my eyes underwater; I get a bad reaction to the chlorine. I wouldn't be able to see it or anything."

"Oh," I said. "I see. You want me to go down and get your top."

"If you would," she said, and now she did look at me again and even managed a smile. "I feel like such a damn fool," she said.

"It could happen to anybody," I said. "Be right back." Which I was, since I forgot to take a breath before diving. I remembered halfway down and went back up, where I grinned inanely at the girl, said, "False alarm," took a deep breath, and headed down again.

I saw the thing almost at once, a bright yellow infinity symbol against the pastel blue of the pool bottom. I kicked down to it, grabbed it in one hand, reversed myself, looked up, and fell madly in love.

I think I could recommend that to all men everywhere. If you want to know whether you really love your girl or not, put her in a swimming pool in just the bottom piece of a two-piece bathing suit, dive to the bottom of the pool, and look up. If you see what I saw, you're lost.

What I saw were long, long legs, sort of waving at me, slowly scissoring in the water. Above them, the yellow trunks of the bathing suit, nicely round behind, beautifully flat before, with the pleasant protrusion of the pudenda to add concavity to the stomach. The ledge of love, someone once called that—a delightful phrase. Then the torso building up firmly from the narrow waist, and the breasts, free of restriction but supported by the water. Not large, not small, not anything but nice. Very nice. Then delicate shoulders, and one long arm moving like a reed in the water, the other arm out of the water as she held onto the side of the pool.

First I had seen only her face and known she was beautiful. Now I had seen only her body and knew she was incredible. I could hardly wait to put the two together.

With a great deal of difficulty, I managed to get all the way up to the surface again without touching any part of her body. To do that, of course, I had to wind up out in the middle of the pool again; I used a sidestroke in swimming to her, so that I wouldn't be lifting a bra out of the water every few seconds. "Here," I said. "The Holy Grail, just as I promised you so many years ago."

She smiled and said, "Thank you. You're really sweet." Confidence was already returning to her face and voice.

But then another problem developed. I saw her struggling and beginning to look worried, and I said, "What's the matter?"

"It takes two hands," she said. "Every time I try to put it on, I sink."

So it wound up with me putting it on for her. It took me two hands, too, and *I* sank, but I didn't mind.

When the operation was finally completed, she turned to me and said, "I really don't know how to thank you."

"Easy," I said. "Take it off again." But then I saw her expression snap shut, and I quickly said, "Hey, don't take that seriously, that was just a joke. Off the top of my head, you know?"

"I didn't think you were that kind," she said.

"Oh, I'm not. Listen, you want a drink?"

"Frankly," she said, "after the experience I just had, I desperately *need* a drink."

"Come with me," I said, and we swam together over to the steps and climbed up out of the pool, and I got to put the two parts together, and I was well pleased with the result. Also with the shoulder-length blonde hair that dropped into sight when she took off the bathing cap. I found myself counting how long it had been since the divorce, and it worked out to be approximately seven thousand years, give or take a couple weeks.

Tables with umbrellas were near the pool. We went to one and sat down and ordered a pair of gin and tonics and I introduced myself as me and she introduced herself as Linda McMahon. How beautiful her slender fingers looked without rings.

"I'm from New York," she said.

"So am I." And I told her about my working for the Network.

She said, "I *thought* I recognized you. Didn't you used to be the emcee on *Husband and Wife?*"

"You remember that?" I knew she couldn't be more than twenty-five, and she was probably less.

"My mother watched it," she said, which made me feel wonderful. I suppose something must have showed on my face, because she added, "I did too, a lot of the time."

"Well, it wasn't so long ago as that, was it?" I said, and sucked my stomach in.

Our drinks reached us eventually, and we spent a pleasant hour talking about this and that. She said she was a stenographer with a firm down in the financial district, and I told her quite a bit about the special I was in Florida working on for the Network. I'm afraid I padded my part a bit, but if you ever have a chance to see Linda McMahon, you in the legal department, you'll understand. Believe me you will.

Finally I asked her for a date for that evening, and she said she was sorry, she couldn't, she'd already agreed to have dinner with a boy she'd met on the plane. "Boy," that's the word she used, and naturally I spent the entire evening replaying that word on the tape recorder in my head, trying to figure out from her inflection whether the word meant bad news for *him* or for *me*. In any event, she sounded sorry when she said she was sorry, so I said, "What about tomorrow night?"

"Well, what about your work?" I'd told her we were only waiting around now to film the guns being loaded on the boat and I wasn't sure exactly when that would happen.

"Let's take a chance," I said. "You're here in the hotel; if something comes up I'll call you."

"All right, fine."

"Dinner tomorrow?"

"Dinner tomorrow," she said, and gave me a beautiful smile, and said, "And to think I almost took my week in Puerto Rico."

"Oh, no, don't do that. And don't misunderstand me, but I've got to tell you, I'm glad you lost your top."

She laughed and said, "Don't *you* misunderstand *me*, and I'll tell you so am I."

We talked a while longer, and then she had to leave to get ready for her date. I didn't have anything in particular to do, so I walked her into the hotel. Then I walked her to the elevator. Then I rode up in the elevator with her. She got out on four, and there was nothing left for me to do but go on up to eleven and into my room, where the message light was on by the telephone. I called to collect the message, and it was Bob; call him. I called him, and he said, "It's tonight, chum. Don't make any plans."

"You mean the boat?"

"Easy. The walls have ears."

I remembered how loose my lip had been with Linda McMahon, and felt slightly embarrassed. "Right," I said. "So it's tonight, is it?"

"We'll have dinner together," he said. "I'll come by for you around eight."

"Fine."

He came by for me a little after eight, accompanied by a girl with hair the oddest orange color I've ever seen. It was sort of like the orange of an orange popsicle, but more metallic. She was also very short and had huge breasts and a huge behind. Men turned to look at her, but mostly because she was so startling, not out of any desire to clutch at her body; she was like a caricature of the things the male is supposed to like best in a woman.

I could never figure out Bob's taste in girls, by the way. Several times in the months I knew him he showed up with girls who were right up there in Linda's class, but other times it was weirdos like this orange-headed dumpling tonight, or else one time it would be a very plain girl with no makeup and wearing flat-heeled shoes, and the next night it would be a brunette in sequined harlequin glasses, and you just never knew what the one after that was going to be like. I don't know if Bob had catholic taste or no taste at all, but I do know I never saw a one of those girls twice. On the other hand, his conversation with the girl of the day usually implied that they were old friends who'd known each other for years. Very confusing.

Anyway, Bob introduced the orange-head as Chuckles, which

was an incredible misnomer since she was the original Great Stone Face and never cracked a smile the entire time she was with us, and then the three of us went down to have dinner in the hotel dining room.

By the way, I have pointed out to the people from the accounting department that I had nothing to do with the expense sheets on that trip or any subsequent trip involved with the making of this special—except, of course, for the Ilha Pombo Island trip—and that a comparison of the expense sheets for the other trips with the expense sheets for the Ilha Pombo Island trip will show that where I *did* have control of the expenses, there were none of the anomalies and oddities and unanswered questions that turned up in the expense sheets on the other trips, and I think it would be a good idea for me to point out the same thing now to the legal department, so consider it pointed out. I did not handle the expenses on any trip but the one to Ilha Pombo Island, and I cannot be held accountable for any expenses on any of those other trips, and I refuse to accept the responsibility.

Anyway, a total of three of us ate dinner in the hotel dining room that evening, regardless of what the expense sheets say, and throughout dinner Bob kept making heavy allusions to the fact that he and I were going to go do something mysterious a little later that he couldn't tell Chuckles about, and she stolidly ate her meal and gave every indication of not giving a damn, and after dinner Bob took Chuckles into a corridor corner outside the dining room and nuzzled her a bit and whispered to her and squeezed her behind and gave her his room key, and then he and I went upstairs to collect the film crew, which had been alerted by Bob earlier.

We were a much smaller crew that left the hotel around ten-thirty that night, smaller than the one that had recorded the arrival of the guns at the flamingo rustlers' camp. Bob and I were in the Mustang with a cameraman with a field camera, of the kind used in Southeast Asia, and Arnold was in the Dodge Dart with two sound technicians. Since what we were going to film that night was clandestine and technically illegal, we had to be more circumspect and not call too much attention to ourselves, and therefore we traveled with the minimum. And even that, as it turned out, was too much.

One sidelight. Nothing on God's green Earth has ever looked

more inappropriate than Arnold in a yellow pullover polo shirt and white slacks. The sneakers looked all right, but the yellow shirt and white slacks were beyond belief. I've tried to find something to compare the sight to, but there isn't anything; Arnold in a yellow pullover polo shirt and white slacks was in a class by himself.

He rolled his cigarette pack in the polo shirt sleeve, by the way.

The Dodge Dart went first, since Arnold was the only one of us who knew exactly where we were going, and I followed in the Mustang. Bob had talked about driving the Mustang, but he'd been building himself another quite a bit today and I decided it was probably safer all around if the driving was done by somebody else. The cameraman wanted to do nothing but sit in back and fuss with his equipment, so by process of elimination the driving devolved upon me. That's why I was driving, and the only reason. I wasn't in charge, I was simply driving.

The cameraman, by the way, was Rudy Patelli, who figures more prominently in this report a little later.

At any rate, we headed south out of Miami on Route 1, and somewhere south of Goulds I followed Arnold and the Dodge Dart onto a scrub road to the left, toward the ocean. We traveled a couple miles, and then Arnold stopped, and I stopped behind him, and he got out of the Dodge and walked back, and I cranked down the side window to let in all the humidity and insects, and Arnold said, "You wait here. I'll see what the story is."

"All right."

"Just wait."

"I'll wait," I said.

He nodded and went away, slapping at his neck. I rolled the window up again and devoted myself to killing mosquitoes and other less-identifiable bugs for a while. Bob, who had been silent until now, suddenly sighed and opened the glove compartment and took out a small brown paper bag. Reaching into it, he unscrewed a top, then tilted the bag up and drank out of it. Grinning at me, his expression weird in the dashboard lights, he said, "Insect repellent. Want some?"

"No, thanks."

"Saved it for an emergency. This is it."

Arnold was coming back, and someone else with him. At first I thought it was my old friend Luis—same barrel shape, same arrogantly lazy way of moving—but when he came into the illumination of our headlights I could see it was an older man, milk chocolate in color, with iron gray hair and an iron gray mustache. He was wearing uniform-type clothing—khaki trousers, web belt with brass buckle, short-sleeved khaki dress shirt open at the collar, cordovan paratroop boots—but without any kind of insignia. Arnold, trotting along beside him, looked faintly worried, like a puppy who vaguely suspects he's about to be blamed for something.

They came up on my side of the car, and I rolled the window down. The older man stood there gazing grimly down the road behind the car while Arnold came over and said, "Colonel Enhuelco says no filming."

Bob shouted, "What? What the hell?"

Arnold leaned down and looked past me at Bob. "The guns were already loaded."

"Loaded? What the hell? That's what we came out here for! Colonel! Colonel?"

The colonel—for indeed it was he—didn't move, didn't react in any way, but just kept on glaring grimly down the road behind the car.

I leaned closer to the window—which meant, unfortunately, closer to Arnold, who had apparently never paid sufficient attention to the breath-mint commercials we show—and called, "Colonel? What's the problem?"

The colonel slowly turned his head and looked at me. He looked at me as though *I* were the puppy and I'd just done something on his uniform. He said, "Those wishing to address me do not sit down." He had a heavy accent, but I couldn't figure out what kind. It almost sounded German.

Bob said, "What did he say?"

"He wants us to stand up."

"Oh, for Christ's sake." Petulantly Bob flung his door open and got out of the Mustang, and I opened the door on my side and also got out.

I said, "What seems to be the problem, Colonel?"

"We do not wish to alert the dictator, Mungu."

"Well, this isn't hard news," I said. "There's no intention to broadcast anything we film tonight for several months."

"No filming," he said.

Bob, on the other side of the car, called across its top, "Goddam it, Colonel, that wasn't the deal! You specifically told me—" He reached one arm across the top of the car to make his point, forgetting that the brown paper bag was still being held in that hand. When he thumped his fist on the car, there was an odd *bonk* sound and liquid sloshed from the bag. A sharp aroma filled the air. Bob, looking very embarrassed, withdrew the hand, said no more, and bent out of sight on the other side of the car.

So it was up to me. The cameraman, Rudy Patelli, was still fussing with his equipment inside the car. It was only later that I learned he was filming this whole thing. Of course, the light was so poor—nothing but moon and stars and the backspill from the headlights—that virtually none of the film showed anything usable, and in fact the only figure who can be identified with any assurance in the film is me, but at least Rudy was trying, he was showing initiative, and that's the important thing.

Enough of Rudy. He doesn't have any problems, and I do. And my problem at that specific moment was Colonel Enhuelco. I said, "Colonel, I give you my promise, and the promise of the Network, that none of this will be leaked, that we won't use a thing until the special itself, and that probably won't be for a year or more."

"You want my men and me to take a bad risk," he said. "So you can make money."

It's always embarrassing to be told that you're doing something for money, even when it's true and it's your job. I said, "Colonel, I know we don't have the same kind of motivation you have, but as I understand it there was an agreement that we'd come—"

"The rifles are loaded."

"Then I don't see why we came out at all."

"Go back," he said, and walked by me, brushing me with his shoulder. He went past me, then turned and looked back and said, "Your Network is rich. Let the Network be a partner in our cause, and we will be more friendly."

Bob, without his paper bag, had emerged once more, and now he called across the hood of the Mustang, "Colonel, we already have a deal. You gave me your solemn word of honor—"

The colonel looked at him. "Words are words," he said. "The deal is not good enough." And he turned and walked away, and if Arnold hadn't leaned across the hood just then to say something to

Bob we would have had at least the colonel's back clearly illuminated on film as he walked away from the headlights, because Rudy was shooting through the windshield at the time. But Arnold did lean forward, so it's that yellow polo shirt of his and his sharp chin we see on film, and in case you'd like to know what urgent statement he had to make to Bob and screw up our filming of the colonel, it was, "I told him we had a deal. I told him before."

"Son of a bitch," Bob muttered. "He wants more money."

And there's something else I think bears repeating. It has been said by all concerned in recent days that Colonel Enhuelco never received any Network money, and it certainly does seem to be true that no Network check was ever made out directly to the colonel. But News and Current Affairs does have its slush fund, and sums of money *were* paid out to Bob Grantham for disbursement as he saw fit, and in any event I know full well that I heard what I heard. Bob Grantham said, "Son of a bitch. He wants more money." He said that on the Florida coast south of Miami, on the night I am describing. He said it, and I know he said it, and I will swear to my dying day that he said it. Whatever *he* says, he *said* it.

In any case, it was still hot and muggy and bug-infested out here in the real world, so we all decided at once to get back into the Mustang, Arnold joining us in the front seat. I said, "Now what?" Arnold was in the middle, we were all very cramped, and it was Bob I was trying to talk to.

Bob said, grimly, "I'll tell you what. Rudy, you worked in Indo-China, didn't you?"

"Sure."

"Think you can follow the colonel? He's going out to his goddam ship. Think you can take some pictures?"

"I can try," Rudy said.

"Good boy."

"I'll need somebody with me to carry the power pack."

"Arnold will," Bob volunteered.

We all had to get out of the car again in order to let Rudy and his equipment out of the back seat, and then Bob and I got back into the Mustang—which by now was as bug-infested as the swamp around us—and Rudy and Arnold walked on up past the Dodge Dart and gradually out of range of the headlights.

Bob was feeling surly, one of the few times I've ever seen him without his cheerful the-hell-with-it personality. He kept swigging at his paper bag and muttering to himself, while I slapped myself all over in a useless attempt to keep ahead of the mosquito birth rate. After a while, feeling lonely in the car there, I switched on the radio, and the only station I could bring in with any clarity at all was carrying an address by Billy Graham. So I listened to Billy Graham: "The *pee*-ple to-*day*—in this *mighty land*—are *sore* af-*flic*-ted—and un-*sure* of the *way*."

Bob grumbled and muttered and finally said, "What the hell you listen to that for?"

"I understand his appeal," I said. "It's really good to hear a voice that's so sure of itself. It doesn't matter what he says, it's the tone of voice. You listen to him, you begin to believe that maybe man *is* the captain of his fate and the master of his soul after all. Listen."

We both listened.

"There," I said. "Doesn't that make you feel better? Don't you begin to think that maybe *you* could be sure of yourself too, someday?"

"Screw," he grumbled. "Give me Galen Drake."

"Well," I said, "you're a sophisticate."

Neither of us had much to say after that, but Billy Graham spoke for all of us. He said that plans *can* work out, that one man can buck the system, that Yankee ingenuity and American know-how can lick wildcats, that self-confidence is not absurd, and that the American way of life marches toward an ever purer tomorrow. His *words* didn't say that, his words talked about Christ.

Finally he was finished, and a really inept local announcer came on to introduce a really inept local choir, which proceeded to fire off some underrehearsed hymns at the heavens. "Christ," Bob said, and swigged.

"Christ was a hippie," I said. "I'm surprised Billy Graham doesn't realize that."

"I hate glib shit like that," Bob said, glowering at me.

"No, it's true. Think about driving the money changers from the temple. Can't you see Jerry Rubin doing that?"

"You're going to get the whole Chicago Seven into the New Testament," he said. "For the love of God, don't. I write that crap all the time; don't make me listen to it."

I was offended and said no more, and a few minutes later Rudy and Arnold came back, and I had to get out again to let Rudy and his equipment and another million mosquitoes into the car, and Arnold went back to the Dodge Dart, and I got behind the wheel again and turned off the choir and said to Rudy, "Any luck?"

"Pretty good, I think."

I've seen the film since then, and it does have its own kind of interest. Rudy couldn't get anything—no light—until the colonel was actually out on the water. A rowboat with one man in it had been waiting for him at a crumbly wooden dock, and while the man rowed, the colonel sat in back. Their destination was an aged fishing boat at anchor offshore, a boat about twenty feet long, with an oversized cabin and a general look of having been made somewhere in the islands and not in an American factory. The film shows the rowboat moving steadily toward the fishing boat. Rudy had a zoomar lens and got as close as he could for greater clarity. No faces can be made out, but there are two people in the rowboat, one rowing and a stocky man sitting in the back.

Then, on the film, the stocky man stands up, and for several seconds it looks as though he's doing an imitation of Washington crossing the Delaware, only backward, and then his stance tells us the truth; he's taking a leak. The rowboat plows steadily along, and the stocky man stands there peeing over the stern. Then he does that half-twitch–half-dancestep we've all done in front of urinals all our lives, and sits down again. Shortly afterward, the rowboat reaches the fishing boat and the stocky man climbs aboard, followed by the oarsman. The rowboat is tied with a rather long rope to the stern of the fishing boat, and then the fishing boat begins to move out to sea. There's no sound with the film, of course, but Rudy told me once that the sound of the fishing boat's engine was one of the worst noises he ever heard in his life. "I kept wanting to clear my throat," he said. "You know what I mean?" I knew what he meant.

And that was our second filming session on the "Sea of Guns" special. All that's left to be said is that I got the Mustang stuck in the swamp while trying to turn around and it took us two hours to get the damn car back on dry land again, and everybody blamed me, which I don't think is entirely fair since Bob was the one outside shouting directions at me when it happened. And the suggestion I've heard—that the incident happened because I'd been drinking—is totally untrue and unfair. It is true I had some Lancer's rosé with dinner, and a couple of drinks with Linda in the afternoon, but this was midnight by now and I hadn't had a drink for hours and in any case I hadn't been drunk all day. *I* wasn't the one guzzling from the brown paper bag.

I'm running out of tape again, goddam it. Well, I have time to do the other side before the six o'clock news comes on, but then I think I'm going to take a break for a while. I can see now that this report is going to take a good long while, and I'm sorry, but for my own protection I think I should mention every detail I can remember. So you'll just have to bear with me, and if that elevator is giving you motion sickness why don't you take a break, too?

Did you ever notice how it's impossible to judge visually how much tape is left? I thought sure we were down to the end, but it just keeps running on and

TAPE TWO, SIDE TWO

THIS, as is clearly marked on both the cassette and the package, is side two of tape two. If you are listening to it out of sequence, don't; it will just confuse you.

When last heard from, I was in southern Florida, covered with mud and mosquito bites, having been along on a fool's errand—only one of many, of course—and it is well after midnight, and I am tired and dirty and itchy and hot, and everybody is mad at me and blames me for getting the Mustang stuck in the swamp, and we are all at last on our way back to Miami and the hotel.

Well, we made it, with no further incident, and several employees and guests looked at us rather oddly as we squished toward the elevators, covered with mud and carrying odd pieces of television machinery. I went up to my room and took a leisurely shower and went to bed and was awakened by mosquito bites all night, and in the morning Bob called to say that he'd been in touch with New York—I assumed at the time he meant Mr. Clarebridge—and we were all going back up there this afternoon. At first I thought *great!* and then I remembered Linda, the girl I'd met at the pool the day before. We were supposed to have a date that night.

I said, "Wouldn't they like us to stick around for some follow-up? Maybe we can get Colonel Enhuelco on film after all."

"Nope, it's back to New York," he said. "What the hell, I'm ready to go."

Well, I wasn't. But I didn't have any choice, so I called Linda's room and told her I couldn't make it for dinner tonight after all, and she said, "But I thought you were going to be here until the guns were loaded on the ship."

It seemed to me that wasn't a subject we should talk about on the phone, but on the other hand the one thing worse than being indiscreet on the phone is to *say,* "Don't be indiscreet on the phone" on the phone, so I didn't say that. I said, "It already happened. Last night."

"Oh. Did you get good film?"

"No, they wouldn't let us."

"That's too bad. So it was kind of a waste, wasn't it?"

"Kind of. Listen, you'll be back in New York eventually, won't you?"

"End of the week. Why, you want to take me to dinner up there?"

I thought, Does she have a boy friend in New York? I said, "Well, you have a sort of rain check."

"Then I have to say yes," she said, and gave me her phone number, and I promised to call her the next week, which I did.

But in the meantime, we left on a charter flight that afternoon out of Miami International, landing in Newark because Kennedy had one of its recurrent nightmare breakdowns—whether that one was of equipment or personnel I no longer remember; they all blur together after a while—and the next morning there was a meeting in a conference room at The Hub.

Now, I want to be as exact as I possibly can about that meeting in February, because I know there are now a lot of different versions of what went on in the course of it, and I want my own version to be as close to the truth as I can possibly make it.

All right. There were five of us present. I was there, of course, and so was Bob Grantham, and so was Mr. Clarebridge. The other two were Frank Dorn, Senior Vice President, News & Current Affairs Department, who was Mr. Clarebridge's immediate boss—Mr. Clarebridge, if you will recall, is Vice President, Special Projects, News & Current Affairs Department—and a guy named Joe Singleton, a recent employee whose background was mostly in ad agencies and who was at that time one of Mr. Clarebridge's assistants.

It turned out that Mr. Clarebridge, the evening before, had gone over the film and tape we'd brought back from Florida, and Mr. Dorn had gone over them this morning, and the question now was whether or not to go ahead and do the special. Up to this point, everything had still been more or less in the exploratory stage.

Now, I can't document this, but I can give it as my opinion that there was never a possibility that the people at that meeting would decide to scratch the project. Mr. Dorn kept talking about how he liked the anti-Communist aspect of the situation, and of course he's one of the few people left who will publicly defend the concept of the blacklist. Bob Grantham called him Frank right away, of course, and talked to him in his own language—Communist enslavement off our own coast, that sort of thing—and I noticed that the facts of the case were already being blurred. The only Communist nation in the Caribbean was Cuba, and these guns weren't going to Cuba. They were going to Ilha Pombo, which was a more old-fashioned tyranny without much by way of political theory behind it, and there was some sort of loose vague notion that after Ilha Pombo was captured by the revolutionaries there would be some further step taken in the direction of Cuba. But all of that was never anything but vague and was never the subject under discussion, except that every time the executives from the Network—meaning Mr. Walter J. Clarebridge and Mr. Frank Dorn and the others who were eventually involved—every time they got together to discuss the special they wound up talking about communism and Cuba. And Bob Grantham led the discussion in that direction every time.

What Joe Singleton was doing there I didn't at first understand. He didn't have a heck of a lot to say, but when he did speak it was always in favor of the project, and he early on gave the impression that he had seen our film and listened to our tape with Mr. Clarebridge. (As a matter of fact, no one at all said anything against the project, I remember that distinctly, though of course at this point everybody else remembers having been extremely dubious. I think that was Mr. Clarebridge's recent phrase: "I was extremely dubious.")

Anyway, it eventually turned out that Joe Singleton was going to be put in charge of the project as producer, if we were to go ahead with it. Bob would remain writer; I would remain interviewer and probably narrator.

The only thing that anybody was dubious about, come to think of it, and while on the subject of being dubious, I do remember that Mr. Dorn was dubious about expenses. He said, "From what Walter tells me, we could run into a number of unusual expenses on this project."

Mr. Clarebridge said, "Nothing we can't handle out of the miscellaneous fund, Frank."

And Bob said, "Frank, I'm keeping it as low as I can. But you know how these people are when they know they're dealing with an American corporation."

"I certainly do," Mr. Dorn said, and sounded ominous about it, as though he'd been done in by barbarians from the outside at some time in the past.

There was nothing specific said about bribery at that meeting, or payoffs, or where any of the money would go. Only what I've just said. "Unusual expenses." "Miscellaneous fund." And what Bob said about people dealing with an American corporation. That was all that was said, and at that I believe I remember more on the subject than anybody else present at the meeting.

Mr. Dorn preferred not to give us a decision immediately, so when the meeting broke up we all knew we were going ahead but at the moment we weren't going ahead. We all went back to what else we had to do with our lives, and I returned to the Townley Loomis lunchtime interviews.

My place at the Townley Loomis lunchtime interviews, both during that first trip and the later ones, was taken by Caryl Ten Broeck, one of the grand old men of radio, a Network man from the Network's very beginning. I can never hear the man's name—Caryl Ten Broeck, what resonance—without hearing in my mind's ear those radio broadcasts during World War II, scratchy and tinny and full of static but endlessly dramatic: "Hello, America. This is Caryl Ten Broeck reporting from London." Those were the days!

Caryl makes his living these days doing voice-overs for a frozen food company, but he still considers himself a Network man—as I do, may I say again—and he's always available to fill in when needed. He usually takes part in our local outlet's election night coverage, for instance, doing the analysis on why Staten Island votes Republican, that sort of thing. We all look up to Caryl; even Townley has been heard to admit that Caryl was one of his boyhood heroes, and I think it's really great that he's available to take over things like the Townley Loomis lunchtime interviews. He doesn't need the money, of course; he does it for love of the medium. And if he drinks a lot, well, the old-time boys all did, and Caryl never lets it keep him from doing a first-rate job, and the suggestion that he drinks because he's unhappy is ridiculous. What the hell has he got to be unhappy about?

Anyway, I went back to the Townley Loomis lunchtime interviews myself for the rest of that week and got somewhat caught up on Townley's letters from listeners—Caryl doesn't do the letters, not since the first day the Network gave him the job and it turned out he doesn't really understand how to be tactful on paper—and on Friday the word came down that the project was officially alive, officially called "A Sea of Guns," and I should hold myself in readiness for further traveling.

That was also the day Linda was supposed to be home, so I called her late in the afternoon. She was there, and we made a date for dinner that evening, and the first thing she asked me about when I picked her up at her place at seven-thirty was the Ilha Pombo gunrunning project, and she seemed delighted when I told her it was definitely on. We had a drink in her living room before going out to dinner and chatted about this and that, mostly the Ilha Pombo special, and I told her what I knew of the project up to that point.

Linda's apartment, by the way, was just exactly the kind of thing I'd been looking for myself after the divorce, when I settled for this concrete carton I'm living in now. She lived down in the West Village, just off Hudson Street, and she had the second floor rear in a walk-up building. The living room was long and narrow, with a floor-to-ceiling window at the end overlooking backyards full of hedges and even some small trees, and the left side wall—which was of exposed brick—had a working fireplace in it, though she was always reluctant to build a fire because of how expensive logs are in New York.

This room was furnished in light and airy things, wicker chairs and glass-topped little tables with black wrought-iron legs and things like that, and lots of potted green plants around, and a print of the unicorn tapestry on the wall opposite the fireplace. Also a pseudo-Persian rug on the floor.

Linda was very proud of the apartment, as well she might be, and with only one small hint from me she showed me the rest of the place. A narrow walk-in kitchen was off the living room through a doorway in the short wall opposite the window; toward the front of the building, in other words. She'd put up bright wall-paper and hung copper pots and generally made a Revolutionary War effect in the room which overcame pretty much the lack of a window.

Everything else was off to the right of the living room, opposite the wall with the fireplace. Starting at the kitchen end of the living room, there was first the triple-locked front door, then the door to the bathroom, and finally the door to the bedroom.

She'd done the least with the bathroom. Showing it to me, she grinned and shrugged and shook her head and said, "It keeps seeming hopeless." And she was right. A grim room, windowless, with a thick coating of high-gloss yellow enamel everywhere, it looked like a place where butterflies are subjected to scientific torture.

On to the bedroom, which was airy and light, like the living room, and also had one of those floor-to-ceiling windows overlooking the greenery. The color scheme in here was pink and white, ballerinas danced all over the walls, and I was interested to note that the bed was a double.

Well. We finished the tour and our drink and went out for dinner. The Three Mafiosi, naturally, though I didn't charge the Network. I wouldn't. But the staff knew me there, and when you want to impress a girl on a first date you can't do better than take her to a top-flight restaurant where the headwaiter and everybody else knows your name.

That was our first date, Linda and me, but it was far from our last. We took our time over dinner, then went to sit for a while in Paley Park and listen to the waterfall—she'd never known about its existence before—then went to my place in the West Sixties, and I very shamefacedly reciprocated the tour. She was unfailingly enthusiastic and kind—even offering to swap bathrooms with me—but I knew there was no comparison between the apartments. Hers had been better to begin with, and she'd done better things with it.

By then it was just about eleven o'clock, and I said something about the TV news. She asked me if I would be on it, and I said no, I almost never did hard news, and then she asked if I would mind if we watched it. I said would *she* mind, and she said not at all, she was wondering if *I* would mind, because the fact was she tried never to miss the eleven o'clock news. "I think an informed citizen is the strongest defense a free nation can have," she said.

"I think so too." So I turned on the set, and we sat side by side on the sofa and watched the news.

I kissed her during the sports. Soft delicate lips, very gentle, very nice. Her fingertips stroked the line of my jaw. I kissed her again and rested a casual hand on her knee. Slender legs. In my mind I saw them moving above me through the water.

During a beer commercial I made progress, though not much, and Linda professed interest in the news story that came on next, which ended progress entirely. I don't remember what the news story was; I was thinking about her lips and so on at the time. But the news came to an end, and she said it was time for her to go home, and a first date seemed just a trifle early to suggest that she stay over, so I took her home, kissed her some more in the doorway, suggested that *I* stay over, and she laughed and said, "This time it's *my* turn to give the rain check."

"I can hardly wait for a sunny day," I said, and kissed her one last time, and she went into her apartment, and I went home through February slush, thinking of sunshine.

That was our first date, and the others were like it, more or less through the rest of February and on into March, three and four evenings a week. The rain check remained uncollected, but somehow that was all right. Linda cooked for me from time to time, either at her place or mine, and we went to the movies and three times to plays, and we necked a lot, and if we never quite got to bed it didn't really seem to matter. Except sometimes, I must admit.

Linda was one of the best listeners I've ever met, and as a professional interviewer believe me I know a good listener when I see one. In the course of those few weeks I must have given her my complete life story, down to my grammar school grades, with endless recapitulations of my marriage and virtually tons of shoptalk about my job and the Network, and I kept pulling myself up short and saying, "You can't be interested in all this." But she'd say,

"No, please, I want to hear it." And she sounded as though she meant it.

As with most really good listeners, she was also a very reluctant talker. I knew that she was originally from Omaha, Nebraska, and that her family still lived back there. I knew that she worked in a firm down in the financial district. I understood from various hints she dropped that she'd had a more or less recent tragic love affair that she was still getting over—which explained a lot about her reticence both to talk about herself and to risk any serious steps physically with me—and I wound up with the opinion that she was beautiful, intelligent, somewhat shallow, very pleasant and easy to be with, and totally without unplumbed depths. Of a mental nature, I mean.

Which is why the Women's Lib stuff absolutely floored me.

This was in early March, just before the Nashville trip. I'd had a Townley Loomis lunchtime interview with a man who'd written a book detailing his theory that the Black Panthers were responsible for eighty-seven political assassinations in the United States since 1960, including all the big ones—his book stated, for instance, that Sirhan Sirhan was hypnotized by a black fortune-teller named Madame Sarah into *believing* himself guilty of murder—and it was nearly three-thirty before I left the restaurant. The reason it was so late, whenever we had a *bona fide* nut on the show we always taped at least an extra half-hour of answers so we'd be able to edit out anything he might say that we wouldn't want to go out over the air. This guy had anti-Semitism, the Black Panthers, and the Crusade Against Communism all intermixed so totally in his head that it was hardly possible to ask him to pass the salt without getting a response too inflammatory to get on a program like the Townley Loomis lunchtime interview. He didn't belong on our show in the first place; he really belonged on one of those late-night radio things with the flying-saucer people and the old troupers who write their vaudeville reminiscences, but this kind of booking goof did occasionally happen, and we just had to live with it.

So it was almost three-thirty when I staggered at last from the General Texachron Building—The Three Mafiosi is on the twenty-first floor there; I don't know if you people in the legal department would be in the economic position to know that or not—and damned if the Women's Liberation Movement didn't have a protest demonstration going on out front, right in the middle of Sixth Avenue, which you people in the legal department probably call The Avenue of the Americas.

Frankly, I like the Women's Lib women. They always make me horny. They move their bodies around a lot and jump up and down, and the more excited and strident they get the softer their bodies look. There's something very interesting in there about opposites, or action and reaction, or something like that. Also, most of them in the midtown area are secretaries or researchers or whatnot in the office buildings, and when they're going to have a demonstration they all take their bras off and leave them in the desk drawer, and when they hit the street their breasts are loose under their blouses or sweaters or dresses, and I kind of like that too. And then when they jounce around, a lot of them get themselves excited, and pretty soon there's all those nipples pressing against cloth everywhere you turn, which is also pleasant.

I would say, generally speaking, that I'm in favor of the things the Women's Lib women want. I think they ought to get equality of the sexes, I think it would make things a lot easier for men as well as women if we all moved through life with an equal handicap—but not yet. I'd like to see some more demonstrations first.

Anyway, this one had that sort of manic imagination that characterizes the Women's Lib, and I stopped—everybody stopped—to watch awhile. They had brought out an effigy of Bluebeard, and a couple of them were shouting about Bluebeard mentalities in the boardrooms of the corporations, and they were building themselves up to set fire to the Bluebird effigy, and I was watching them all and smiling happily, and there was Linda!

I didn't recognize her at first. She was bouncing around with the best of them, her face flushed with excitement, blonde hair swirling around her head, some of it plastered by perspiration to her forehead, and I gazed upon her with both astonishment and a suddenly developing lust. For the first time in the month or so I'd known her, I actively craved to possess the body of Linda McMahon.

I hope I'm not embarrassing you, there in the elevator, and if I seem to be going into extremely private detail on this subject, I think you will understand; as it eventually turns out, there's a reason for it. I want to be just as explicit about my developing relationship with Linda McMahon as I am with anything else that happened in the last several months. So if you feel the need to stop the elevator and this tape for a while so you can go take a cold shower and jog up and down the legal department halls for a few minutes, I'll certainly understand.

However. The point I want to make right now is a perhaps delicate one, and also a bit tricky. I fell in love with Linda down in Florida, underwater, but somehow it was an ethereal love, not really a very physical love at all. I am not a sexual maniac or a victim of satyriasis, but on the other hand I wouldn't say I was particularly undersexed either, and I think my former wife, Marlene, about to become Marlene Bricker, will if necessary corroborate that statement. Our problems weren't in bed. In fact, until Linda entered my life I had been undergoing rather severe withdrawal symptoms which had shown no sign of easing, and I had seriously contemplated three or four times the possibility of lifting my self-imposed lifetime ban on paying for it, and only the thought of what I would think of myself the next day dissuaded me. But Linda seemed to cool my fevers without actually treating them. She herself was so cool, so neat, so white-glove *trim* that sexual desire was only a sonar echo of its former submarine self. Linda looked, in fact, like the kind of girl who sings with patriotic choruses that wear straw hats, blue blazers, and white skirts, and who ever lusted after any of *them?*

But. Seeing this impassioned, red-faced, yowling girl in the middle of a mass of wriggling humanity on slushy Sixth Avenue in the middle of the afternoon on a sunny but blustery March day, I suddenly felt the jolt of lechery in my innards, and the submarine reappeared and at once began to surface.

As I stood there, slightly dizzy with this unexpected burst of passion inside my skull, Bluebeard too was set on fire, and an instant later the cops came. And there I saw the one exception to the cops' elbow-plucking rule; when the object of their attention is a good-looking girl without a bra on, they will not grab her elbow.

Well. A lot of the women decided to get the hell out of there, and a lot of the women went as limp as their physical properties permitted, and some of the women—Linda was an instigator, one of the instigators, of this group—decided to fight back and went surging into the line of police with fingernails flashing.

It was going to be trouble. In fact, it was trouble. Without a thought for anything in my head, not even remembering that as a reporter—more or less—I was committed to a life of noncommittaldom, I surged at once into the melee, fought my way to the side of my love, put my arm around her waist from behind, lifted her in the air, and struggled backwards out of the mass of punching people again, Linda riding my hip and slugging it out with people as we went by.

There was a phone booth straight ahead. I made for it, evading both Women's Lib women who wanted to scratch my eyes out and cops who wanted to grab my elbow, reached it at last, pushed open the folding door, shoved Linda inside, followed her, and slammed the door shut behind us. We were now in a rectangular fishbowl, glass on all four sides of us, struggling men and women careening and carrying on all around us.

Linda, gasping, panting, still struggling, almost let *me* have it before she realized who I was. Then she stared at me and said, "Jay!"

"I just rescued you," I said, and leaned against her, pressing her into the closed door of the phone booth while I kissed her more meaningfully than I'd ever done before.

Passion is passion, and it changes from one objective to another in the twinkling of an eye. Linda, her adrenalin already flowing with the prospect of a fight, remained startled and unresponsive to my kiss for a second or two, but then abruptly shifted gears, threw her arms around me, and returned the kiss in a way I hadn't known she was capable of.

The next couple of minutes were half animal, half divine. Linda squirmed her body against mine, I stroked her braless breasts, I held the pert moons of her behind, I rested my palm on the ledge of love. People thumped and bumped into the glass walls all around us, but they were too busy to care about us, and we were too busy to care about them. A group of male spectators had waded in to fight with the cops by now, the Women's Lib women had for the most part become the spectators, and a donnybrook was developing between attaché cases and nightsticks.

I had Linda's skirt up, and I was trying to get her panties down. She was gasping and groaning and biting my lips and my jaw and my neck, and at the same time one of her hands was trying to fight me off, and I don't know what would have happened in the next couple of minutes if the phone hadn't rung.

She at once went rigid—I had been rigid for quite a while—and pushed away from me, saying, "You better answer that." She didn't meet my eye.

I didn't want to lose the moment. I still held onto various parts of her. "It isn't for *me,* for God's sake," I said, and tried to pull her close again.

"You never know," she said, plucking my hands from her body.

"Nobody knew I was going to *be* here!" It was an insane conversation, and I knew it, and the phone constantly ringing in our closed close quarters didn't help much.

"Well, maybe it's for me," she said. "But you answer it, I don't want anybody to know I'm here."

"I—" But there was nothing left to say, and finally it was easier to just answer the phone; at least it stopped it from ringing. "Hello?"

"Delicatessen?" A woman's voice, middle-aged.

I raised an eyebrow at Linda. "No, it isn't the delicatessen," I said. "You've got the wrong number."

"Are you sure?"

"Am I sure? Of course I'm sure! Wrong number!" And I hung up, and tried to recapture the moment with Linda, who had cooled a hell of a lot faster than I had. "Hey," I said. "Where were we?"

"About to make a terrible mistake," she said. She still looked fevered but also now somewhat frightened and not really passionate in any way anymore.

"Love is never a mistake," I said, and reached for her, and the phone rang. "Oh, *damn!*" I cried.

"I'm not here," she said.

"I know, I know." I answered the phone. "Hello?" I don't believe I sounded very friendly.

"Hello, delicatessen?"

"Lady, this isn't the delicatessen!"

"But it has to be the delicatessen. The delicatessen is what I dialed; the delicatessen is what you got to be."

"This is not a delicatessen. It's too *small* to be a delicatessen!"

"I know I dialed the delicatessen," she insisted.

I thought of hanging up; no, she'd just call back again. Could she be persuaded? I doubted it. I sighed and said, "All right, it's the delicatessen."

"I knew it," she said; she was very calm in victory. "You got a pencil?"

"You want to give me an order?"

"Why would I call the delicatessen if I didn't want to give an order?"

So I took her order. It went on and on, and I tried reaching out and stroking Linda to keep her attention, but it was already lost. She shrugged my hand away and continued to look through the glass at the mob surging and struggling all around us. She was no longer a passionate part of that mob—or of our private mob in the phone booth—but seemed a deeply absorbed spectator, interested in watching it the way some bright children are interested in watching chemistry experiments.

"You got that?"

Was she going to ask me to read it back? "I've got it," I said. "I've got to hang up now, the phone is ringing." And I hung up.

Linda glanced at me. "What are you going to do about the order?"

"Fill it, naturally. I think I've got a sideline."

She nodded, her attention still mostly on the chaos outside, and then she did a small double take and looked at me and grinned broadly and said, "Well, hello!"

"Fancy meeting you here," I said.

"Just what I was going to say. Oh, you mean—" She gestured at the melee outside.

"You never told me you were in Women's Lib."

"Well, it didn't seem like a boy-girl kind of conversation topic."

I had to agree with that, and to applaud a mind that could become deeply involved in an issue like this and still know when it would be inappropriate to talk about it. I said, "You get into this sort of thing often?"

"Not this far uptown."

"I think you need me around as a permanent rescuer."

"Usually it's much more peaceful than this," she said, and looked outside again. Sirens were wailing in the distance, a dozen people were sitting on the curbs holding their heads or lying full length on the sidewalk, and the fighting seemed to have settled down. "I'd better get going," she said. "I'm hours late for work."

We had attained something there in that phone booth, a new level in our relationship, and I didn't want it to get lost again. I reached out and touched her arm and said, "I like you when you're liberated."

She blushed, hot and red, and looked away from me. "I was—excited."

"I know. I liked it."

"Well— I've really got to—" She struggled to open the door behind her without getting any closer to me, which wasn't possible, and I did nothing to help. "I'm really awfully late and— I do thank you for rescuing me, I— Why don't you call me tonight?"

"Here?"

"No, at— Oh!" Her laughter had something hysterical in it, and she finally lunged the door open and burst out onto the sidewalk. "Call me!" she cried, blinking furiously in embarrassment and nervousness, and waved a nervous hand at me and hurried away along the sidewalk, southbound.

I came out of the phone booth and stood on the sidewalk and watched her, enjoying the way she moved, the way she looked, until there were too many other people in the way and I couldn't see her anymore. And then a cop grabbed my elbow and said, "I said to move along."

"Oh," I said. "Certainly, officer."

"And none of that wise-ass back talk," he said. He was very irritable.

I walked away, thinking about various things, and when I got back to The Hub there was a memo on my desk that Joe Singleton wanted to see me in his office. Joe was now officially the producer of the "Sea of Guns" special, and I took it for granted he wanted to see me about the next step in that project, and he did.

"Bob Grantham just called from Nashville," he said. "There's a shipment of guns going through near there tomorrow. He's set it up so we can film and also do some interviews. We'll take a late flight out tonight."

Which we did. I called Linda at her place that evening and told her about it, and the news seemed to excite her, anything about the "Sea of Guns" special always excited her, but as for myself I felt lousy. I had really been looking forward to going over to her place that evening and finishing what we'd started in the phone booth that afternoon, and now of course it wasn't going to be possible. But I'd see her in a couple of days, when I got back from Nashville. "I can hardly wait," she said.

"Neither can I," I said.

I don't know, I suppose I could describe all these other trips in minute detail, but unless I draw the line somewhere I'm never going to get finished with this report, and I can feel my voice getting hoarse already. Frankly, the trips between Florida in February and Oklahoma in May all pretty much blended in together. They were all like the Florida trip, really, except shorter and duller. We have film and we have interviews from all the trips, and you can take a look at them if you want, but nothing really very interesting happened in the course of any of them. I never heard anybody talk about money; I never heard anybody talk about anything that would now be of interest. Joe Singleton and I always traveled together on these trips, and our cameraman was usually though not always Rudy Patelli, and sometimes Bob was with us from New York and sometimes he was already at the other end when we got there, and Arnold appeared and disappeared in odd and unpredictable ways and didn't seem to do much of anything.

We made four trips, all in all, between the beginning of March and the end of April, and we gradually worked out the route of the guns, though our trips weren't in proper sequence to follow any one shipment of guns from beginning to end.

The shipments began in a place called Herkimer, Oklahoma, which isn't very far from Oklahoma City. They traveled via truck on Interstate 40 and US 64 to a small town near Little Rock, Arkansas, where they were stored for a while in a barn on a farm that seemed to specialize in lima beans. Then other trucks picked the cases of guns up and took them via Interstate 40 and US 70 northeast to the vicinity of Nashville, where they were kept on the premises of a bankrupt tractor dealership. From there, yet different trucks took the guns via US 41 and Interstate 75 to an abandoned railroad station outside Atlanta. (We got some nice film here of the rusty abandoned railroad tracks and the little green railroad station building and the weeds growing up everywhere.) Then it was Interstate 75 to Gainesville, Florida, where the cases were stored in a shed out behind a country bar-restaurant, until more trucks would pick them up and take them down to the flamingo rustlers' camp below Miami.

From all the different shipments we filmed over those two months, I began to believe that eventually every rifle in the world would wind up on Ilha Pombo Island, which might not be such a bad thing when you stop to think about it. But the notion of following one specific shipment of guns from beginning to end never did work out in practice, and we wound up with film showing different shipments at different times on different stages of the route.

Not that it made that much difference. We could very easily have rearranged the film segments to imply one shipment moving from stage to stage, and I'm sure that's what we would have done if the special had ever actually been made.

Anyway, the main trip we were all waiting for was the one to Herkimer, Oklahoma, to see Mr. Jaekel "Jack" Grahame, the licensed arms-dealer from whom the rifles were coming. It was apparently very difficult to get Mr. Grahame to go along with the idea, because Bob and Arnold made half a dozen trips to Oklahoma before finally, in early May, a firm appointment was set up with him and we made our arrangements to fly out to Oklahoma.

During these two months, by the way, I went on seeing Linda between my Ilha Pombo trips, but the fire we'd ignited in that phone booth in early March was out again, and nothing I could seem to do would stir it up once more. She was the same cool, friendly, lovely, intelligent, pleasant but somehow nonsexual girl she'd always been. I talked with her about Women's Lib, but her responses were always reasonable instead of impassioned, which wasn't what I wanted. I considered following the Women's Lib demonstrations around Manhattan in hopes of re-establishing the laboratory conditions that had produced such good results the last time, but male intuition told me the same stimulus wouldn't work twice; I knew now that a really lusty wench lived down inside cool, calm Linda McMahon, but it would take something other than a Women's Lib brawl to drag her to the surface a second time, and I just couldn't seem to figure out what that something might be.

Along about the middle of May, we finally took off for Oklahoma. Joe Singleton, Rudy Patelli, an assistant cameraman, two sound technicians, Bob Grantham, a lot of equipment, and me. We landed in Oklahoma City at four-thirty in the afternoon, which meant we drove to our downtown hotel through the rush hour, which meant we were all irritable and hot and tired by the time we got to the hotel, where we discovered that no one had made the reservations that were supposed to have been made for us. Angry phone calls to our Oklahoma City affiliate. Angry phone calls to The Hub in New York. Angry scenes with assistant hotel managers. And finally Bob said, "Let me call Jack," meaning Jaekel "Jack" Grahame, the man we were here to see. He borrowed an assistant manager's office, made a phone call, came back out a couple minutes later, and said, "It'll be okay. Just wait a couple minutes."

We did, and it was. The assistant managers, who had been relishing up to that point the chance to be snotty to people from New York, suddenly became obsequious and rubbed their hands together a lot. We got suites, we got half a high floor to ourselves. Everybody loved us. The management sent up baskets of fruit.

"I want to meet this guy Grahame," I said. I was impressed.

"That's what we're here for," Bob said.

After dinner we got into three rented cars and drove out to Herkimer, through that sleepy little town, and out a blacktop road until we came to a turnoff on the right barred by a tall wrought-iron gate with brick gateposts and wrought-iron fencing that stretched away along the roadside to right and left. Triple strands of barbed wire topped the gate and fence.

There was a small metal box attached to the left gatepost; Bob got out of the lead car, opened this box, and spoke briefly on the phone inside it. As he was getting back into the car, the gate slowly swung inward, all by itself, without a sound.

As we drove on through, Joe Singleton, who was in the same car with me, said over his shoulder to Rudy Patelli in the back seat, "You'll want to come back here in the daytime tomorrow and shoot some film of this."

"Huh," Rudy said. "Why don't we just use some footage from a James Bond movie?"

It was hard to see much, in the darkness. We drove amid stately trees, oaks I think, along a fairly narrow blacktop road, until we came to a large, sprawling brick building, two stories high, with four white pillars across the front and an impressively large main entranceway. We stopped the cars and climbed out and walked up the slate steps onto the slate veranda, and as we approached the wide white front door it opened and a man in green velvet livery invited us in. "Mr. Grantham," he said, "Mr. Singleton, Mr. Fisher, if you would come with me, Mr. Grahame is expecting you. If you other gentlemen will go with Albert, you will find beer and sandwiches in the kitchen."

Albert was also in green velvet livery. Looking blankly at one another, the crew members went off in Albert's green velvet wake, while, looking blankly at one another, Joe Singleton and Bob and I went off in the other one's green velvet wake.

Damn. I'm running out of tape again. I did an interview with Grahame during that trip, and I want you to listen to that before you go on with the rest of my report, but I'd like to describe Grahame a little bit on this tape first. I'll do it fast; maybe I can fit it in.

Jaekel "Jack" Grahame is six feet seven inches tall, approximately fifty years of age, is in perfect physical condition, has silver gray hair—a lot of it—a firm square jawline, and piercing steely blue eyes. I never saw him when he wasn't holding a rifle in his hands, just as there are people you never see without their pipe. He walks around with a rifle as though it were a walking stick or a pencil or nothing at all, and he sort of strokes it while he talks. He met us in the downstairs library of his home, a large echoing room with a tile floor and floor-to-ceiling bookcases full of army officers' memoirs, histories of wars, volumes of battle memorabilia, and an incredible variety of books about guns. He was born and raised in the United States and has no particular accent, but he always struck me as somehow more European than American. Perhaps Prussian.

The interview I want you to listen to wasn't done that night but the next afternoon, with the two of us sitting beside the swimming pool out behind his house, while his servants showed our crew around the warehouses tucked away in the woods out ahead of us. The first evening, we just talked and he showed me around his estate a bit, but I won't be able to describe that on this tape. I'll put it on the beginning of the

APPENDIX THREE

Jay Fisher Interview with Mr. Jaekel "Jack" Grahame, at the Grahame Estate Known as "The Oaks," May, Current Year

Q: It's really beautiful here, Mr. Grahame.

A: Thank you, I think so. One likes to visit the metropolitan centers from time to time, but it's always good to be home again.

Q: You visit the metropolitan centers often?

A: Business carries me, from time to time.

Q: Which gets us to our topic for today—your business. You are in the business of selling guns.

A: And other military equipment, yes. I am a private munitions dealer, licensed by the United States Government.

Q: I take it your usual customer isn't, say, the weekend deer hunter.

A: No, not quite. My usual customer is a government, in fact, though I do sell to private citizens. I sell to those who have the purchase price, like any businessman, if their patronage will not endanger my license.

Q: Could you tell us some of the governments that have been your customers in the past?

A: Frankly, I'm reticent to name names. Not that anyone has done anything wrong, but governments—like private citizens—prefer to deal with a man who can keep his own counsel.

Q: Then you wouldn't want to talk about where your guns have gone in the past.

A: Well, they're not *my* guns actually. I don't manufacture them. I am the well-known middleman; I operate between the manufacturer and the consumer. And as to where they've gone, most of my customers over the last several years, I would say, have been in South America.

Q: South American governments.

A: And other groups in that area, yes.

Q: Other groups? Would Communist guerrillas in Peru, for instance, have been doing any of their fighting with guns bought from you?

A: Well, it's difficult to tell, of course, in this turbulent world of ours, where one's guns might eventually turn up. I do not sell directly to pro-Communist insurgency groups—our own government would frown on that—but I have no doubt a shipment now and again finds its way into the hands of Castroites and other leftist revolutionaries to the south. It would be pleasant, of course, if we could keep them from getting arms—we could pick them off at our leisure then, couldn't we?—but I'm afraid it rarely if ever works out that way.

Q: What would you say, Mr. Grahame, is the morality of the gun?

A: The morality of the gun? What an odd phrase. I would say— I would say that the morality of the gun is the morality of its user, wouldn't you?

Q: Then guns themselves have no moral value? It depends how they're used.

A: Guns . . . The fact of the matter is, you know, the gun is the cornerstone invention of our civilization. I've heard the argument that the automobile is the center, and I've even heard that television, your medium, is the center, but in point of fact the center is the gun.

Q: Really?

A: The gun is power, that's obvious. It is the raw material of power, and power is ultimately the only civilizing influence in the world. It was the handgun that brought civilization to the American West, for instance. The gun is the primary tool in situations of mob control, which is to say, in the formation of societies. The gun determines territorial claims, which is to say national boundaries. The gun determined that you and I would speak English now, rather than French or Spanish or Portuguese. The gun determined that we would be here at all, and that the Indian would not.

Q: The Indian is still here, though, isn't he?

A: Herded into reservations, by men with guns. If there were no guns, men would not be able to build cities, because all the bricks would be stolen the first night. If there were no guns, estates like this would be overrun by the scruffy mob. And as population gets more and more out of hand, the gun will be increasingly the only determinant of which of us will live which sort of life.

Q: You credit guns with the sort of power that most people give to money.

A: Without the gun, most people wouldn't have their money. Not for long. And with the gun, it is possible to get money, women, or whatever else you fancy in this life.

Q: Excuse me, Mr Grahame, your words could be misinterpreted there. I know you don't mean to imply approval for armed robbery or rape or—

A: Why not? I am hardly in a position to favor arms restrictions. Once we accept the idea that society is valuable, that our civilization was worth the building and continues to be worth the saving, we must take the next step and agree that the tool which built our civilization is also valuable and, to use a moral term, good. That tool is the gun, and no usage of the gun could be considered evil. Now, if some dolt takes a pistol and holds up a bank, I would disapprove, but only of his tactics, not his choice of equipment. His tactics will put him directly in opposition with a superior force of men armed with more guns; that is to say, he will be caught and perhaps shot. The gun is power, true; it is the central tool of human civilization, true; but as with any tool and any form of power, some intelligence must be employed by the operator.

Q: Well, then, what should he do instead of robbing a bank? He wants money, he wants a better life, and your prescription is that he go out and get a gun. What should he do with it?

A: He should first learn military science, which is, after all, the science of the use of the gun. And one of the first lessons in military science is, Never attack a superior force.

Q: Except in guerrilla warfare.

A: Hit and run, exactly. Rather than robbing banks, our dolt, if he is a determined loner, would be much better off mugging stray citizens in dark alleys. You notice how many of our fellow beings in the major cities have independently come to this same conclusion; bank robberies are down, muggings are up.

Q: And you don't disapprove of mugging.

A: Certainly not, unless I am the one mugged. But if I strongly needed money, and I had a gun, and you had not, I would certainly mug you.

Q: Heh heh. Well, then, I guess it's lucky for me you're doing well in your business.

A: Yes, it is.

Q: Yes. Well— Uh—

A: Of course, there are other things our hypothetical dolt can do. If he can find a sufficient number of individuals who agree with him that he should be wealthy and powerful, and if *they* are armed, he can mount a revolution and overthrow the government of the United States and set himself up as dictator. On a smaller scale, he can still do what any number of American adventurers used to do, which is take his gun to South America, overthrow a government down there, and either become dictator himself or put a local figurehead up in front.

Q: All of these are unlikely, uh—

A: Yes, of course. But possible. And there are still the more direct ways to turn the gun into power, money, influence, and the good life. One can become a Mafia killer, a Medal of Honor winner, a circus sharpshooter, a Presidential bodyguard—the list is really quite long.

Q: And you disapprove of none of these occupations?

A: Certainly not. They employ the equipment I sell.

Q: Not even Mafia killer?

A: Why pick that one out? The purpose of a gun, of any gun, is to project at high speed a piece of metal into a human body in such a way as to stop that human body from functioning. The Mafia killer is certainly employing his gun in the precise way the manufacturer had in mind.

Q: Wouldn't munitions manufacturers generally say they have self-defense in mind?

A: And quite properly so. All shootings are self-defense. Self-preservation requires that we keep ourselves alive and struggle to attain our goals. No one has ever fired a gun at anyone else with any other purpose in mind.

Q: You mean if a Mafia killer knocks on my door and shoots me when I open it, it's self-defense? Even if I'm not armed and he never saw me before in his life and is just doing it for money?

A: You've just answered your own question. Money. What the gun is to civilization, money is to the individual. Most thinkers on the subject, it seems to me, have reversed the functions of the two, by claiming that guns protect the individual and money is the fuel of society, whereas guns keep society moving and healthy and money gives the individual what he needs to sustain his individual life. If someone shot you for money, whether he intended to collect from an enemy of yours or out of your own pockets, his need for money is a simple, clear-cut demonstration of self-defense in action.

Q: Well—I'm kind of at a loss. I never heard quite this argument before.

A: Possibly not. We all live by this creed, but it's entirely possible you've never heard it articulated before.

Q: We all live by it?

A: We live in a world in which individuals who consider themselves to be in opposition to the war in Vietnam can use the phrase "inflated body counts" without ever being appalled by the linguistic ghastliness of what they have done.

Q: I'm not sure I follow you.

A: If human beings truly opposed war—any war—as these individuals claim, they would be unable to *consider* counting bodies, much less counting inflated bodies. The only true war protest would be to continue vomiting until one had sickened and died. I have not as yet heard of this happening.

Q: What about the people who burned themselves to death?

A: It would have been more humane for them, and more profitable for me, if they'd shot themselves.

Q: Uh. Yes, uh— A couple of, a couple of minutes ago you said something about guns being manufactured to shoot human beings. But what about hunters?

A: I believe the psychological term is "sublimation." The desire to kill people is very strong in these individuals, and they ease the pressure somewhat in a more or less socially approved way. It has been remarked in the literature that man is virtually the only animal that kills its own kind. Ants, too, as I remember. But no one seems to have noticed that man is interested *exclusively* in killing his own kind. He will kill other animals for food or to counter neuroses, but throughout human history most of our race's time and energy and resources have been devoted to killing one another. We even teach our children all about it in school and call the topic history.

Q: You talk as though this isn't just a job to you, but as though you came to it out of conviction.

A: In a way, I did. The family has been in munitions sales for three generations. My grandfather sold rifles to the Indians out in these parts.

Q: Wasn't that illegal?

A: Not according to Indian law.

Q: In any case, you yourself grew up surrounded by guns.

A: Not precisely. My father wouldn't permit firearms in the house.

Q: He wouldn't?

A: He believed power shouldn't be handled carelessly.

Q: But you have guns in the house.

A: There are no children in my house. The line ends with me.

Q: And will your business end with you?

A: Hardly; it's too profitable. I am only a shareholder now, actually. I sold a controlling interest in the company to a New York–based syndicate in 1956.

Q: Oh, really? But you remain active in the company.

A: I remain the company. The majority stockholders furnish capital and contacts and frequently smooth the way with our government and other governments, but this is still, at the sales level, very much a one-man operation.

Q: You do all the selling yourself.

A: Yes.

Q: And what is the company name now?

A: The same as ever—Grahame Arms Sales, Incorporated. Of course, now we are a subsidiary of a much larger firm, a conglomerate.

Q: Oh, really? Would you have any objection to mentioning which firm?

A: It's complicated, actually; I have trouble with it myself sometimes. The hierarchy of angels in heaven is no more complex. We are a subsidiary of a company which is a subsidiary of a holding company which is—I'm not sure I'm remembering all the steps here—a subsidiary of a conglomerate called General Texachron.

Q: Is that right! I have lunch in their building a lot, in New York. The Three Mafiosi.

A: An adequate menu.

Q: Gee, I think it's— Uh. So. In this out-of-the-way corner of Oklahoma, a one-man operation turns out to be a part of a giant American corporation.

A: We are all parts of giant American corporations these days. The world alters, and we all adapt to the new conditions. As a matter of fact, I foresee the day—probably not in my own lifetime, but perhaps in yours—when the question of money versus guns as the seat of all power will be given its decisive test. The conglomerate corporations, which are already interindustrial and international, will eventually begin to think of themselves as having formed a new kind of social structure making national boundaries obsolete. Those whose survival depends upon national boundaries, such as generals and senators, will naturally reject this idea, and the inevitable result, it seems to me, will be a new kind of war. Between, say Chrysler Corporation and France.

Q: Who will win?

A: Who won the Hundred Years' War?

Q: Well . . . I don't know.

A: No one. They're all dead. And something else came along—us.

Q: That's what will happen again?

A: That's what always happens. We kill one another, and more come along to take our place. And for one period of history the Grahame Arms Sales company will continue to be here to expedite the process. And now I believe I've had enough sunlight and enough questions. Shall we go indoors?

Q: Yes, of course.

TAPE THREE, SIDE ONE

THIS IS THE BEGINNING of tape three, God help me. If you've started it out of sequence, stop at once and find the right place in all these tapes.

Will I ever get finished? I was going to eat dinner, I put a TV dinner in the oven, and when I took it out and lifted the foil off it, a puff of steam rose up full of the smell of wet garbage, and I just couldn't do it. The food's still out in the kitchen, cooling in its aluminum tray, and I'm back here in the living room, brooding at my blank television screen and talking talking talking into this little microphone here.

I hope you took the time to listen to the Grahame tape, you in the elevator, because I'm going to refer to it from time to time. Like for instance, his mentioning General Texachron. At the time of that interview, I didn't yet know that the *Network* is a subsidiary of General Texachron, meaning that Jaekel "Jack" Grahame and I are essentially co-workers for the same company.

I find that difficult to think about, by the way. I suppose medieval man found the stars difficult to think about in the same fashion; too high, too far away, too incomprehensible, too huge, too nonhuman. I have thought of myself as a Network man for the last twelve years, and I'm going to go on thinking of myself that way. The Network is large enough for me to think about; to think of myself as a Texachron man would require a leap of imagination, or faith, or religious frenzy, that I'm just not capable of.

Well, that's neither here nor there. The interview with Grahame speaks for itself, and— Sorry, I didn't mean that the way it sounded.

Actually, the most interesting thing he said to me isn't on the interview tape at all. He said it the night before, when I first met him, in that odd library of his full of gun lore and yesterday's military campaigns. He wanted to chat with us New Yorkers about New York—the weather, the latest strikes, that sort of thing —and volunteered the information that he himself traveled to New York constantly, primarily for cultural enrichment. Then he said, and this is the line I remember, "I believe I have seen every program S. Hurok has ever presented." And he smiled, and added, "Except circuses."

I remember what Joe Singleton said in reply, too, because it was the first time Joe became truly a part of our growing little group, with a personality and a point of view and some problems of his own to contribute. What he said, in a wry sort of tone, was, "But that's our future, isn't it? Bread and circuses?"

"Oh, a little wine too, I hope," Grahame said smoothly, and Bob Grantham said something forceful about guns being in the forefront of the attack on atheistic communism everywhere, and Grahame said something back about guns being in the forefront of most attacks whatever the politics, and then he offered us a tour of the house.

And the Joe Singleton nightmare began.

Up till then, Joe Singleton had been the closest thing to an unperson you can get without having been Russian Premier first, and my assumption all along had been that Mr. Clarebridge had chosen him simply because he was so malleable and unimpressive, to act as sort of an extension of Mr. Clarebridge during the development of the "Sea of Guns" project. The last thing I'd expected was Joe Singleton as a single-minded moralist.

Jaekel Grahame is what touched him off. Looking back on it afterwards, it seemed to me that the ironic condemning expression of face that I most remember Joe for began even before we entered Grahame's presence, back on the short drive from the electronic gate to his plantation-style house. Something in Grahame's manner or life-style or both had pressed a button in Joe's head, and he became somebody else. Or that is, he became somebody.

Grahame, as I said, took us on a tour of the house, and at every stop Joe had a remark to make, and they were all in the same mode, and none of them was particularly bright. Not considering the fact that we were this man's guests, and that we wanted to do filming and interviewing here tomorrow.

The wine cellar. It was a large, cool, low-ceilinged subbasement, with arched sets of pillars everywhere and thousands of bottles nesting in the bins. "Ah," Joe said snidely. "The wine for the circuses, eh?"

"The wine is for the bread," Grahame said, and smiled condescendingly at him.

But Joe didn't see the smile. He was looking around, his expression bitter-ironical. "Make a nice fallout shelter," he said. "If you could keep the local peasants out."

"Fallout shelters are a bit obsolete, don't you think?" Grahame said. "I believe what killed that market was the offering to the public of fallout shelters that could be purchased with thirty-year mortgages. In any event, no sane man would wish to outlive his own civilization. Why enter upon the living hell of someone else's world? Having taken the stairs down, we shall take the elevator up."

We took the elevator up, arriving in the kitchen, a huge spotless room surrounded by white tile and polished chrome, with a great butcher-block table in the middle. "And here's where we operate on the natives," Joe said.

Bob and I looked at each other. A pall settled slowly on our heads.

But Grahame smiled and said, "No, actually this is the kitchen. We prepare our meals here. Should operations be necessary, a small but adequate hospital is available in Herkimer. Or one could, of course, travel on to Oklahoma City. This infrared oven was a great disappointment to me; slower than advertised, and meat cooked in it tends to taste flat."

A corridor, rather wide, lined on both sides with paintings. We entered at one end, and Joe said, "Ah, the family portraits. Ancestral gunrunners, painted in whiskey and blood."

"Actually," Grahame said pleasantly, "they're landscapes for the most part. I have a very old-fashioned liking for the traditional, the classical. No member of my family ever sat still long enough to be painted." And he led us down past pastoral scenes, all in greens and blues, very thinly populated by people. Here and there a white pillar rose surrealistically in a forest glade, proving that the painter lived before Freud.

A record library with a built-in stereo system, all in a smallish square room of its own, the records stacked in rows all around the room, reminding me of the radio station in Peoria where I first went to work for the Network. And Joe said, "Sounds of Vietnam, I suppose. In stereo."

That was the time both Bob and I tried to talk over him, Bob saying something inane about the lighting in the room, me saying something inane about the stereo system; but it was Joe's remark that came through.

And Grahame was still amiable and easygoing. "Bach, in fact," he said. "Brahms, Mozart, Vivaldi. I do have the 1812 if you'd like to hear it, a very old recording made in Boston, with sixteen real cannon. Shall I put it on?"

Joe said, "No, thanks. I'd prefer to never hear a cannon again."

"Particularly in the middle of a symphony orchestra, I quite agree."

Well, I could go on, but it's almost as painful to recall as it was to live through. Grahame has a very large home out there in Herkimer, Oklahoma, and he showed us the entire first floor and the basements. He apologized for not taking us up to the second floor, explaining, "My second and fourth wives are up there, both visiting at the moment, and they prefer privacy. I hope you'll understand."

Even Joe didn't have a response for that one.

Which made it the highlight of the evening, the only moment during our hour and a half there that Joe didn't have something awful to say.

We crossed paths with Rudy and the other technicians at one point. They were in a beautifully appointed small dining room, all in light shades of green and yellow and white, and they were wolfing sandwiches and swilling beer and playing poker with the two boys in green velvet.

Joe, of course, had something to say: "What, still alive? I was afraid you'd been thrown to the alligators by now."

"We prefer to make our guests feel at home," Grahame said, his manner still bland, still patient, still easy. "I believe that even in New York alligators are still not a part of the average man's home."

"Average man?" Joe's voice dripped with undiluted if unfocused scorn. "You consider yourself the average man?"

"Well, no one is entirely average, really. But I do consider myself a fairly average wealthy man, yes. Don't let us disturb your game, gentlemen, we're just passing through."

And so on. You talk about mixed emotions. On the one hand, Grahame was so baffling a character and his house was so tastefully rich that I was prepared to let the tour go on forever. But Joe was being so goddam obnoxious I kept hoping the tour would hurry up and finish so we could get out of there and Bob and I could kick the meatball's head in for him.

I'm still sorry we didn't.

Anyway, the ordeal did finally end, we gathered up the crew—Rudy was the only winner from our team—and it was arranged we would go back out the next day for filming and interviewing.

Joe was in a different car from Bob and me, which meant we couldn't murder him, but we could assassinate his character, which we did. Bob broke out an emergency brown paper bag from the glove compartment, and for one of the few times in our career together I matched him drink for drink.

The result was, Joe drove faster in his car than we did in ours and was nowhere to be found when we got back to the hotel. Bob and I went to Bob's room, he sent a bellboy to get us another brown paper bag, and we went on drinking and grousing together until around four in the morning, when the phone rang and it was Joe. *"Here's* our story!" he yelled. "You wanna *hear* something; come on down *here!*" And he hung up, without telling us where *here* was.

I'd answered the phone, because Bob was in the bathroom at that moment, and when he came out he asked me who it was and I said, "Joe."

"That clown. Wha'd he want?"

"I don't know."

"That's just like him," Bob said, and sat down and built himself another.

Joe called back about half an hour later, and this time Bob answered the phone. He said, "Hello?—Down where?—Hold on."

He put his hand over the mouthpiece and said to me, "He wants to know why we're not there."

"Because he didn't tell me where there was."

"Oh." Into the phone: "Because you didn't tell us where there was."

I said, "He hung up."

"You hung up." Hand over mouthpiece, to me: "Says he didn't."

"Lemme talk to him."

I went over and took the phone and heard Joe saying, "—tradition of newspapermen! You want the facts? You want to rub the public's nose in the truth? Here it is, right here!"

I said, "You keep saying here, but you don't say where. The tradition of newspapermen is who what where when why, the five double-u's. All you've told us so far is who. You. And besides that, we aren't newspapermen."

"We're *news*men! Get out front of the hotel; I'll send a cab for you. You and Bob and Rudy and everybody. And all equipment for a filmed interview. Get right on it!" And he hung up.

"I don't believe it," I said, and looked at Bob. "He wants us to go interview somebody."

"Who?"

"What where when why."

He was baffled. "What?"

"Where when why. Excuse me, I got to wake the boys."

It turned out nobody was asleep. The poker game was still going on. One of the green velvet boys from Grahame's estate, the big winner, had come on to the hotel with us, and our gang was still trying to win its money back. And still losing, by the way; nobody wound up very happy from that trip to Oklahoma.

Anyway, the boys had been drinking while card playing, so nobody was very sober, and nobody really minded going out at four-thirty in the morning to film an interview with who knew who at who knew where about who knew what for who knew why. We all just trucked on downstairs, carrying television equipment and playing cards and six-packs of beer and brown paper bags, and found a cab waiting for us out front. We rescued our rented cars from the hotel basement and followed the cab to a dingy hotel in a dingy section of town, where a dingy desk clerk looked at us and said, "My God, it's true!"

Bob said, "Where is he?"

"Twenty-seven. Just up them stairs."

We went up them stairs, and down that hall, and room twenty-seven had a green-gray door with metal numbers nailed to it. Bob knocked, Joe opened, and we all trailed in.

The room was square, bare, and awful. A sink in a corner had a light fixture over it, sticking out from the wall with a milk-glass shade. The bed was old but would never be an antique, and the faded pink blanket stretched tight across it looked as though it was intended for covering dead bodies.

The girl sitting on this bed didn't look all that lively herself. Pudgy, pale, wearing a faded flower-print dress approximately the same color as the blanket, she made me think of uncooked bread dough with too much yeast in it. Everything about her was faded —the blonde hair, the blue eyes, the pink mouth—and she couldn't have been more than twenty-two, twenty-three. Her legs were chunky, and her shins were covered with red bites and scratches. She was possibly the least appealing female I had ever seen.

And what did Joe say? Joe said, "There she is!" As though unveiling Miss America.

"There she is, all right," Bob said. He looked at me, shook his head, and lifted the brown paper bag to his mouth. Behind me, I could hear the popping of beer cans being opened.

I said, "What now, Joe?"

"Now you interview her," Joe said. "Just follow her lead, Jay, you know how to do it. Let her tell her story. We may be jaded New Yorkers, we may be hard-bitten, tough newsmen, but I tell you now there won't be a dry eye in this room when this little lady is finished. Set up, boys, set up! This is Pulitzer Prize country!"

We weren't drunk enough to believe him, but we were drunk enough to go along with him. The boys set up, I sat down on the bed beside the girl—she just sat there and phlegmatically watched us, speaking only when spoken to and never becoming animated at all, which the little holes in her upper arms may have had something to do with—and I said, "What's your name, dear?" I can be very avuncular when called on.

I'm almost tempted to lie right now and make up a name. "Judy," she said. Or, "Mary," she said. But I might as well plow on through, being truthful one hundred per cent of the way:

"Beulah," she said.

I looked over at Bob. He was drinking from the brown paper bag. I wanted to drink from the brown paper bag, too, but they were setting up the camera and some things shouldn't be put on film.

Including the forty-five minutes that followed. If you're completely insane, you in the elevator, you can go to the files and find that film and show it to yourself. Frankly, I advise against it.

Myself, I don't remember very much of the damn thing. It was late, I was tired, I'd been drinking, and the whole episode had a weird aura of unreality about it which kept me from permitting very much of it into my brain. I do, however, remember very vividly the first exchange between the girl and me:

"Well, Beulah, what happened?"

"Welfare made me a hoor."

Yes, indeed. I knew better than to look at the camera, or Bob, or Joe, or the lights, or anything but Beulah. I looked at her, and I gave her my interested smile, and I swear to God what I said was, "Tell me about it."

And she did. It was long, it was rambling, it was full of low-key spite, it was delivered with virtually no emotional impact at all, and it made absolutely no sense. None. Joe Singleton, when we got back to New York, screened the interview four full times, trying to make sense out of it so it could be used somewhere and therefore justify his having done it, and *he* finally gave up.

If you do watch it, by the way, against my advice, let me explain the startled look that crosses my face at one point, since nothing you can see or hear will account for it. It was a shout I heard from the hallway, which becomes only an indistinguishable burr on the sound track, and it is the sound man's assistant shouting, "Hey! This place is a goddam whorehouse!"

When a project starts at such a low point as this one, it's hard to say that it thereafter goes downhill, but that's just what happened. While I sat there on that lousy—I mean that literally—bed with Raggedy Ann the hooker, looking interested while she maundered along like a William Burroughs book read backwards, a goddam bacchanal was taking place just the other side of the camera. Joe, with that unerring instinct we all came to know and love before we were finished, had chosen the only true beast in the joint; there were a lot of surprisingly good-looking heads jumping around out there in the hall, in their nighties. They'd thought the day's work was done, and here the joint was full of men again. As a matter of fact, their profitable day's work *was* done, since our crew stiffed them, in a manner of speaking. But while it was going, it was going good. Poker became strip poker, booze flowed all over the place, and enough pubic hair flashed past the hall doorway to wear out two pairs of censors' scissors.

And through it all, I sat there beside that humorless child and listened to the drone of her voice and pretended enthrallment. I couldn't even drink.

The reason the camera bobbles a lot, by the way, is that people kept handing it to each other, everybody wanting to get a piece of the action, in a manner of speaking. The last twenty minutes, the camera is being held by Joe Singleton, which could have gotten us all in a lot of trouble with the unions if anybody had given a damn, which nobody did.

Well, let's ring down the curtain on that, Joe Singleton's first—but not last—venture into the heady highlights of *Front Page*. The film was shot and so were we, and dawn was coming up like thunder when we staggered back to our own hotel, some of us carrying new little friends who would travel with us all the way to the hardened metropolis of New York.

The next morning, Joe and Bob and I rode in the same car, me driving, and Bob started to give me his usual list of questions about the Communist menace that I should feed to Grahame, but Joe said, "Come on, Bob, the hell with that. That's fifties stuff."

"It's coming back," Bob said. "Believe me, it's coming back."

"It's as dead as the New Look," Joe said. A prophet ever. He said to me, "I have some questions for you, Jay. Now questions. Today questions."

The morality of the gun—that was one of Joe's now questions. And since Joe was more the boss than Bob, it was Joe's questions that I asked, and I must admit they worked out. Joe, like most people, is a monomaniac; when he's right it's beautiful, and when he's wrong it's something else again.

So I did the interview, and while I was doing it the boys were scouting around for other things to film, like Grahame's arsenal. He had this long Nissen hut in the woods out behind his house—you could just see it, brown and anonymous amid the trees, from the swimming pool area—and inside it was full of guns. Not just the building itself, but two levels of basements built under it. Aisles of shelves and bins, and all full of munitions. Rifles, handguns, cases of bullets. Bazookas, small artillery shells, all sorts of weaponry. The aisles, both above and below ground, were lit by rows of fluorescent lights, giving a very inhuman glare to everything. Two sullen local citizens were employed there, and they stood about flexing their muscles and glowering at us and waiting for the fags from New York to make a false move. Their power was older than either guns or money, but held in check by their dim comprehension of the strictures of civilization.

Most of the weapons underground were lying open, but the ones at ground level were for the most part in cases, either because they had just recently arrived or would shortly be on their way again. The smell of creosote was strong in the air, and my earlier image of rifle crates as coffins came back to me again, turning the Nissen hut into a mortuary.

Grahame gave us all an open-air snack near the swimming pool when we were finished our work, and while we were feeding our faces two beautiful women walked out from the house, both of them putting one foot directly in front of the other the way models do.

They were like models in every way, actually. Tall, very slender, coolly good-looking, expensively dressed, moving their arms and their heads in the artificial ways that models do when displaying what they're wearing. These two women came out simultaneously, not quite in step, and it was as though they had come out not to join the group but to show the new fashions. Grahame introduced them, and they were wives number two and four, naturally, and the reason I promptly forgot their names was because I couldn't tell them apart. I found myself looking them over for their numbers, as though they were race horses.

Yes, that's it, race horses. Thoroughbreds. I know there are people who claim they can tell race horses apart, but us ordinary people find it impossible. And numbers two and four were like that, identical the way race horses are identical, delicate and graceful and well bred the way race horses are delicate and graceful and well bred, and in a strange manner they were even beautiful the way race horses are beautiful.

One of the great unanswered questions of my life has to do with wives one and three. And five, if there is a wife five. Were they race horses, too? Or did Grahame have a fluctuating taste; were wives one and three of a totally different type; does he live his life leaning first one way and then the other? I will never know, and whenever my mind has nothing else to plague me about, it nags me with that unresolvable question.

Anyway, two and four joined us, and the atmosphere became more garden party, and we stood around eating and drinking and chatting together, until Rudy Patelli took me to one side and murmured, "Come on with me, Jay, I want to show you something."

"What?"

"Just come with me."

We slipped away from the group and headed through the woods. Half a dozen times I have seen movies or television shows in which the botched attempt to assassinate Hitler is portrayed, and it always shows that one-armed colonel with the bomb in the briefcase going through woods just like Grahame's toward a hut very like Grahame's, and I suppose that's why a heavy aura of foreign intrigue settled over me as I followed the suddenly mysterious Rudy Patelli amid the tree trunks.

The locals barred our way. They gave us angry grins that implied that civilization was suddenly rather far away, and they flexed their muscles some more, and they insultingly suggested we force our way past them. They wanted us to try it, and we chose instead to retreat. They didn't laugh at us as we backed away, they just stood there like leashed mastiffs and watched us go.

Back in the woods again, I said to Rudy, "What was it? What did you want to show me?"

"I have it on film," Rudy said. "Never mind those bastards, I'll show you when we get back to New York."

And he did. About four days after we got back he came into my office, where I was answering some of the Townley Loomis mail, and he dropped a photograph on my desk and said, "Take a look at that."

I took a look at that. It was a color blow-up of a still from the film he'd shot back in Oklahoma, and it showed half a dozen rifle crates in two stacks on the concrete floor of the Nissen hut. I looked at it, and looked at it, and finally shook my head and said, "I don't get it."

Rudy patted one of the crates with a fingernail. "See that crate?"

"I see it."

"Look at the corner."

"The one that's dented?"

"That's the one."

I looked at the dented corner of the crate. Then I looked up at Rudy. "I still don't get," I said.

"It's the same one," he said.

"The same what?"

"The same *crate!*"

"The same crate as *what?*"

"The same crate as the guy dropped in Florida!"

"What sa—?" I stared at him. I looked at the photo again. I said, "Are you sure?"

"You're goddam right I'm sure," he said. "If those palookas hadn't kept us out, you'd of seen it yourself. It's the same crate."

"But that doesn't make any sense," I said.

"I tell you what sense it makes," he said. "We haven't been filming a lot of different gun shipments, we've been filming *one* gun shipment, and the damn thing wasn't going from Oklahoma to Florida, it was going from Florida to Oklahoma!"

"But—but why?"

"How the hell do I know why? They're *doing* it, that's all."

"But it doesn't make sense."

"You said that."

"I still say it," I said. I shook my head at the photo some more. I said, "Maybe they return the crates and fill them up again. Like deposit bottles."

"Sure," he said. I believe the expression is, "His voice dripped scorn." I think that's the phrase I want.

"If there was only some reason for it," I said. "Some logical explanation. What are they doing it *for?* What do they *get* out of it?"

"That's not my department," Rudy said. "My department is to see. Me and my camera, we see things. You people decide what they mean."

"We better take this to Joe," I said.

"You take it," he said. "I've done all I want to do."

"But you're the one who found this."

"It's all yours," he said. "Rudy Patelli doesn't make waves."

"But if the Network is being conned and you found out about it, you should get the credit."

"Rudy Patelli takes the cash," he said, "and lets the credit go."

And he refused to come with me. Now, this is *exactly* the way it went, and I don't care what anybody thinks he remembers or doesn't think he remembers, this is what happened. Rudy Patelli came to me with that photo and refused to go any farther with it. So *I* took it to Joe Singleton, and I told him what Rudy had told me, and I showed him the photograph, and I described the incident in Florida when the crate had been dropped—he hadn't been with us yet at that time—and he frowned, studying the photograph, holding it in both hands, listening to me, and when I was finished he said, "Are you sure of this, Jay?"

"Rudy's sure," I said. "And to tell you the truth, it does look a hell of a lot like the same crate. But it's tough to be sure from just a photograph."

"I'll take it from here, Jay," he said. The fit hadn't hit the shan *in re* his Oklahoma City hooker yet, and he was still being forceful and firm-jawed.

"Fine with me," I said, and I left the photo with him and went back to work. And it was my private opinion, as of that moment, that the "Sea of Guns" special had just hit a reef and sunk without a trace. I was, unfortunately, wrong.

That was a very dull period for me. Neither Linda nor Bob was around, and I was used by now to the two of them pretty well filling up my evenings. Though not simultaneously; I made sure that Bob never saw Linda, and vice versa, expecting the effect would be bad on both of them.

I knew where Bob was, and about Linda I found out later, when she came back and called me and told me she'd been home to Nebraska for a week because an uncle had died. Her mother's kid brother. Lung cancer, you know, the usual. As to Bob, the minute he'd gotten back to New York he'd started making the rounds of the publishers and had lined himself up a contract to do another book: *The Illustrated History of The Rifle*. He was a houseguest at Grahame's estate back in Oklahoma for ten days, researching the book. Arnold, believe it or not, had gone along to take the pictures.

With nobody around, there was nothing for me to do evenings but watch television. That was the main week of the trial of the St. Louis Thirty-seven, a group of demonstrators who had, among other things, pumped two tank-truck loads of fertilizer into the main St. Louis Army–Air Force Recruiting Station one night, which turned out to be a not entirely happy surprise for the sergeant who opened the front door the next morning. The main focus of the trial, however, was their attempt to remove the roof from Kiel Auditorium, "to let God's light," as one of the priests in the group described it, "shine full on the heads of the Establishment." Speedy action by the police had saved the auditorium roof and had also resulted in three of the St. Louis Thirty-seven attending the trial in wheelchairs. Four policemen had already been brought to trial on charges of overexerting themselves, in the usual attempt to show fair play in the courts, and had been acquitted. And now it was the turn of the Thirty-seven.

Anyway, it was one of the most interesting political trials of our time, and television was full of it all week, and I wound up more or less saturated by the trial before it and the week and I were all finished. The St. Louis Thirty-seven were mostly found guilty, of course—four weren't, none of them wheelchair cases—and were given the usual bewildering variety of sentences, some suspended and some not.

Photographs weren't allowed to be taken in the courtroom, of course, so it was the usual display of pastel watercolors that carried the visuals into homes across the nation, including mine. And there they all were; the craggy-faced judge, the blonde and beautiful girl agent provocateur turned informer, the one-time governor of Rhode Island or someplace appearing as a character witness for the Thirty-seven, the sullen, baffled, badly shaved subliterate policemen all looking like *Tarzan in New York,* the whole bunch that we'd seen already in city after city across this mighty land, till I began to suspect it was one huge traveling carnival playing in town after town, like the old O. C. Buck shows. Looking at the watercolor drawings, who could be sure it wasn't the same judge; this one says his name is Masengotti, the last one said his name was Fuller, and there's no way to say for certain they aren't one and the same. The beautiful girl agent provocateur and informer? Mary Marie Conroy this time, Cindy Lawson last time, and as alike as Jaekel Grahame's wives. And none of them anxious to have their pictures taken.

Except the defendants, of course. We had tons of footage of them, massed together like a lacrosse team gathered for the yearbook picture, saying impassioned things and looking as unlikely a group to be mixed up with one another as those assembled for somewhat different purposes by Agatha Christie.

Doing my Townley Loomis interviews, believing the gun-running special was dead, settling into a solitary life once again, I found myself taking more of an interest in that dumb trial than in my own daily concerns. And so I provided a beautiful example of mixed emotions when, the following Monday, Joe Singleton called me into his office and told me "A Sea of Guns" was still very much alive, thank you, and that nothing was going to stop it from being done and that the word had come down from on high that the priority on our project was triple A triple One. Or would have been, if we graded priorities around The Hub.

I said, "But what about the dented crate?"

"Doesn't make any sense," he said. "So you must have been mistaken."

"Me? It wasn't me, it was Rudy Patelli."

"Whoever it was," he said, brushing the question of responsibility away as though it didn't matter, "it had to be a mistake. That's the word, so that's what we'll act on."

"The word from Mr. Clarebridge?"

"Above," he said. And then he leaned forward and looked very confidential and said, "Can you keep something under your hat, Jay?"

"Sure," I said.

"The CIA is interested," he said, and looked meaningful.

"Interested in what?"

"In this show. The word I got, the CIA wants us to go ahead."

"Why the hell would the CIA care whether we went ahead or not?"

"The idea I got," he said, "and don't quote me on this, but the idea I got is that we're funneling funds to the revolutionaries."

"Funneling funds," I said. Some phrases are just too absurd to be encompassed the first time around and have to be repeated aloud, to give the meaning a chance to filter through.

"That's right," Joe said. "But don't quote me."

I promised him I wouldn't quote him, but the time has come to break that promise, and now I am quoting him. I understand that Joe has already denied that this conversation ever took place, but it did take place, and I am quoting what he said, and he said everything that I just reported, including the business about the CIA, and that the word on the CIA had come from above Walter J. Clarebridge.

Now, I don't say that what Joe told me is true, and in fact I have a theory of my own on that. It all depends how much money the Network had paid out by that time. Slush fund moneys apparently had been going to Bob Grantham on a more or less regular basis for six months by this point, but how much it added up to is anybody's guess. Bob's own estimate of twenty-five hundred dollars seems somewhat low, but the FBI's estimate of forty thousand dollars, on the other hand, seems a bit high.

But let's say the amount was somewhere between those two estimates, which would make it an amount of money worth thinking about. Nobody, it seems to me, would want to take the responsibility for *saying* that that money had been thrown down a rathole. I'm not making any suggestion as to where the breakdown in communication occurred, but I have the feeling a breakdown did occur somewhere, and that the reason for it was that nobody wanted to be the messenger with the bad news. In olden days, kings sometimes killed the messenger who brought the bad news, and in subtler fashions the practice is still very much alive in American business. Did *no one* realize ahead of time that the Edsel was going to lay an egg? I don't believe it. But nobody wanted to be the first to spoil the fun; everybody said to himself, 'Gee, all the other guys seem to think it's a good idea, maybe I'm wrong; I better keep my mouth shut.'

Did Joe Singleton actually pass the story of the dented crate on to Mr. Clarebridge, or did he tell me that stuff about the CIA just to keep me quiet? I don't know. I do know the temptation must have entered his mind to let the thing slide and hope for the best; it would only be natural.

But say he did pass it along, say he decided it would be safer in the long run to tell the story to his boss, if only so he'd be protected should the thing blow up later on. Now, how does he tell the story? Does he make it sound like trouble, or does he downplay it a little?

Hell, *I* downplayed it. I gave it to Joe with a lot less heat in it than when Rudy gave it to me. So why shouldn't Joe cool it down even more when passing it on to Mr. Clarebridge?

So say the story did get to Mr. Clarebridge, regardless of what he says now and whether or not he can remember it. What does Mr. Clarebridge do? He is the guy, after all, who's been disbursing the money. He can't call the deal off on his own, he has to talk it over with Frank Dorn first, the Senior Vice President, News &

Current Affairs Department. Does Mr. Clarebridge talk to Mr. Dorn? Or does Mr. Clarebridge make up the CIA story to keep *Joe* quiet?

We can go right on up, to Mr. Dorn and above, and we can ask the same questions at every level. And there's always still the possibility that everybody did what he should, everybody passed the dented-crate story on, everybody discussed it in a calm, rational manner without giving too much consideration to the money that had already been spent or the egg that might wind up on various individuals' faces, and that the CIA *actually was* involved.

An involvement, by the way, that they would very naturally be in no hurry to admit to at this point, not the way things stand now.

So all I'm trying to make clear here is that the temptation to cover up the signs of trouble was strong at every level of management from Joe Singleton on up, that the same situation could have arisen if we were an automobile company or a computer manufacturer or a processor of frozen foods. Nobody wants to take the individual responsibility for pointing out a team goof; that's the flaw in the American way of doing things, and it has gotten the nation and the world into a lot more hot water over the last few decades than this comparatively minor flap over Ilha Pombo Island.

Comparatively minor, I mean, in comparison with some other things I could mention but won't. Not minor from the Network's point of view, God knows, and not minor from my point of view either.

Well, anyway. This first wave was a small one; it didn't engulf us, it didn't sink our ship. "A Sea of Guns" was alive and well and doing just great. Bob was still away when I got that news, but Linda was back, and she was pleased for me because I told her I was pleased, but the truth is, I had a funny little sensation in the back of my head; I had this very strange feeling that a heavy safe had just fallen out of a very very high window way way up in the sky somewhere and that wherever on earth it landed was where I was going to be. Under it.

But I didn't say anything about that to Linda. Mostly I was trying to recapture that phone booth mood with her, and I didn't want any distractions. Not that I seemed to be getting anywhere, but my hope at least was high.

I didn't mention my premonition to Bob either, when he got back from Oklahoma. He was happy the project was still alive, and I saw no point in telling him anything about my own uneasy feeling; it was all too vague and unfocused. The hell with it, is what I thought.

So Caryl Ten Broeck was brought back in to do the Townley Loomis lunchtime interviews again, and I spent the next couple of weeks doing interviews for "A Sea of Guns" set up by Joe and Bob. Mostly this was filler stuff—talk pieces with experts. I interviewed a well-known pacifist on the subject of just revolutions—I don't mean mere revolutions, I mean just revolutions as opposed to unjust revolutions—and I interviewed a retired Marine general about the history of gunrunning, and I interviewed a man from the State Department about the legal questions involved, and I interviewed a man from the Israeli mission at the UN who reminisced about his own career of smuggling guns into Palestine in the late forties, and so on and so on.

And then one day in early June I was called in to see Joe Singleton, and Bob was with him, and Joe said, "Jay, we've gone over all this stuff we've done, and the actual gun movement footage and interviews with the people handling the guns—that's all great stuff, very toothy, very real. But this other crap, this head in front of a bookcase stuff, this stuff is crap."

"It's standard," Bob amplified. "Very standard usual pat stuff."

They were talking as though the interviews had been *my* idea. No, sir, I'm as quick to pass the buck as anybody, particularly when I'm lily white, which I was at that moment. "I had the same feeling," I said. "Every time you guys sent me out to see another of those bald people it kept striking me how tame the stuff was in comparison with what we already had from the field. But it's your ballgame, I'm just the voice, so I didn't feel I should say anything."

They looked at each other, and I could see them both deciding to find another patsy. Each other, if need be.

Joe cleared his throat. "Well, we're in agreement," he said. "That's good."

"That's fine," Bob said. He smiled at me.

"Because here's what we've come up with," Joe said. "We're all going to take a trip. We're going

TAPE THREE, SIDE TWO

SORRY ABOUT THAT. I didn't realize I was coming to the end of the tape. This is the second side of tape three, by the way; be sure you're listening in sequence.

Ilha Pombo Island. That's where Joe said we were going, to Ilha Pombo Island, the damn place the guns were supposed to be headed for.

Let me tell you a little about Ilha Pombo Island. It is a huge bird dropping in the blue Caribbean, and I don't know which is worse, its history or its geography.

History first. Ilha Pombo Island was deserted until 1598, when a Spanish ship landed there for the purpose of depositing a sailor who had been caught by the captain doing something unspecified with a mule they had on board. This is the extent of the Spanish involvement with the island, which makes it something of an oddity in the Caribbean, most islands there having been mugged pretty completely by the Spanish three or four hundred years ago. The sailor, whose name is not known to any of the source books I have looked in at the library, left no trace of himself on the island, apparently having flung himself into the sea rather than live there.

The Portuguese came next, in 1601. With practically everything else already snapped up by the Spanish, the Portuguese really had to scrape the bottom of the barrel to find islands *they* could occupy, and at the very bottom of the barrel was this piece of, uh, coral, and they occupied it and gave it its name, Ilha Pombo, which means Pigeon Island. Actually it means Island Pigeon, but they were trying to say it the other way around. Nobody knows why they named it Pigeon Island, since the place had no indigenous birds at all except a particularly ugly kind of carrion gull that doesn't look anything like a pigeon and lives on dead fish.

Anyway, the Portuguese landed a few of their own number to start plantations and a lot of black African slaves to run the plantations, and for fifteen or twenty years they all tried to make a living off the island together, which was impossible. And the reason it was impossible is geography, which I'll have to bring in now, and then get back to history later.

There are two kinds of islands in the Caribbean, volcanic and coral, which means there are islands formed from inactive volcanoes and there are islands built up of coral formations. Volcanic islands tend to have rich soil and high mountains. The high mountains attract rain clouds, the rich soil grows jungle, the jungle rots and makes the soil richer, and these days those islands grow sugar, lots and lots of sugar. Coral islands tend to have poor soil and no mountains, which means they don't attract rain clouds, coral doesn't filter sea water the way rich soil does, and generally speaking coral islands are poor and desertlike and no fun to live on.

Ilha Pombo, need it be said, is a coral island. It is, however, a very old coral island, meaning rather large, meaning that in the interior of the island there has been enough scrub growth rotting away over the last several thousand years to produce some kind of more or less useful soil and even provide filtered water underground that can be tapped by a well. So life is not impossible on Ilha Pombo, just unlikely.

Well. The Portuguese and their slaves led a hand-to-mouth existence on the island for twenty years or so, and then the Dutch came. The Dutch shot almost everybody—as though life weren't tough enough—enslaved the slaves who'd survived, and built a port. The Dutch weren't dumb enough to try to live on the island; they just wanted it for a way station amid the Dutch West Indies. They'd arrived in June, which happens to be the rainy season on Ilha Pombo, and didn't find out till later that the other eleven months of the year it doesn't rain at all. Their mistaken impression of the place is indicated by the name they gave the port when they'd finished building it—Schlamm. Which means Mud.

Well, the mud dried, and life went on, and all of a sudden the French attacked with a bunch of warships. They stood offshore and blew up everything in, on, and around Schlamm, and then steamed in to enslave the surviving slaves, rebuild Schlamm, and rename it Schlammville.

Schlammville got slammed again about thirty years later, by the English, who were going through the Caribbean picking up everything in sight, like a late starter in a Monopoly game, and who kept the name of Schlammville for the island's only town, but who renamed the island. Ilha Pombo became Ilha Pombo Island, which means Island Pigeon Island, which makes about as much sense as anything else in this life.

The seventeenth century was limping offstage around this time, full of musket shot, and the eighteenth century was crawling on, clutching a rope and a sword. For the next two hundred and fifty years, the big struggles of the big world powers tended to find their reflection in the tiny prism of Ilha Pombo Island, with one fleet after another steaming in to have at Schlammville, but for the most part the flag flying from her stump of a flagpole was the Union Jack, and for the most part the survivors continued to be the descendants of the African slaves originally imported by the Portuguese, with some infusions of this and that kind of European blood from time to time, so that by now the average Pombian, which is what they call themselves, thinks of himself as black but is actually a sort of milk chocolate in color.

Since the end of the Second World War, the European colonial powers have been unloading their colonies as quickly as possible, and Ilha Pombo Island became an independent state in the fraternity of nations in 1952, retaining some ties with the British Commonwealth, and with her foreign policy—if any—to be handled by Great Britain. In an election in April of that year the island's thirteen thousand citizens elected their first President, Dr. Martin Chiswick-Smythe, an Oxford-educated general practitioner in medicine, milk chocolate in color, with a round bald head, round smiling face, and round metal-framed eyeglasses. In October of the same year, two army colonels—the army was too small to have any generals—overthrew Dr. Chiswick-Smythe in order to save the nation from a Communist takeover, and set up a military dictatorship in his place. No one has heard of Dr. Chiswick-Smythe since.

The two colonels were named Colonel Dewrane Mother and Colonel Padigard Enhuelco. They survived as a team about as long as Kosygin and Bulganin did, and it was Colonel Mother who struck first. Colonel Enhuelco managed to escape with his life, though very little else, and made his way to the United States, where, fifteen or so years later, I met him, as already recorded, late one night on the Florida coast. Colonel Mother changed his name to Mungu, which in Swahili means God, and settled back to enjoy life as a dictator. Under his reign, the average individual annual income on the island dropped from approximately thirty-four dollars to approximately fourteen dollars and fifty cents, the tourist trade dropped from about fifty overnight guests a year to zero, and the United States has so far pumped in approximately twenty-two million dollars in foreign aid to keep the island from going Communist. It must have been money well spent, because the island hasn't gone Communist; it's still run by Mungu.

Anyway, various malcontents on the island have been trying to put together a revolution for a long time, but Mungu rules primarily by torture—he likes to set fire to people, burn a couple of fingers or toes off, put out the fire, and then start asking questions—and it makes it tough to put an organization together when you're afraid to talk to anybody.

Though we've managed here at the Network, haven't we?

Well, never mind that. About Ilha Pombo Island. Malcontents have tended over the years to make their way off the island, most of them with fingers and toes missing, and by now several hundred of them are in the States, working at jobs that don't require ten fingers. Most of them would be very happy to see a revolution in their homeland, and, they'd like it so much they don't even care if it's led by Colonel Padigard Enhuelco. One problem at a time, that seems to pretty well sum up the islanders' attitude about things.

Well, that's the island. It's down there in the Caribbean, too small and grim and unhappy to have been heard of by the average American, and it was the final destination of the guns we'd been photographing *en route*. Which made it, according to somebody's bright idea, our destination, too.

Joe and Bob together explained it to me, that June day in Joe's office. The idea was, instead of trying to fake up a survey of gunrunning as an entire subject, why not *concentrate* on this one *specific* incidence of gunrunning in the very backyard of the United States, and only lightly demonstrate how it connects with gunrunning generally? Everybody, apparently, agreed that the idea was a first-rate one and therefore we should all go to Ilha Pombo Island, to film its isolated coves, where guns *might* be smuggled ashore, to film its capital city, which one day *might* be embroiled in civil war, and for me to interview the island's president, Mungu himself, who one day *might* be overthrown.

Was this the safe, and was it even now landing on my head? I hated the idea from the first minute I heard it, and demonstrated my dislike by simply saying nothing about it. By that I mean, the decision had already been made, somewhere above me in the chain of command. My opinion didn't matter, and therefore I didn't offer it. My not offering it, however, made it plain to Bob and Joe that I was not delirious with joy, and they spent a lot of time explaining to me what a great idea it was. They never convinced me.

Well, at least we weren't going to have to *stay* on the island. An island with zero tourists has, of course, zero hotels. We would stay instead at a place called Carefree Beach Hotel on the island of Abulia, a former French colony twelve miles away from Ilha Pombo. And an advance man—another of Mr. Clarebridge's assistants—was already on the way down there to set things up for the interview with Mungu and the stay at the hotel, and everything else.

Ultimately, five of us made the trip. Besides Joe Singleton and me, we had a three-man technical crew; Rudy Patelli for camerawork and Hank Tashwell and Irv Berg for sound. We would pick up other assistants locally.

It turns out, as you'll notice, that Bob didn't accompany us. There was some sort of trouble about visas, some reason why Bob's name was on several lists, and he was going to be refused entry by both Abulia and Ilha Pombo, so he stayed home. He saw us off at the airport, though, saying, "Boy, I wish I were going with you fellows."

"That's funny," I said. "I wish I were staying here."

So none of us got his wish. We five boarded a commercial flight for the first leg of our journey, to San Juan, Puerto Rico, and Joe made me feel a lot better by saying, as the plane lifted into the June sky, "Now, if we get hijacked to Cuba, I'm going to want a lot of film, a lot of coverage. Jay, I want you to interview everybody in sight, starting with the hijacker."

I said, "And Castro?"

"If he shows up."

Well, we didn't get hijacked, which is about the only disaster that missed us. We landed in sunny San Juan on schedule, off-loaded ourselves and our luggage and our equipment, and had a hell of a time finding the charter flight that was supposed to be waiting for us. Joe Singleton bustled back and forth, paging people and buttonholing people, and the rest of us stood around in the muggy heat for a while, until Rudy said to Hank and Irv, "Watch the goods, will you?"

"Sure," they said, and Rudy made a head motion at me, and the two of us strolled away.

I said, "What's up?"

"I figured it was time for a drink," he said.

I looked at him. Had the spirit of Bob Grantham entered into him; was Bob among us after all? But then I thought it over and realized that it wasn't Bob talking through Rudy's mouth; it was sanity speaking. The only sensible thing to do, while the muggy heat lay all about us and Joe Singleton scoured Puerto Rico for our pilot, was to go have a drink. Something very tall, with ice. And limes. And alcohol.

The bar was air-conditioned, though open all along one wall. We could sit there and drink our long cold drinks and watch people trot up ramps with heavy luggage, shortening their lives.

The bar was dim, particularly after all the sunlight, and only sparsely populated, mostly with people in airline uniforms. Rudy and I sat at a table and quietly shared a drink together, and I said, "By the way, I did pass on what you told me about the crate." This was the first I'd seen him since.

He nodded, gazing out at a fat woman carrying two fat babies up the ramp. "I figured you did."

"They decided you were mistaken."

He nodded again. "I figured they would." And that ended that conversation.

We ordered a second round and sat there in companionable silence, and I glanced around at the other customers in the tranquil bar with us, and over to one side I saw a man in a dark blue uniform with wings over the pocket chatting expansively with two girls in stewardess uniforms. He was a stocky man, with a round, florid face and a thick black mustache and sparkly eyes, and his cheeks had a ruddy red glow that seemed to light up that corner of the room. He too was drinking something long and cool, with limes in it, and he was ordering them four at a time, one for each girl and two for him. He had a hearty manner and a robust laugh, and his eyes didn't seem to be quite in focus.

I said to Rudy, "Excuse me," and he looked at me in surprise and said, "You farted?"

"No," I said. "I'm getting up for a second. I'll be right back."

"Go ahead," he said, and went back to watching people climb the ramp. Rudy is one of the world's champion watchers.

I got up from the table and walked over to the man in blue with the two girls and said, "Excuse me." He looked at me, and before he could ask me if I'd farted I said, "Would you by any chance be Captain Archer? Of Straight Arrow Airways?"

He gave a big, happy smile, pointed at me, and said, "You must be the TV people!"

"I'm just one of them," I said. "There's another one over there. We also have a couple watching the luggage, and our producer is running all over the place trying to find you. Paging you, and like that."

"They don't have a loudspeaker in here," he said. "I can't hear a page. Tell your friend to come on over."

"Okay. Rudy!"

So Rudy brought our drinks over, and we joined Captain Archer and the young ladies, and about an hour later Joe Singleton staggered in, looking harried, and plopped himself at a small table near the entrance, where the air conditioning was the least effective. He ordered a drink about the way the man crawling through the desert asks for water, and then sat gasping and panting and staring frenziedly out at Rudy's ramp.

Rudy said, "Shall we tell him?"

Captain Archer said, "You know that fellow?"

"He's our producer. The guy looking for you."

"Does he have a drinking problem?"

"Not yet," I said. "Excu— I mean, I'll be right back."

I went over and sat down across the little table from Joe, and at first he just sat there and panted and looked at me. Then his waiter brought him his drink, and he slurped at it, and then he said, "I can't find him. I just can't find him."

"He's over there," I said.

Joe turned his head and looked. Captain Archer gave him a big grin and a wave.

I said, "There's no loudspeaker in here. You can't hear a page."

Joe slowly swiveled his head back around until he was looking once more at me. "That's him over there?"

"That's him."

"Do you suppose we could get him to fly us away from here?" Joe sounded piteous, really piteous.

"I'll go ask him," I said.

"You do that," he said, and buried his nose in his drink.

I went back over to the other table and said, "Captain Archer, our producer would like to know if you'd be willing to leave now."

"I don't see why not," the captain said amiably. "Hey, José!"

That was the waiter, who pirouetted in response. "*Si?*"

"Give the bill to that fellow there." Meaning Joe.

While Joe paid the bill, looking dazed, Rudy and Captain Archer and I said so long to the girls, who weren't stewardesses at all but were actually tourists from Cicero, Illinois, who had discovered they could meet a better class of male on their travels if they hung around airport bars in stewardess uniforms. We exchanged addresses and phone numbers, but so far neither of them has called me and I haven't called them. Maybe they're still in San Juan, at the bar.

Anyway, Captain Archer and Rudy and Joe and I left the cool bar and went through the hot terminal building to the impossible outdoors, where Hank and Irv were melting over the piles of equipment. One sniff of our breaths, and they became at once indignant and irritable, which they remained for the rest of the trip, adding just one more fun element to an already enchanting voyage; two people going around permanently miffed at the other three. I'm going to include a tape of my interview with Mungu, and if you notice that I sound oddly like Donald Duck on that tape, it is because of this rift in our ranks that started in Puerto Rico, the two sound men, Hank and Irv, on the one side and Rudy and Joe and I on the other.

Well. These things happen. To return to my narrative, I was totally surprised when Captain Archer's plane turned out to be a perfectly acceptable twelve-seater aircraft with shiny new white and blue paint gleaming in the sunlight, and when his copilot turned out to be a neat and dapper little Oriental gentleman with wraparound sunglasses, a clipboard, and a look of no nonsense. Straight Arrow Airways was not the disaster I'd been prepared for, though just about everything else on the trip was.

Abulia, for instance. I have remarked earlier that this trip took place in June. I have also remarked earlier that Ilha Pombo's one and only rainy season is June. And I have in addition remarked earlier that Abulia is twelve miles away from Ilha Pombo, which isn't very far. Both islands can fit very handily under the same rain cloud.

We landed in a cloudburst, and a short milk-chocolate-colored man in a gray uniform came out from the tiny shedlike airport building, carrying a huge black umbrella up over his head, boarded our plane, and charged us one hundred fifty dollars import duty on the television equipment.

Joe said, "But we're not importing this stuff! It's tools, we're going to *use* it."

"To bring in," the short man said, "is to import."

"But we'll bring it all back out again when we leave."

"You needn't pay the export duty until that time. But the import duty you pay now."

"*Export* duty!"

"No, import duty. The export duty you pay on the way out."

I may be wrong, but somehow I have the feeling that if Bob had been along with us something would have gotten worked out. But all poor Joe could do was look astonished and offended, wave his arms over his head, express indignation and outrage, and finally pay the hundred fifty dollars. The short man took the money with a secretive little smile that told me at least some of it was never going to get to the Abulia Treasury Department, and he and his umbrella went away again.

None of us had umbrellas. Because of the rain, none of the locals hanging around the airport had any desire to come out and help us off-load the plane. To this day, I can still feel soggy and soaked just thinking about that next ten minutes. I've had less water land on me in the shower.

Oh, well. We finally transferred ourselves and our luggage and our equipment to the little airport building, and Captain Archer and his faithful Oriental companion lifted their big bird into the black clouds, and we were alone in a wooden room with a lot of milk-chocolate-colored natives in ripped polo shirts and baggy trousers and no shoes. Nothing happened for a minute, and then the short man reappeared, without his umbrella, and went around behind the counter to sit on a stool and laboriously write our names and home addresses and purpose of trip in a big ledger he had there. For various reasons, we described purpose of trip as "to film travelogue."

It turned out that two of the barefoot loiterers were cabdrivers, one possessing a beige Simca and one a black Simca, and between them they managed to get us and all our junk away from there when the short man was done. Hank and Irv were having nothing to do with us, of course, so they and their equipment went in one car and Joe and Rudy and I and our stuff went in the other.

It might be interesting to know what Carefree Beach Hotel looks like when the sun is shining. For all I know, it's one of the beauties of the world. When I saw it, however, all the jungle greenery around it was sagging and drooping, the vines all over the pink stucco walls had been beaten leafless by the rain, and a temporary wall of rough unpainted plywood had been run across the end of the lobby that was normally left open to the sea breezes.

Inside, water stains discolored practically every ceiling and wall, and here and there thin rivers of water meandered across floors like the Mississippi through delta country. The desk clerk, a thin man with a ferocious mustache, was in an even worse temper than Joe, and between them they practically got us thrown out of our reservations. Rudy was back talking with the cabdrivers, and Hank and Irv weren't talking to anybody, and Bob wasn't with us, so it became up to me to soothe the desk clerk's ruffled feelings and cool Joe out until we were safely in our rooms. It is, by the way, from that incident that Joe dates his awareness of the fact that I was his enemy and out to make trouble for him. You'll see it in statements of his about the Ilha Pombo Affair—how he'd known for some time that I was out to do him harm in any way I could—and if you question him on the subject—as I have done—you will discover that in his mind it all began when I, in his words, "sided against me with the Carefree desk clerk." That's the level of sweet reason we're all working at these days, and if you people in the legal department manage to distill Truth from your post-morteming you'll be better than Solomon.

Well. We got to our rooms at last, five in a row on the upper floor, with windows overlooking a sheet of rain. Occasionally one could get a glimpse of the roiling ocean out there, being beaten like a flank steak by the rain, and the strip of murky amber-white nearby was probably Carefree Beach.

I was wet to the skin, of course. I stripped off everything and dried myself with the one clammy hand towel I found in the bathroom. When that wouldn't do the job—face and hands and it was ready to be wrung out—I used the thin cotton blanket folded at the foot of the bed. It was clammy, too, but at least it was big, and I managed to get fairly dry.

The word "clammy," as a matter of fact, covers just about everything I encountered at the Carefree Beach Hotel, from the floors and sheets to the food and employees. It was like being a houseguest of Bela Lugosi. Rain drummed everywhere, as monotonously and boringly as a salesman rapping his knuckles on his sample case in a waiting room, and one kept expecting Maugham characters in dirty white suits to stagger down the hall clutching bottles by the neck.

A little rain had seeped into my suitcase, naturally, but I found enough dry things in the middle to dress myself, which I was almost finished doing when a knock sounded at the door and Rudy called, "Joe wants to see you when you're ready."

"One minute," I said, and one minute I took, and went next door to Joe's room, where Rudy was pouring bourbon over ice in three glasses. "Civilization," I croaked, and the three of us lifted our glasses in silent toast to adversity—Joe and I still continued to have moments of being on the same team—and then we sat down to talk. Hank and Irv had been invited to join us but had declined.

"We'll want to get over to Ilha Pombo Island as soon as we can," Joe said. "And we'll want some locals to help out with the equipment. Jay, you seem to be on good terms with the desk clerk, why don't you go talk to him about it?"

"I already worked it out with the cabdrivers," Rudy said. "They know a guy with a boat, and they'll sign on themselves as our assistants. They'll be back around five."

It was then about twenty past four in the afternoon. Joe and I looked at Rudy with astonishment—a cameraman isn't expected to be an organizer, particularly not when the producer is along—and then Joe began to ask searching questions about the arrangements Rudy had made, details of price and how much time the cabdrivers would be available for us, all trying to find imperfections in Rudy's work, but there were none, and it's from *that* moment that Joe knew Rudy and I were in a combine against him.

I don't want to overstate that, by the way. For the most part, Joe continued to get along with both Rudy and me for quite some time after the episodes I'm recounting here, but *these days,* when he talks about the people who are trying to stab him in the back, he dates Rudy's and my betrayals from our first day at Carefree Beach Hotel.

Anyway, we discussed our present situation and immediate plans, the three of us, until about quarter to five, when Rudy was sent to relate the details to Hank and Irv. It was felt that Rudy, being a technician himself, would have a better chance of getting along with those two than a pair of white-collar workers like Joe and me.

While Rudy was off with Hank and Irv, I went to see the desk clerk and find out whether we could borrow or rent raincoats from somewhere. As it turned out, borrow, no; rent, yes. Five heavy black rubber raincoats with hoods were found for us, each one weighing about as much as a portable camera. At ten past five, when the Simcas rearrived at the hotel entrance, we all put on these raincoats, gathered up the equipment, and staggered out into the rain to bundle ourselves with a great deal of difficulty and discomfort into the two cars.

Nothing on earth is as hot and uncomfortable as a black rubber raincoat in the tropics, in June, inside a Simca. I felt like a baked potato in aluminum foil. We drove for fifteen minutes, and at the end of that time I was wetter inside the raincoat inside the car than if I'd been naked outside running along beside the car in the rain, the only difference being that I'd manufactured all this moisture myself.

Rudy summed it up for us, while tearing the raincoat off the instant he got out of the car: *"Christ!"*

Exactly. All five of us stripped the raincoats off, and we left them in the beige Simca, and somebody stole them while we were gone, and the Network paid an outrageous price for them later on.

The boat was what I'd expected the plane to be, only larger. It was a big, ungainly thing that looked as though the builder had been inspired by photographs of the dodo. It was all wood, it was of local manufacture, and at some time in the dim past it had been painted most of the colors available from Sherwin-Williams. A lot of this paint had chipped off since then, and some of the rest was grease-covered, but here and there one saw a length of bright blue railing or a touch of green on a doorjamb or a winking ruby of red on the mast.

This was primarily a fishing vessel, which meant it had an unfortunate aroma, and so did anyone who stayed near it for more than thirty seconds. It also meant the thing was mostly a big hollow storage area, with a prow in front, a smallish cabin on top, and a big greasy grindy noisy inefficient engine in the back. The crew consisted of three men and seven boys, of whom one man did the steering and the yelling, one boy kicked and spat at the engine, and everybody else stood around coiling rope.

We were making some attempt to keep our equipment moderately dry, though it was all the same sort of stuff that was even then being dragged through rice paddies all over Southeast Asia. In any event, once we'd piled the equipment in the cabin with the steersman, there wasn't any room left for people, so we five joined our two cabdrivers and the eight standby members of the fishing boat's crew out on deck, where the rain could have at us without restraint.

Joe yelled—we all had to yell to be heard—"How can it keep coming down like this? When does the goddam sky *empty?*"

"July," one of the cabdrivers yelled, and grinned and shrugged.

It was about five-thirty when the last rope was undone from the dock and our boat sagged seaward. I never entirely understood the word "wallow" until that trip, and now that I do understand it I hope I never have the opportunity to use it again. The boat floundered forward through the waves like an exhausted swimmer, seeming as though at any instant it would run out of strength entirely and simply sink under its own weight. The steersman yelled constantly, the standby crew rushed about coiling lengths of rope, the engine boy steadily kicked and spat at the engine, and we seven passengers huddled together on the foredeck in the rain and watched Abulia slowly fade behind us while nothing at all appeared out in front. *How does he know we're going in the right direction?* I wondered, but I didn't ask aloud, for fear there would turn out to be no answer.

We traveled a good half-hour through an impressionistic Japanese movie, the whole world reduced to this sort of blue and gray bowl of water through which we perhaps moved, our tiny shouts disappearing in the immensity of water surrounding us, nothing to be seen anywhere but the gray-black clouds above, the slanting gray rain all around us, the blue-gray-black roiling ocean for a floor, and we symbols of the Human Condition hopelessly adrift in the middle of it all.

But then we saw it. Something, some low something, out there ahead of us through the swirling sheets of rain. Low, featureless, colorless, spread across our path. We stared at it, and one of the cabdrivers said, "There it is. Pombo."

And there it was. We chugged forward, and imperceptibly the island came closer, and I thought, *Hell, I could swim it from here!*

Later, as they say in the ladies' novels, I was to recall those words.

In the meantime, though, our ship slowly attained shore, and at last we could see Ilha Pombo Island, the prize that was going to be fought over with those guns we'd been filming. One look, and I knew it wasn't worth it.

Ilha Pombo may look somewhat better in sunshine than the way I always saw it, but it can never look good. You know the kind of rag rug everybody's grandmother used to make, and it would wind up out on the back porch? That's what Ilha Pombo looked like. You can shine all the sunlight you want on a rag rug on a back porch, it still isn't going to look great.

As to Schlammville, I could see at once why practically every nation in Europe used tax money at one time or another to send a fleet over here to blow the place up or burn it down. Corrugated metal, odd pieces of wood, and lengths of tarpaper were the principal building materials. A couple of very, very old trucks were parked near the quay we were approaching, and so far there were no people at all in sight.

It was already easy to see why no tourists came here. I'm sure it wasn't my imagination, and I'm sure it wasn't just the rain; a very mean aura of cruelty and pain completely encircled Schlammville.

As an individual I would never have willingly gone near the place, and even with the weight of the Network behind me I was apprehensive.

The first Pombians I saw didn't do much to reassure me. Decrepit people dressed in rags, many of them missing fingers and toes, they sort of oozed out of doorways as we reached the concrete pier, and stood watching us, silently. Beside me, Rudy had commandeered one of the cabdrivers to assist and was busy at work with his camera, getting footage of everything in sight. If you want to look at it sometime, go ahead, but you'll find it depressing. I've heard people suggest that the Ilha Pombo Affair is basically comic, and so I suppose it is, the farther you get away from it. But not on the island itself; comedy withdraws, and shields her eyes.

The crew of rope coilers uncoiled all its rope and attached us to the pier, and as we were stepping ashore a bright pink Chevrolet sedan, about ten years old, appeared amid the shacks and squelched through the mud toward us, coming to a stop at the edge of the concrete. I noticed that most of the Pombians, with no fuss, oozed back into their doorways again and out of sight.

Three men emerged from the pink Chevvy, all of them tall, all of them fat, all of them wearing modified US Army uniforms with lots of vegetable salad, and all of them sporting sunglasses. *Sunglasses!*

And arrogance. They practically goose-stepped in their paratrooper boots, they were so full of themselves as they marched to our sodden little group out on the pier, and the tallest and fattest of them barked, "Entrance visas!"

Joe had all that stuff, and I saw him bracing himself to refuse to pay import duty on the television equipment, but oddly enough nobody suggested that money change hands. What these three were mostly concerned with was assuring themselves we were neither impostors nor spies. The notion that anybody would try to get on this island at all was incredible enough; the idea that anybody would be so anxious to come here as to do so under forged credentials was staggering. Still, that was the assumption those three were working under, and it was their island, so we had to play along, each of us in turn holding his face up to the rain so they could compare it closely with the picture in the appropriate passport.

We five Network men finally passed inspection, but there was immediately trouble about our cabdrivers. Joe kept explaining that they were assistants hired on Abulia to help out, and the leader of the Sunglass Brigade kept insisting Abulians couldn't come ashore without visas, and furthermore visas were never given to Abulians, and in any case Pombians could certainly be found to act as assistants, so finally Joe gave in and it was decided the cabdrivers would wait with the fishing boat until we returned and we'd pay them just as though they'd been able to do what we'd hired them for.

Now there was some confusion as to what was going to happen next, and finally Joe went off alone with the three men in their Chevvy, and the rest of us continued to stand around on the dock in the rain. Joe looked a little nervous about being cut out of the herd that way, but there didn't seem to be any alternative, so he went.

Rudy was grousing. "It's gonna get dark," he said. "I can't get any decent footage in all this rain anyway, and now it's gonna get dark."

"We'll just wait and see," I said.

Hank looked at Rudy and me and said, "Why don't you two guys go get yourself a drink?"

Rudy said to him, "Can't you forgive and forget, Hank?"

Hank gave him a dirty look and said, "Can't you shtoop yourself if I fold you?"

"You try it," Rudy said.

I immediately said something soothing to Rudy, and Irv said something soothing to Hank, and we managed not to have a brawl there on the dock in the rain on Ilha Pombo Island with the Pombians watching from their doorways and the Abulians watching from their fishing vessel. We managed not to, I say. America *has* progressed since the days of Wallace Beery.

And Joe progressed, too. We stood around for about twenty minutes, and then an army truck with a canvas top came slipping and sliding down through the mud and stopped where the pink Chevvy had been before, and out of the passenger seat came Joe, smiling, looking happy and relieved. "They laid on transportation for us," he said.

Meanwhile, out of the back of the truck were jumping four skinny Pombians; all of whom looked terrified and went on looking terrified for as long as I saw them. They came trotting over, double-time, and picked up our equipment with careful haste, or hurried caution, and carried it to the truck.

I said, "What's happening?"

Joe said, "We'll drop you and Hank and Irv and the sound equipment at the palace, to set up for the interview tomorrow. Meantime, Rudy and I will go do some location shooting."

And that's what happened. Rudy and Hank and Irv and the four terrified Pombians and all our equipment and I got into the back of the truck and sat on the metal floor, and Joe sat up in the cab with the driver, a younger version of the three army types we'd met before, not as tall, not as fat, but also wearing sunglasses. And off we went to the palace.

And that's what it is, all right. A palace. If you want to know where the twenty-two million dollars in American aid went, take a look at Rudy's footage of that palace. Seventy-three rooms. The outside completely built of white stone imported from Europe. Muzak throughout. Fifty Coca-Cola vending machines strategically placed. Persian carpets, French antiques, Scotch whiskey, American plumbing. Twenty-eight television sets, and a master antenna on the roof tall enough to pick up San Juan *and* St. Thomas *and* Havana. A movie screening room and an extensive library of very recent American and European movies. I could go on, but I don't think I will.

Hank and Irv and I debarked from the truck at one of the side entrances to the palace, where three more skinny terrified Pombians leaped out to carry the sound equipment. Another tall, fat boy in sunglasses and army uniform escorted us all to a big airy room with a conference table in the middle and a lot of pornographic photo blow-ups on the walls. Hank and Irv forgot all about being mad at me—and also all about setting up the sound equipment—while they browsed along the walls in concentrated imitation of life at the Louvre. Unusual positions, unusual participants. I believe Rudy shot some footage of those walls, but I don't think they're in our files. I know that during the interview with Mungu the next day, tall screens were set up around the walls so nothing would show in the background of the footage we shot then.

The entire palace, of course, was air-conditioned; the only time I didn't feel soggy and clammy during that trip was when I was in the palace.

I kept expecting Mungu himself to put in an appearance that first day, but he never did. It was just the three of us Network men, the three Pombian porters, and the army man. Hank and Irv weren't talking to me, and none of the Pombians were talking to anybody, so it made for a pleasant interlude all the way around. Hank and Irv finally finished their study of the walls and set their equipment up at one end of the conference table, with wires running down to the two lavalieres at the other end. Sullenly, speaking to me only the absolute minimum necessary, they had me sit where I would sit during the interview tomorrow, put the lavaliere on, and do some talking so they could check their levels and equipment and all that stuff they do. Then I sat where Mungu would sit tomorrow, and put *his* lavaliere on, and talked some more so they could do the same thing all over again. Usually in those circumstances I recite the Gettysburg Address, but in the present surroundings I had the feeling it might not be a diplomatic move on my part, so instead I recited *The Night Before Christmas.*

Sound men take forever to become satisfied with their equipment, and Hank and Irv are as finicky as any of them, but even so we were finished setting up quite a while before Joe and Rudy came back. I sat there and played with my lavaliere while waiting, and Hank and Irv went back to memorizing the walls, and eventually they came to the Coke machine in the corner and Irv called to the army type, "Okay if we have a Coke?"

The army type didn't know but wasn't willing to admit ignorance in front of foreigners. "You will wait," he said, trying to put a lot of menace in it, and marched out of the room. I could hear him making a phone call next door. Hank and Irv went back to the walls, I continued playing with my lavaliere, our three Pombian assistants huddled together in a corner, and finally the army man came back and ordered, "You may have Cokes."

"Thanks," Irv said, and opened the machine and took a bottle out—no money was needed—opened it and passed it to Hank. He took another one out, opened it, hesitated, then came over and without a word put it on the table in front of me.

"Thanks," I said, but he'd already turned away again. He went back to the machine, took out another bottle, opened it, and headed for the three Pombians in the opposite corner.

The army man barked, "No. Cokes for visitors only."

Irv looked at him. "I'll give you the dime," he said.
"Cokes for visitors only."
Irv looked at the Coke, at the three Pombians watching him with terrified expressions on their faces, at the sound equipment scattered all over the room, back at them again, and finally shrugged and said to them, "It's your country." Which was probably a dangerously subversive thing to say, all in all.
So we sat and drank our Cokes, and the three Pombians continued to huddle in a mass in a corner, and the army man stood with feet spread and arms folded over by the door, and it gradually grew dark outside and was completely night before Joe and Rudy got back. Another army man came to tell us our transportation was here, and we three Network men followed him away, leaving No-Cokes and the three assistants back in the conference room. I never saw any of them again and can only assume that No-Cokes ate them.
The truck was at the side entrance again. We climbed into the back, and Rudy said, "Well, I got footage, but it probably stinks."
Hank said, "Good, you putz," and Rudy looked at him and considered going over there and unscrewing Hank's head. Irv talked to Hank and I talked to Rudy, and nothing happened.
At night, Schlammville was both better and worse than in the daytime. You couldn't see most of the poverty and meanness, but on the other hand the small bits you could see served as a wonderful spur to imagination.
The rain, naturally, was still coming down. It didn't stop, it didn't slow down, it didn't even falter, not once during the entire time we were on the islands. It was just there, a fact you got used to after a while, like being dead.
A few lights, most of them candles, shone in windows of hovels we passed. The palace, of course, was bathed in electric illumination, possessing the only generator on the island and keeping all the resulting electric power for itself. Spotlights shone on the walls all the way around, and most of the rooms were kept lit all night long; Mungu, it was said, didn't much like the dark.
The fishing boat was waiting for us, the Abulian crew and the cabdrivers all crowded together into the small cabin amidships. They came bounding out when we appeared, delighted at the prospect of going home again, and Rudy's camera equipment was loaded aboard lickety-split.

It was amazing how one's spirits lifted, despite the rain, despite everything, the instant the ropes were loosed from the pier and the fishing boat began to sag seaward. Hank and Rudy even smiled at each other, and all the rest of us—Network men, rope coilers, cabdrivers, steersman, engine kicker—all smiled cheerfully at one another in a general wave of good will.

The ship turned slowly, reluctantly, and finally pointed its nose toward Abulia, invisible a dozen miles away. Looking back, I saw that Ilha Pombo at night, from a distance, gave a deceptive appearance of beauty, the squat dark village backlit by the brightly illuminated palace a mile inland; it was like some grim kind of Disneyland.

I made my way sternward, around the cabin and over the coils of rope, wanting a better look at the island before we got too far away. My toe caught in a length of rope, the ship sluggishly shook against a wave, and I flipped very neatly and quietly over the side.

TAPE FOUR, SIDE ONE

THIS IS SIDE ONE of tape four. Do not listen out of sequence. This is a recording.

Yeah, I know, there was some tape left. Tape three, side two, the one just before this, I quit with a couple minutes' tape left. But let's be honest about it, I've been in this business long enough to know a lead-in for a station break when I see one, and that finish was a natural, so I took a station break.

As a matter of fact, I took a break entirely. This is a new day, though I don't expect it to be much different from any of the old days, and I am starting afresh this morning. I talked my way through six sides of cassette tape yesterday, and I could feel my voice going toward the end there, and I decided it was time to quit for a while. So I did. I threw out the TV dinner, took some Alka-Seltzer, and watched television until my eyes closed.

Well, you don't want to hear about my troubles; you're from the legal department, not the medical department, you want to hear about the Network's troubles. When last heard from, I had just fallen into the Caribbean, at night, in the middle of a rainstorm.

And nobody noticed me leave. I sank for a while, I surfaced again at last, and when I stared around frantically for the boat it was going away from me. I tried yelling, but even I couldn't hear me, and every time I opened my mouth I took on several gallons of sea water—it doesn't taste like salt, it tastes much worse than that, like the bottom of an overshoe—so I quit yelling and started swimming. After the boat, at first, as though there were a chance in hell I could catch up with it. I swam a few strokes, and looked, and the boat was farther away. Almost out of sight. Out of sight. Back in sight briefly, as both it and I were lifted by waves, and then out of sight for good and all as the waves dropped us again.

Now what? I'd been soaking wet anyway, so that didn't bother me, and I knew I was a pretty good swimmer and wasn't in any immediate danger of drowning, but on the other hand the boat was gone and I wasn't capable of swimming any twelve miles all the way back to Abulia, not even if I could find the damn island in the rain in the dark. So now what?

The ocean lifted me, and turned me around, and showed me Ilha Pombo, the faint line of white light from the palace giving the place the appearance of some sort of Nordic Heaven.

So. There was nothing else for it. I swam ashore.

That sounds easy, doesn't it? "I swam ashore." What a brief little bit of tape that uses up, to say those three words. Believe me, it was a bit tougher to do than to say. And if I hadn't finally abandoned the struggle to keep my shoes I wouldn't have made it at all. The weight of the shoes dragged me down and dragged me down until it became obvious they were determined to go to the bottom of the Caribbean with me or without me.

Did you ever try to take your shoes off in the middle of the ocean at night during a cloudburst? To start with, wet laces don't untie; we all know that, it's one of the first traumas of childhood, one of the first hints of what adult life is going to be. Besides that, the only way human beings can reach their shoes at all is by sort of curling up a little, and when you curl up a little in the ocean you become a ball, and the ball promptly rolls over and puts your head at the bottom—that is, underwater. I can't think why my head would be my heaviest part, but apparently it is.

Well, I got them off. Obviously I did, or I wouldn't be here talking into this goddam microphone and wondering what my stomach will accept for breakfast. I have a Sara Lee cheese danish coffee ring in the freezer, and I'm trying to forget it's there. It's absurd to live on ice cream and pastry and Diet Pepsi, ridiculous and unhealthy and fattening.

So I got ashore. I'm back in the past now, back to the narrative. I finally reached shore, more dead than alive as they say, and went crawling up onto the weedy mud not far from the pier where we'd had the boat docked. I lay there for a while, trying to get my strength back, and I guess I fell asleep. Or passed out, it's all the same thing.

And I dreamed—I remember this vividly—I dreamed I was back in the house in Wilton, in bed, asleep, in the summertime, and the air conditioner was going and had made the room too cold, and Marlene had taken all the covers over onto her side of the bed, and when I tried to get them back she poked and tugged at me, pulling the covers away again, and I pushed at her hands, and she punched me a very hard, bony punch in the mouth, and I woke up. And it was pitch dark, and raining, and somebody was taking my pants off.

"Hey," I said, and sat up, and got punched in the mouth again. There was movement all around me, maybe half a dozen scampering forms in the darkness, and somebody decided to strangle me. Others were holding my wrists and sitting on my stomach and yanking at my trouser legs, but the main one had his hands around my throat and was strangling me. Fortunately he didn't have enough fingers to really do the job right, or I wouldn't be here now to describe all this.

Fortunately, also, my one shout of *hey* had been heard in the right quarters. I was lying on my back with all these thin bodies holding me down, my pants had been stolen, I was breathing very hoarsely through my incompletely closed windpipe, I was trying unsuccessfully to thrash around, I was in terror of my life and convinced it was all over for me, and a tiny white light came bobbling from far away, an angry voice began shouting over the drumming of the rain in the mud beside my head, and the thin bodies abruptly faded into the night. The fingers clutching my throat left last, and most reluctantly, and then I was alone. Without my pants. I was wearing now white socks, white boxer shorts, and a pale green pullover shirt. And I wasn't feeling good.

The white light came closer, becoming a flashlight, and more angry voices shouted. Confusion took place all around me. Slowly I rolled over in the mud onto my stomach, got my hands under me, and lifted myself with great difficulty to my knees. The flashlight was in front of me, pointing at me, and I can't have looked very appetizing—wet, muddy, bloody from the punches in the face, half-dressed, groggy. I looked up above the flashlight, at the patch of blackness approximately where a face would be if I wasn't talking to a midget—I could see nothing at all beyond the light—and I said, "Thanks. I think you saved my life." And he kicked me in the stomach. I said, "Oof," and doubled over, and something very hard hit me on the back of the head, and when I woke up I was tied to a table in a room with paneled walls.

Let me try to make clear just how odd that was. I am talking about wall paneling, ordinary sheets of wall paneling such as suburban men all over this mighty land do-it-themselves in the basement playroom on weekends. Paneling. Walnut, with the vertical black lines that are supposed to imitate the spaces between boards and give the illusion that you have a wall made out of boards. It was exactly like waking up in somebody's basement playroom, and in a way I suppose that's really what it was; somebody's basement playroom. Mungu's basement playroom.

There was also the normal dropped ceiling; you know what I mean—two-foot by four-foot sections of soundproofing fiberboard set on a metal gridwork—you see those ceilings all over the place these days. And the tile floor, you see that a lot, too. And the recessed fluorescent light fixtures with the things across them that look like giant ice cube tray inserts.

But instead of the usual dart board on the wall there was an iron maiden. And instead of the card table a whipping post. And this wasn't a Ping-Pong table I was strapped to, it was something else entirely; white porcelain, with a groove down the middle of it and a pour spout at the end, past my feet. I had no idea what the thing was at the time, but since then I've described it to a few people and I've found out what it is. An autopsy table. Except that most of them don't have straps that hold the customer rigid in one position, since most of the people who use autopsy tables don't have the problem of keeping the clients from going away.

If I'd known at the time that I was lying on an autopsy table, I probably would have dropped dead of fright. As it was, I had an idea my condition wasn't exactly enviable.

I was not alone in the room. Three army types were there, identical with all the others I'd seen earlier today—tall, fat, khaki-uniformed, beribboned, sunglassed. Even here, indoors, underground, at night, during a rainstorm, there were the sunglasses.

Unfortunately, they almost at once noticed that I was awake, and they came smiling over to discuss the situation with me. With sunglasses and uniforms it's hard to tell, but I didn't think I'd met any of these three before, which was a pity. In any event none of *them* recognized *me,* and that was the important part.

One of them leaned over me and said, "So Colonel Enhuelco's spy awakes." He kept smiling. They all kept smiling, all the time.

I said, "I'm not a spy." What with the exposure, and the salt water, and the being strangled, my voice wasn't at its best.

He had a night stick in one hand, the kind police carry in big cities, and he tapped me on the lower ribs with it. Just a tap, but my ribs went on aching for an hour. "Don't lie," he suggested, and smiled at me.

A second one had come around to the other side of the table. He said, "Is Colonel Enhuelco still in Florida?" He had a small metal hammer in his hand.

"I don't know."

Smiling, he tapped me on the forehead with the hammer. "Ignorance can be a painful problem."

Somebody was touching my toes. I couldn't lift my head, but I could strain my eyes and look down over my cheekbones, and way down at the far end of the table was the third one, smiling at me. Between finger and thumb he was holding the big toe of my left foot. My socks were gone. So were my shorts and my shirt. He said, "Please hold out as long as you possibly can. It gets so dull around here."

"Get him ready," the first one said, looking at his watch. He suddenly sounded a little nervous.

"Listen," I said, "you're making a big—"

The one on my right tapped a kneecap with his nightstick. "Say nothing," he said.

"But—"

The one on my left tapped my other kneecap with his hammer. "Be silent," he said.

I was silent.

The third one, meantime, was doing something uncomfortable to my toes, and at first I couldn't figure out what it was. Then I realized he'd taken some adhesive tape and was curling the toes of my left foot and taping them down to be as small and unobtrusive as possible. All but the big toe. Meanwhile, the other two stood on either side of me, smiling at me and patting their weapons into the palms of their hands.

My big toe got very cold. I squinted down over my cheekbones again, and he had a little can in his hand, flat, and was squirting something from it onto my big toe. I sniffed. I smelled it. It reminded me of—Wilton. It reminded me of Wilton. The backyard. Summer. Barbecues.

Charcoal starter! The stuff similar to lighter fluid that you squirt on charcoal before you light it, to make it burn right away.

"Oh," I said, and got both kneecaps tapped.

I lay there blinking a lot, looking up at the dropped ceiling, wishing it would really drop and kill everybody, including me. And then a door opened, and I swiveled my eyes around and looked, and an enormously fat man in a uniform more resplendent than a Fifth Avenue doorman came waddling in. He too wore sunglasses, and was smiling, and he held a huge cigar in his left hand. It wasn't, I noticed, lit.

This was Mungu. It had to be. All the really nasty dictators in the world rolled into two.

He came forward, smiling, waddling, and I noticed that my three friends were suddenly all very nervous, their hands visibly trembling, their smiles obviously forced and strained, and I thought, *If his own assistants are that afraid of him, I should probably faint now.* But I didn't. I would have loved oblivion, if only for a little while, but I remained insistently awake.

Mungu approached the foot of my table, and the army man there stepped nervously to one side. Mungu smiled at me, holding up his cigar for me to see, and said, "Would our guest be kind enough to light my cigar?"

"He would love to, sir," said the army man down there, the one who'd prepared my toes, and he hurriedly brought a Zippo lighter out of his pocket.

I took a deep breath. I yelled, *"I'm Jay Fisher!"*

Hammer and nightstick lifted, but Mungu frowned at me and said, "What?"

The hammer and nightstick were still poised. Shaking, sweating, I said, "Jay Fisher. From the Network."

Mungu's frown deepened. "I'm not supposed to see you until tomorrow," he said.

The reason for that pause there is that I'd come to another natural station break and I could sense it, and I just automatically stopped talking. Then I realized the tape was going around and I wasn't saying anything, so I switched it off. And have been away eating Sara Lee cheese danish coffee ring and Diet Pepsi. For breakfast. Soon I'll be having some more Alka-Seltzer.

All right. Back to the autopsy table. As soon as the mix-up was brought to light I was freed from the table and allowed to wash my face and hands and big toe. In fact, I was allowed to shower—I half-expected gas instead of water—and was then given brand new clothing in my own size. Mungu had disappeared immediately upon finding out who I really was and giving new orders about me, and I didn't see him anymore that night. Nor my three friends from the playroom. A slender Frenchman in a black suit and white shirt and narrow black tie and open-toed brown sandals was put in charge of me. "I am M'sieu Mungu's correspondence secretary," he said, and would say no more. When I tried to tell him what had happened to me—not to mention what had almost happened to me—he professed total ignorance on the subject. When I asked him his name, he said, "I am insignificant, unimportant, not relevant." And when I asked him questions about Mungu and Ilha Pombo and just about anything else, he went back to being ignorant again. He was possibly the least-informed individual on any and all subjects I have ever met.

But he was, for all that, an excellent guide. Dressed in proper-fitting and nicely tailored new clothes—down to expensive black oxfords—showered, fed beef stew and beer, my basic optimism, crushed to earth, began slowly to rise again.

And in the last analysis, I did get a much better ride back to Abulia than if I'd stayed with the fishing boat. The Frenchman took me up and down long, brightly lit corridors in the palace to a room with a Cadillac Eldorado in it. I don't mean a garage, I mean a room. True, it had an overhead garage door at one end that opened onto a blacktop driveway, but it also had carpets on the floor, paintings on the walls—French impressionists, not for Hank and Irv at all—Louis XVI chairs and tables, floor lamps, a Coke machine, and a television set.

There was a chauffeur already in the car, an army man in the inevitable sunglasses, but younger and thinner than any I'd seen up till now. He was sitting at attention, staring straight ahead out the windshield, and gave no indication of awareness of our presence when the Frenchman and I arrived and climbed into the back seat, except that as soon as we'd shut the door he started the engine, pushed a button on the dashboard that opened the overhead door at the end of the room, and we drove out of the palace and into the continuing rainstorm.

An interesting trip. We were on blacktop the whole way—earlier today we'd driven on nothing but mud—and we didn't go down into the town of Schlammville at all. It was maybe three or four miles—absolute silence in the car, but outside, rain noises: tires on wet roadway, windshield wipers clicking back and forth, raindrops thrumming on the roof—the Frenchman and the chauffeur both staring straight ahead, me looking out the window in a vain attempt to see what we were driving past, and then we came to a stop. I looked out front, and the headlights showed me another garage door. The chauffeur pushed his button, the door lifted, and we drove into another room. I knew it was different because the furniture here was American Colonial.

The Frenchman pointed. "You go through there," he said. "So nice to have met you."

I said, "By myself?"

"Yes. You go through there."

Reluctantly I got out of the car. The chauffeur had left the garage door up, and now I realized the Eldorado had been discreetly air-conditioned, to dry the air more than to cool it. Mugginess poured in through the open door.

I was no sooner clear of the Cadillac when it backed briskly out again, making a tight backwards U-turn out there in the rain. The overhead door slid down again while the Cadillac was still making its turn, and I was alone. Just me and the air conditioning, which was busily restoring the atmosphere to its proper calm.

So I went over to the door the Frenchman had pointed at, opened it, looked through, and saw a yacht. Indoors. An outsize boathouse, that's what it was, with a medium-size white yacht floating in it.

A milk-chocolate-colored young man in a sailor suit trotted over, saluted, and said, "All ready to go, sir."

"Back to Abulia?"

"Yes, sir. Gangplank this way, sir."

I followed him aboard, and I assume someone pushed a button somewhere, because a *huge* overhead door at the far end lifted, and out we sailed into the night and the storm. The young man in the sailor suit had brought me into shelter before rain could land on me, though, and I looked around to find myself in a sort of New York singles' bar without people. Except for the bartender, a burly red-haired man in a white apron, drying glasses with a small white towel. "Yes, sir," he said. "And what's yours?" He had a deep Irish brogue.

I went over and sat on a barstool. "Nepenthe," I said.

"Yes, sir," he said. He put a newly dried glass on the backbar and used the towel to wipe the spotless surface in front of me. "Would that be Irish nepenthe, Scotch nepenthe, or Kentucky nepenthe?"

"Kentucky nepenthe," I said.

"Very chauvinistic," he said, "but the customer is always right. And what would you like with it, sir?"

"A glass," I said. "And some ice."

"No sooner said than done." But first he whipped from under the bar a bowl of cashews and put them by my right hand. I munched cashews, listened to the rain beating on the windows, felt the throb of the mighty engines down below—or the galley slaves, I'm not entirely sure which it was—and watched the barman build me my first drink. But not my last.

We only had twenty minutes together, he and I, and we discussed nothing but the lore and learning of alcohol, but I found him a fascinating and soothing presence in my life, which after all is precisely what a bartender is supposed to be. "Have one with me," I said after a while. As though I were buying.

"Thank you, sir." Also as though I were buying. "I believe I'll have Irish," he said.

"Very chauvinistic," I said.

"Ah," he said. "But I have justification. Your health, sir."

"Your health."

He drank his neat, all at once, from a shot glass, so for the rest of our time together we discussed the various ways of drinking various liquors and the advantages and disadvantages attendant upon each. And then the young man in the sailor suit popped his head in and said, "All here, sir."

"Right," I said, and got off the stool. I was feeling much better. "Well, good night now," I said.

"Drop in anytime," he said.

The young man had a big pink umbrella he insisted on holding over my head as we went down the gangplank together to a covered wooden pier, where he pointed to the right, said, "Down there, sir," saluted me briskly, and hurried back up the gangplank again.

I went down there and found a black Citroën sedan waiting for me, with a chauffeur holding the rear door open. I slid in, he shut the door, he trotted around and got in behind the wheel, and in ten silent minutes he was trotting around to open the door again at the entrance to Carefree Beach Hotel.

The desk clerk was flipping through stacks of flimsy paper. He looked up, saw me coming, and was very pleased to be able to announce, "No more dinner, sir. Too late for dinner. Dinner all finished."

"So am I," I said, and went on by him and turned left at the temporary plywood wall and walked down to the bar, which had temporary plywood over its glassless windows, making it look like a correspondents' hangout in a war zone.

There were three people in there. The first and most important was the bartender, a local citizen, a distinct comedown from my Irish friend on the yacht; this one had been permanently embittered by something or other in his past, apparently, and could neither forgive nor forget. The second, sitting at a table over a planter's punch, was Joe Singleton, looking impassioned as usual, and the third, sitting over another planter's punch at the same table, was a man I'd never seen before—fortyish, broody-eyed, with thick black hair and a full black beard. He was wearing a Harry Truman-type Hawaiian shirt, faded dungarees, and black sandals.

Joe looked up and saw me and said, "Hi, Jay. Come on over and sit down. Want a planter's punch?"

I went over, but I didn't sit down. I said, "Are you kidding?"

"No, they're good," he said, and held his glass up toward me. "Here, try it."

I said, "Didn't you even *miss* me?"

"Well, I figured you didn't want dinner, and believe me, Jay, you were right. Have you ever had—what is it?—plantain?"

Well, I won't repeat the whole conversation. In sum, nobody had seen me fall overboard. In the darkness and the rain, with all the confusion of people and equipment, nobody noticed that I wasn't among those present when they landed at Abulia. After that, everybody assumed I was in the other car—two Simcas, remember?—and then everybody assumed I didn't want dinner, and then everybody assumed I was taking a nap or something in my room. God knows how long it would have been before everybody ran out of assumptions.

In the course of all my baffled questioning and Joe's baffled answering, he introduced his tablemate: "Oh, by the way. Jay Fisher, Harvey Osgood."

"Hi," Harvey Osgood said. He had very bright eyes above the beard, and he was watching our conversation with a great deal of interest.

"Hi," I said. "But, Joe, didn't anybody *notice*—" And so on.

But nobody had noticed.

In the middle of all this, the embittered bartender came over with three more planter's punches, and rather than add another burden to his heavy load by pointing out I hadn't ordered a planter's punch, I sat down at the table and began to drink one of them.

Anyway, eventually I finished with my questions, and then Joe started with his, beginning, "Well, if you weren't with us, where were you?" And I told him. And Harvey Osgood sat there fascinated, and Joe sat there getting more and more excited and indignant and enthusiastic, and by the time I was finished he was practically jumping up and down on his chair.

"We've got to get that on film!" he shouted. "Before it fades in your mind, we've got to get it on film!"

"It will never fade in my mind," I said.

"Nevertheless." He was up in arms again, the same as in Oklahoma City. "Now's the time to put that story down in living color," he told me. "Still steaming from the jungles of reality. Excuse us, Harvey."

"Sure," Harvey said, and Joe got to his feet and dragged me away from the table and the planter's punch and upstairs to Irv's room, where the poker game was going on. Hank and Irv had called a temporary truce with Rudy for the sake of having enough people to make an interesting game, and the two cabdrivers were also sitting in. Joe burst in on this friendly session, towing me behind him, and gave a highly dramatized yet encapsulated version of the story I'd just finished telling him, adding that we were going to film me telling that story right now, right this minute.

Hank gave it as his opinion that the whole story was bullshit, that I hadn't fallen overboard at all, that I'd been in the hotel the whole time and had probably simply been drinking again. Irv presented a more cogent argument against the filming: "We left all our sound equipment over on the other island."

"There must be *something* around!" Joe wailed, and after he'd wailed it five or six times it turned out there was something after all—a cassette tape recorder, very much like this one. "We can sync in the lab later in New York," Joe said. "The important thing now is to get the thing down on film and tape."

"Sync or swim," Rudy said irritably, "let's get it done and over with. I had a good hand."

"And that's bullshit, too," Hank announced.

Anyway, we set up a thing in a corner of the room, where two plain white walls met, with an interesting water stain on one wall that looked like a map of Laos—to give that news analyst effect—and I sat down on a chair in that corner, and Rudy aimed his camera at me, and every light we could get our hands on was aimed at me, and I held the cassette mike in my hand—just the way I'm doing now—and I told my story. I still remember the opening lines: "Jay Fisher reporting. I have just returned from Mungu's dungeons, on the island of Ilha Pombo Island, here in the Caribbean. I wasn't in those dungeons in my accustomed role as reporter. I was there as a prisoner."

And so on.

I did the thing at some length, with interesting details and appropriate pauses, retaining a journalistic calm throughout, and when I was finished Joe leaped forward and embraced me—Hank and Ive exchanged a glance—and cried, "I've seen News Department history made tonight!"

"Yes," I said, getting out of his embrace. "Thanks, uh."

Rudy said, "Can we go back to the cards now?"

"I want to thank you boys," Joe told them, and they all backed up a bit. "You helped to create history tonight."

"That's fine, Joe," Irv said, and it seems to me I heard Hank mutter, "Bullshit."

So we finally let them get back to their game—it turned out the next day the cabdrivers took our team to the cleaners, even worse than Jaekel Grahame's green velvet mob—and Joe and I went down to the bar again, where Harvey Osgood was sitting where we'd left him, with what had to be a different planter's punch in front of him. Harvey looked at us and said, "Everything okay?"

"Just fine," Joe said. "You should have been there."

"I wasn't invited," Harvey said.

Joe didn't notice. "We made News Department history tonight," he said. "Bartender!"

"He's bringing them," I said.

"Oh."

The bartender put down three planter's punches, looked at me as though it was all my fault, and scuffed back to his place behind the bar. Joe proposed a toast to the Pulitzer Prize, Harvey and I drank to it, Joe swigged deep, we all sighed with contentment for a few seconds, and then Joe said, "Actually, Harvey is an interesting fellow in his own right."

"Well, not really," Harvey said.

"Is that right?" I said.

"He's one of the original Beatniks. He's writing a novel here."

"Is that right?" I said.

"It's just a book," Harvey said.

"He hung around with Kerouak and all those people," Joe said.

"Oh, well," Harvey said.

"Is that right?" I said.

"He's one of the whole original mob," Joe said.

"Oh, I wouldn't say that," Harvey said. "I was just on the fringes, you might say; I didn't really know the guys all that well. Jack and Greg and Allen and them, I wouldn't say I was ever real close to them."

"Is that right?" I said.

"His novel's about all of them," Joe said. "He's been working on it for fifteen years. All over the Caribbean."

"Just the smaller islands," Harvey said.

"No kidding," I said.

"Actually," Harvey said, "the book isn't so much about the guys I knew in those great days as it is about the gut issue of our time."

Joe leaned forward and said, "Sounds like you're onto something, Harvey."

"Alienation," Harvey said.

"Is that right?" I said.

Joe frowned and said, "Alienation, Harvey?"

"That's it," Harvey said. "Modern man is alienated from the technological civilization he himself created."

"Well, that's all true enough," Joe said dubiously.

"Oh, it's true," I said. I was happy to be able to join the conversation. "We ourselves have done several specials on the subject."

"That's just the problem," Joe said. "Harvey, I hate to say this, but I have the feeling that just isn't the gut issue of our times anymore."

"Of course it is," Harvey said. "Why do you think I've been writing the book on all these stinking islands?"

"Yeah, but, Harvey," Joe said, "the problem is, we all *know* about alienation now. Christ, buddy, we've had alienation drummed into our heads for so long now people show up to class reunions under assumed names. When you talked about the gut issue of our times *I* thought you meant the New Morality."

Harvey frowned at him. "The what?"

"You don't know anything about that down here? But that's where it's at, man. The New Morality, *that's* the subject of our generation!"

"What the hell's the New Morality?"

"No bras," I said.

"*And* no war," Joe said to me. To Harvey he said "A hundred generations grew up believing that war was beautiful and sex was obscene. The New Morality says sex is beautiful and war is obscene."

"Wait a second," Harvey said. "Where's that leave Hemingway?"

"Hopelessly outdated," Joe said.

"I can't go along with that," Harvey said. "Hemingway was sort of our, I don't know, our scout leader. We can build from him, we can go on and explore avenues he merely suggested, but to *deny* him?"

"He believed war was beautiful," Joe said. "And sex obscene."

I said, "You know, if Bob were here—"

"The writer on our special," Joe explained to Harvey. "Bob Grantham. He's done some books himself; maybe you know the name?"

"I don't think so," Harvey said.

"Different kind of book," I said. "Anyway, if he was here he would say the gut issue of our time is the struggle between communism and anticommunism."

"The Cold Warrior mentality," Joe said scornfully. "That's deader than alienation."

"Alienation isn't dead!" Harvey was beginning to get irritated.

"The New Morality is where it's at!" Joe shouted. He was getting a little bugged himself.

"It's an honest difference of opinion," I said, not wanting them to really get angry with each other. "Just as Bob would have his own opinion about the menace of Godless Communism."

Harvey said to me, "What about you, Jay? What's your opinion?"

"Oh, I don't have an opinion of my own," I said. "I go along with everybody. I'm just filling in for Bob because he isn't here to state his position for himself."

So for the next couple of hours, we three sat in the bar on the island of Abulia and discussed what was the gut issue of our time, and never did come up with a final answer.

We did salt away a lot of planter's punch, however. And finally staggered away to bed. And then the next morning we all got in the two Simcas and rode back to the fishing boat and traveled over to Ilha Pombo Island again. All of us except Harvey, I mean. I assume he spent the day working on his book.

Oh, and the cabdrivers. Since they weren't going to be permitted to get off the boat at Ilha Pombo, there was no point their getting on at Abulia, so they didn't. Just us five Network men.

The truck was already waiting for us when we got to Ilha Pombo, with several of the usual tall, fat, sunglassed army men, all standing around in the rain as though there weren't any rain. But there was. At least as much as yesterday.

I peered closely at the army men, but none of them seemed to be my friends from the playroom. We piled ourselves and our equipment in the back of the truck again, with another bunch of skinny terrified Pombians along as bearers—I looked them over, in hopes of finding one of them wearing my pants—Joe sat up front with the driver again, and we jounced through the mud amid the shacks once more to the palace.

The screens were set up in front of the art exhibit in the conference room, so there was nothing for Hank and Irv to do but fuss with their sound equipment, all of which had been fussed over at great length already yesterday. Rudy set up his camera and the lights, the Pombians huddled in a corner, two army men stood with folded arms by the door, and Joe kept peering around screens, trying to get a look at the gallery, about which he had only heard yesterday. As for me, I spent my time going over the script.

We'd had to present Mungu with our questions in advance, of course, and Bob and Joe had worked out the script together. Looking at the script now, seeing the interplay of values among the various questions, I was only thankful that Harvey Osgood hadn't been asked to toss in a few questions, too.

Mungu made us wait forty-five minutes, and when he came in he was surrounded by army men. He was also smoking a large cigar, and I wondered who'd lit it for him.

Last night I had been too frightened to take a really close look at Mungu in the short time he was in the playroom but today I did look, and it was amazing just how ugly he was. He was the fattest man I ever saw, and it was *soft* fat; he looked like a baked potato. He was the usual milk chocolate color, but with him it looked as though the chocolate had been left on a sunny windowsill too long. He looked as though if you touched him he would be unhealthily warm, and somewhat oily or moist, and you would come away with chocolate stains on your fingers. He looked like a cartoon character, really; the evil King of the Candy Bars.

And his voice was amazingly mellow, a resonant yet light baritone—chocolate syrup pouring from a chocolate egg. A smiling, sunglassed, incredibly nasty chocolate egg.

Who pretended, when Joe introduced me to him, that we'd never seen one another before. "Very pleased to meet you," he said.

Well, the hell with that. "We met last night," I said. He didn't offer to shake hands with anybody, and nobody offered to shake hands with him.

He was smooth and slippery, and he kept smiling all the time. "I meet so many people," he murmured, and turned away to be introduced to Rudy by Joe, who at the same time gave me a quick dirty look.

Finally we sat down facing one another at the end of the conference table. I put on my lavaliere, and Hank came down to put Mungu's on for him, and when he reached to put the thing around Mungu's neck one of the Army men rushed forward, raising his truncheon to beat Hank with it, and as he started his swing, Hank straightened, saw him, and gave him a hard left to the nose that broke his sunglasses, knocked out a front tooth, gave him a nosebleed, and rendered him unconscious.

"What the hell," Hank said.

The other army men were advancing. Joe was wringing his hands. Rudy and Irv and I were making fists. Mungu very quietly and mellifluously said, "Wait." And everybody stopped dead.

Mungu said to Hank, "You perhaps were improperly or inadequately briefed before coming here. No one is permitted to touch my person."

Hank gave him a flat look and said, "If you can put the mike on yourself, go ahead. I get the same crap from actresses." He stepped over the body on the floor and walked back down to Irv and the equipment. They shook their heads together, giving one another meaningful looks, as blue-collar workers in the same union tend to do.

I see I'm coming to the end of the tape. All right, before you play the other side of this, I'm including the tape of the Mungu interview; you might want to listen to that.

Anyway, in the tape I have left here, let me finish setting the scene. Mungu had his fallen comrade carried away, and then he held the lavaliere in his hands and looked at me and said, "Please take yours off and put it on again, so I may see how it's done."

He said *please*. "Sure," I said, and did. He watched, nodded, and followed suit. And then we did the interview.

I still have tape left. Let me tell you what was going through my head throughout the interview. I was sitting there facing this really gross human being, about the size of Rhode Island, and I still had very fresh in my memory the events of the night before, and one thing just kept circling and circling in my head the whole time of the interview. It's one line from the giant's rhyme in *Jack and the Beanstalk*:

"I'll grind his bones to make my bread. I'll grind his bo

APPENDIX FOUR

Jay Fisher Interview with Mungu, President of Ilha Pombo Island, at the Presidential Palace, June, Current Year

Q: Mr. President, there's a great deal of concern in the United States that the Castro regime in Cuba will export revolution to other nations in the Caribbean and in the Latin American area generally. Do you believe that Castro-type Communist revolutions can indeed take place in Latin America, and do you think such a revolution could gain a foothold here on Ilha Pombo Island?

A: Well, of course, fertile soil for revolution is an area where the people are discontent. I cannot speak for the Caribbean area generally, but insofar as the people of Ilha Pombo are concerned, may I say that I know the hearts and minds of my people, they have opened their hearts to me, and I know that here we have no fear of revolution, neither from the left nor from the right. I am like a father to my people, and the children do not have a revolution against the father. Oh, they may grumble sometimes, they may think the father is too severe sometimes, but they do not have a revolution.

Q: Mr. President, there have been reports that guns and weapons have been smuggled into Ilha Pombo to a revolutionary group here. Representatives of these revolutionaries in the United States protest that they are not Communist-inspired or Castro-inspired but that they are in fact anti-Communist.

A: Do they suggest that *I* am a Communist?

Q: No, sir. They say that they are neither right-wing nor left-wing but middle-of-the-roaders. They claim there is no true democracy here in Ilha Pombo.

A: Unfortunately for them, the fact is, there are no true revolutionaries here on Ilha Pombo. No weapons have been smuggled onto this island for the simple reason that no one here is interested in obtaining any such weapons. There are no revolutionaries on this island, not left-wing, not right-wing, and most certainly not middle-of-the-road revolutionaries, and the reason there are no revolutionaries here is that this *is* a democracy, a true democracy under my paternal benevolence. Democratic institutions are zealously maintained here, and the contentment of my people is the clearest indication of that.

Q: Mr. President, in light of what you've just said, allow me to bring up the question of elections. The only election in the history of Ilha Pombo's independence took place in April of 1952, when Dr. Martin Chiswick-Smythe became your nation's first President. He disappeared in October of that same year, and there has been no election since.

A: In itself, the clearest indication of the democratic peacefulness and harmony that maintain on this island. When Dr. Chiswick-Smythe absconded with seven hundred thousand dollars from the national treasury in the fall of 1952, as you just pointed out, our poor island trembled on the brink of chaos. I was fortunately able to step in and right the ship of state. I have been open to the question of elections from that day to this, but the fact of the matter is, the people are so satisfied with my handling of national affairs that no other candidate for the Presidency has ever come forward. It is a Communist trick to hold a fake election with only one slate of candidates on the ballet. In a true democracy, that sort of sham election is unnecessary. We don't need to prove anything to the world; our affairs are an open book. This is a democratic nation, peaceful and prosperous with an enlightened government and a contented citizenry.

Q: And if opposition to your policies did arise, you would not stand in the way of an election?

A: Certainly not. Of course if opposition arose from a criminal element, from Communists or from those who would simply want to raid the treasury as Dr. Chiswick-Smythe did, it would be a cruel farce to hold an election. Such individuals should simply be arrested and tried for their crimes.

Q: Mr. President, the leader of the forces opposing you in exile in the United States—

A: There are no Pombians in exile. No Pombian needs to fear this government for honest political differences. There are certain criminal elements which have fled their homeland's justice and who are presently at large in your hospitable land, but to call these people exiles implies a dignity they don't deserve. They are simple cutthroats.

Q: Well, Mr. President, the leader of this group of people in the United States, Colonel Padigard Enhuelco, claims that—

A: Precisely the sort of individual I had in mind. This Enhuelco, who has the gall to consider himself a colonel even though the Pombian Army long since cashiered him *in absentia*, was a crony of Dr. Chiswick-Smythe and in fact assisted him in his raid on the treasury and his subsequent escape. I can only assume that he has squandered all his loot and that that is why he is now attempting to raise a mercenary army in the United States to attack his homeland. I tell you, and I warn this fugitive from justice Enhuelco, that the honest citizens of Ilha Pombo will rise as one man to fling back into the sea any gang of hirelings and toughs he may lead against us. The United States is perhaps overly hospitable to allow such a dangerous man freedom of movement on her territory, and I have just recently sent an urgent communication to your President asking him to have this Enhuelco arrested and returned to his homeland for trial, and to further investigate to discover from whom this Enhuelco is receiving monetary assistance. Someone in the United States, some group, is financing Enhuelco's attempted piracy against a sovereign nation friendly to the United States, and I believe your government should act swiftly against these people before irreparable damage is done to the relations between our two countries.

Q: Well, Mr. President, Colonel Enhuelco claims that you—

A: He is not a colonel.

Q: I'm sorry. Mr. Enhuelco claims that you are illegally at the head of government, since you never ran in any election, and that you maintain your power through intimidation, torture, and ruthless suppression of your political opposition.

A: Exactly the sort of thing that a scoundrel like Enhuelco might say, in an attempt to inflame the sympathies of Americans, who are known to be a freedom-loving and tyrant-despising people. The fact that the American government maintains friendly relations with my government is itself a crushing answer to this sort of scurrilous attack. Beyond this, unfounded allegations of torture and intimidation are easy to make, but where are the proofs? It is claimed that we have torture rooms, that I myself engage in torture of prisoners. But where is the proof of these absurd allegations? Who has ever come forward to claim personal knowledge of such torture rooms? No one.

Q: Me.

A: I beg your pardon?

Q: Last night you and I met—

A: Last night I was on my yacht, returning from a conference on Caribbean economic matters held at Kingston, Jamaica. I did not return to Ilha Pombo until half-past nine this morning.

Q: But you—

A: I do not know to what you are referring, but I must point out that I am the head of a sovereign state, and as such I do not expect my word to be questioned. It is possible that enemies of Ilha Pombo staged some sort of playlet for you or other reporters at some recent time, but if so, I am certain no responsible journalist would wish to bandy accusations without proof. If, on the other hand, a journalist were to accept a bribe from enemies of this or any other sovereign state to spread scurrilous lies, I would expect the journalist's employer and government to take swift action to see to it that his crime did not go unpunished.

Q: But—

A: Have you no more questions?

Q: I have more—There are more questions, yes. Uh, Mr. President, it has been suggested that the revolutionaries, should they take over from your government, would—

A: An obvious impossibility.

Q: Yes, sir. But if they should, assuming it were possible, it's been suggested that they would take a more active role in the effort to rid Cuba of its present Communist masters and end the enslavement of the Cuban people before it can spread to other parts of the Caribbean and Latin America.

A: One would assume that individuals who would attack one sovereign state would not hesitate to attack another. But if these people are attempting to gain support among Americans by claiming to be anti-Communist, let me reassure your viewers that the very opposite is the truth. The corruption and thievery and scandal which these people would bring to this island is the very breeding ground of Communist revolution. Were these people to force their will on the Pombian people, I would not be at all surprised to see Communist sympathies quickly take hold in the minds of the simple peasants. Plain, honest, legitimate, democratic government is the strongest defense against communism. As to these people claiming they would go on from Ilha Pombo to attack Cuba, isn't that in itself proof that they are not patriots but merely adventurers, pirates, freebooters? If they would overthrow true democracy on Ilha Pombo, how could anyone expect them to introduce democracy in Cuba? I deplore the current government in Cuba and the illegal overthrow of my good friend Batista as much as anyone, but were I to attack another sovereign state, how could I then claim sanctity from attack myself?

Q: Mr. President, the world today is in turmoil, and much of this has been reflected by the New Morality. The various nations of the world are lining up for or against the New Morality, the Scandinavian nations in the forefront of acceptance while nations such as Greece do such things as ban the miniskirt. The government of Ilha Pombo Island has made no official announcements on such matters as the miniskirt, the Vietnam War, birth control pills, and so on. Would you say where Ilha Pombo stands on these matters?

A: Ilha Pombo is a democracy and therefore does not attempt to legislate the minds and hearts of its citizens. But I would say that generally the people of this nation, and certainly the government of this nation, are firmly in favor of the tenets of traditional morality—hard work, truth, justice, equality of opportunity, and peace.

Q: Thank you, Mr. President.

TAPE FOUR, SIDE TWO

DID YOU LISTEN to the Mungu tape? I hope so. I also hope you're bearing up under all this better than I am. These tapes just keep going on and on, and I never seem to get to the end of the story. We haven't gotten to Base Camp One yet, and Ernesto Rivera's ear, and Richard Conford and Customs.

All right. I'll go as fast as I can. Which is the way we left Ilha Pombo, by the way. If you listened to the Mungu tape, you'll notice that long pause in it, and I suppose you can figure out for yourself that during that time I was considering calling Mungu a lying sack of shit to his face, and of course as you notice I didn't do it. And the reason I didn't do it, the vision of that autopsy table rose before me, and I contemplated it while considering the fact that we were five unarmed men in this maniac's palace, on this maniac's island, and a little scenario opened itself out for my inspection. In that scenario, I *did* call Mungu a lying sack of shit, following which hundreds of fat, tall army men in sunglasses descended on us and bustled all five of us downstairs to the playroom, where various things happened to us on the autopsy table—the groove and pour spout are for blood, of course, and other bodily fluids—following which the various remaining pieces of our various bodies were assembled and placed with our equipment in a truck, which was driven into a tree and set fire to, following which a telegram sadly reporting our fatal accident was sent off to the Network, following which there was absolutely no investigation.

When I was a kid, books and movies constantly came to moments like this, with the fearless American face to face with the foreign tyrant in his palace, and the way the story always went from that point on was that the fearless American told the foreign tyrant off in no uncertain terms, slugged three or four guards, and loped around the palace for a while having duels with various uniformed chunks of ineptitude, until the foreign tyrant fell off a handy balcony. Then the fearless American unlocked the door behind which the heroine was imprisoned—no autopsy tables, just a stone-walled cell—and the two of them embraced as the now-free citizens of the foreign nation skipped singing to the polling booths. I had the very strong feeling that I was betraying my heritage when I didn't do any of that, but I had the stronger feeling that I didn't want to see that autopsy table anymore. The fearless American today allows a long pause to go by while he thinks about things, and then he reads a couple more of the prepared questions, and then he leaves without even asking all the questions he brought.

That old story was a nice blueprint when I was a kid, but it doesn't cover autopsy tables. In today's story, the fearless American maintains a low profile. Which is better than no profile at all.

Wouldn't it be nice if we could go on believing that we could fix things?

Well. Outside, the rain continued to rain. The truck drove us around the island here and there, and Rudy took some footage of isolated coves and places like that—the army men wouldn't let us film any local citizens, including themselves, or any of the hovels we passed—and I stood out in the rain at one point and did some patter for the camera: "Here on this island a new crisis in pan-American relations may be brewing. To an isolated stretch of beach such as this someday soon a band of men may—" And so on.

So. We then traveled to the town of Schlammville again, where Rudy surreptitiously took some footage of the natives and their huts, and we transferred to the fishing boat and went back to

Abulia, and I managed not to fall overboard. We stayed overnight on Abulia, and this time we all got into the poker game, even Harvey Osgood, who alienated us from a whole bunch of our money, and the next morning Straight Arrow Airways dropped out of the clouds right on time and we all clambered aboard, to be welcomed by Captain Archer and his Oriental guardian angel, and off we flew, with absolutely no regrets, to San Juan, where it was also pouring. And where we transferred ourselves and our equipment to a commercial flight to New York, where it was also pouring. The rain got to be a pain in the ass after a while, to be frank.

There's very little left to be said about that episode. Except for the final disposition of the film Joe shot the night I was introduced to Mungu's playroom. He showed it with some excitement to Mr. Clarebridge, who showed it with less excitement to Mr. Dorn, who showed it very dispassionately to some other people. Joe kept wanting us to put it on our seven o'clock news and kept cutting across command channels to talk directly to the hard news people—we were all special events people, of course—but for a long while no decision was made, and then at last the news filtered down to Joe that the decision *had* been made, and it was "not to use the film in question at the present time." Joe got excited all over again and asked a lot of people if censorship was being forced down our throats by somebody, and was assured it was not, and finally he got somebody in hard news interested enough to want to see the film, and they went to the film library and it wasn't there. Nobody seemed to know where it was. Joe told me about this and he swore he wouldn't rest until he found out what happened to the film. About a week later I asked him how he was doing on finding it, and he said, "We've all got plenty to do, Jay. Let's not let egotism interfere with getting our jobs done."

I said, "What egotism?"

"I realize you take a personal interest," he said, sounding a bit angry and impatient with me, "in film in which you appear, but a Network is larger than any individual in it." And so on.

So I didn't ask him any more. And so far as I know the film never did get back into the film library. I say "so far as I know" because I haven't asked anybody. You could ask, if you want, but I don't recommend it.

Anyway, the other film we shot down there did remain in existence, and everybody loved it, and especially Bob, who told me my interview technique was brilliant. But then nothing happened for quite a while, except that I'd run into Bob at The Hub every once in a while, with Joe or Mr. Clarebridge or Mr. Dorn or some combination of them together, and we'd all be friendly, and nobody ever invited me along to wherever they were going. I was back doing the Townley Loomis lunchtime interviews, and dating Linda, trying unsuccessfully to get her to stay overnight at my place, or at least spend half an hour in bed, and for a long while it seemed as though nothing at all was happening in re "A Sea of Guns." Linda and I talked it over, and she was just as baffled as I was, and we wondered if maybe something was happening behind the scenes.

Something was. I arrived at the office one morning, and there was a memo on my desk which told me to come to one of the twelfth-floor conference rooms at three-thirty that afternoon for a discussion of the future of the special titled "To Free an Island." That was the absolute first time I ever heard that title, but I knew at once it had to be "A Sea of Guns" under an alias.

What I didn't realize until I got to the conference was that the change of title meant a change of concept as well.

There was quite a group there. Joe Singleton, our producer. Bob Grantham, our writer. Mr. Clarebridge, the vice president in direct charge of the program. Mr. Dorn, the senior vice president in general charge of all Mr. Clarebridge's projects. And some others. Phil Bifrat for one, a writer under salary to the Network, who was being added to the project as a co-writer with Bob Grantham. Gwen Morrisey, a tough middle-aged lady, an assistant of Frank Dorn's who has a reputation around The Hub of not only being Mr. Dorn's eyes and ears but his brain as well. And Mr. Theodore Pshaw, an Executive Vice President of the Network, meaning a more important man even than Mr. Dorn; in fact, only one or two people at the Network are more important than Mr. Pshaw.

Mr. Clarebridge made the first speech. He said that we had started to do a special about gunrunning in our time and that the project had gradually focused on one specific area of gunrunning and that from that we had just about inadvertently found ourselves with a front-row seat on the early stages of a revolution in the making. "And a revolution, I might add," he added, "of which we can all be proud."

He went on to explain why we could all be proud. Because, he said, these were *our* revolutionaries. He didn't mean they were Americans, and he didn't mean we were responsible for them in any way; what he meant was that they were revolutionaries who were pro-American, which is very rare in the world today. Some Cubans, and that's about it.

"We know what Ilha Pombo Island is like," he said, "and we know that the violent overthrow of that government by force is long overdue. We have exclusive information now that the overthrow is going to happen very soon. We have assurances from the proper quarters that it is an overthrow our own government will look kindly on. And we are in on the ground floor. The Network has an opportunity at exclusive coverage of the preparations of the revolution, and the departure of the revolutionary force."

He talked on a little longer, expanding on what I've already reported, and then he introduced Bob Grantham, calling him "the crusading young journalist who brought this story to our attention in the first place."

Bob stood up and told us his contacts in Florida had told him a revolutionary army was in the process of being trained right now, as we sat there, at camps in the swamp country south of Miami. He told us that the revolutionary army consisted of exiled Pombians, anti-Communist Cubans who were offering their assistance in return for Pombian assistance of a similar nature at a later date, and miscellaneous freedom-lovers and patriots who were there simply because of the obligation they felt to strike a blow for liberty and justice and against atheistic communism wherever it should raise its head.

"And now I would like to introduce someone to you," Bob said. "Wally Clarebridge has already met him, of course, but the rest of you will, I guess, be seeing him for the first time." He went to a door—not the one to the hall but one that led to an inner room—and opened it, and a heavy, brooding man walked in, milk chocolate in color, wearing an ill-fitting black suit and a badly knotted black tie. "Miss Morrisey, Gentlemen," Bob said, "may I introduce the next President of Ilha Pombo Island, Colonel Padigard Enhuelco."

Of course! I'd thought I recognized him. It had been night time down in Florida the one occasion I'd seen him before, but he wasn't a man one forgot all that easily.

And I'd like to point out that Bob Grantham in his introduction of the colonel *stated* that Mr. Clarebridge had met him before. I know everybody denies that now, but nobody denied it then, and when Colonel Enhuelco was shaking hands with everybody he certainly gave the impression he was meeting Mr. Clarebridge for something other than the first time.

In any event, the denials came much later. And Bob did say it, I heard him.

Colonel Enhuelco shook hands with everybody—I didn't remind him of our previous encounter—and then he made his own speech: "I want to thank you," he said, in his very gruff and expressionless voice, as though he were reading a prepared statement and would rather have been off somewhere breaking people's arms, "I want to thank you for the interest you and your Network have taken in the plight of my people on the island of Ilha Pombo. If it weren't for your interest and your support, the future of my people would look much more grim than it does at this moment."

You'll notice he used the word "support." I'm sorry, I know that can't make you legal department people feel very happy, but the truth is the truth. He said support.

And he went on to say that as a result of our support, we were being granted exclusive rights to film the training sessions, to interview the trainees, and to film the actual departure of the invasion force from American shores. He then said several words about freedom and the rights of all peoples everywhere to self-determination, and finished by saying that he was looking forward to being elected president of Ilha Pombo in a free and open election just as soon after the revolution as possible. Then he shook hands all around again—I noticed that his eyes didn't have any expression; they were just wet marbles in his head—and Mr. Clarebridge said to him, "I'll be along in a little while."

That's what he *said*.

So Colonel Enhuelco left, by the door through which he'd entered, and Mr. Pshaw got to his feet to make a little speech in which he congratulated Mr. Dorn for obtaining the Network a project that would at one and the same time advance the cause of world freedom and make a stirring special for the Network. Then

Mr. Dorn got to his feet and thanked Mr. Pshaw and in his turn congratulated Mr. Clarebridge for having the clarity of vision to see the potential in this project when it was first brought to the attention of the Network. Then Mr. Clarebridge got to his feet and thanked Mr. Dorn and Mr. Pshaw for their confidence in him and said he hoped it would turn out to be justified, and he didn't mention me at all. Though he sure does now.

Well, that was the end of the speeches, though there was general conversation for a while afterward, and the meeting broke up at about quarter to five. I went home and got ready for my evening date with Linda, and we discussed the events of the day, and we both thought it was an encouraging sign that even though a second writer had been brought into the project I was still the only interviewer/announcer. To be the man in front of the camera on a major special like "To Free an Island" would be a feather in any man's cap.

Though for the next few weeks there was nothing for me to do. Bob Grantham and Joe Singleton both went down to Florida with a film crew—including Rudy Patelli—and the new writer, Phil Bifrat, went along. But they were just filming training sessions at Base Camp One, which is what the flamingo rustlers' camp was being called now, so they didn't need an interviewer along. I know Mr. Clarebridge spent some time down there too, in June and July, though I don't know how much, and whether or not he stayed at the same motel as Colonel Enhuelco I can't say.

Linda was much more agitated about all this than I was, but of course she didn't understand the way the Network works. She'd say, "Are you *sure* they don't have somebody else taking your place?"

"I'm positive," I'd say. "I know all the guys the Network might pick, and I know they haven't picked any of them."

"You ought to try to find out what's going on down there," she'd say.

"I'll know when the time comes," I'd say.

The fact of the matter is, I really didn't know what was going on down there. I know this is the crucial time, but I just wasn't there for it. Did cars rented by the Network transport guns and ammunition and trainees and food out to Base Camp One? I don't know. Did the Network rent the fishing vessel the trainees used for practicing amphibious landings? I don't know. I wouldn't even want to guess whether those allegations are true or not.

In fact, on that subject, I'd like to make a statement. I do not believe the *Network* was culpable of anything. I think it's entirely possible that executives *within* the Network made errors of judgment and perhaps were even guilty of technically illegal acts, but the Network itself is bigger than any individual and will survive this current mess with its initials unsullied. And I also believe that any man who tries to shunt responsibility from his own shoulders and hide behind the anonymity of the Network is not a true Network man; he is putting his own petty transitory personal concerns above the concerns of the Network.

I name no names.

Anyway, June and July went by, and then in August, Mr. Clarebridge came back from Florida and called me into his office and told me, "Well, Operation Torch of Liberty is just about ready to go."

I said, "Sir?"

"You know what I mean," he said meaningfully.

"I do?"

"Ilha Pombo," he said.

"Oh," I said.

"It is now," he said, "called Operation Torch of Liberty."

"The program, sir?"

"No, the operation. The program still has the same name we discussed before. But we've given the operation a code name, and from this point forward you are to use that code name exclusively."

"Yes, sir."

"Not the name of the island, not the title of the special, not the names of any individuals. Just Operation Torch of Liberty."

"Operation Torch of Liberty," I said.

"Very good," he said. "We don't want to alert the enemy. Surprise is on our side; let's keep it that way."

"Yes, sir."

"Loose lips sink ships."

That sounded like the kind of thing you're not supposed to be able to say three times fast, but I knew what he meant. "Yes, sir," I said.

"You'll be flying down Wednesday," he said. "You'll be briefed at that time."

"Yes, sir," I said, noticing how military his language had become lately. I very nearly saluted when I left the office, but managed to force my arm to stay at my side.

Linda, of course, was delighted. "They still want you!" she cried.

"I told you there was nothing to worry about," I said.

She said, "This must mean they're going to start the invasion soon."

"Well, sure," I said. "The idea was that I'd go down just before they leave and do some interviews—how they feel on the eve of departure, that sort of thing."

"That's thrilling, Jay," she said. "Will you go along on the boat with them?"

"Hardly," I said. "I've seen Ilha Pombo all I want to."

"Well, but the Network will send a cameraman along, won't they?"

"Not on your life." I could just see Joe Singleton telling Rudy he was going to Ilha Pombo with the invasion fleet. I could just hear what Rudy would say back.

"Still," she said, "it'll be thrilling to see them off. I wish I could come along."

"You could," I said, and leered as suggestively as I knew how. Maybe in Florida, in adjoining motel rooms, I could at last attain my heart's desire with that girl.

But she said, "Oh, if only I could. But I used up all my vacation time in February; I just couldn't get away from work again so soon."

"Then come to bed with me here," I said.

"Oh, you," she said, and giggled, and slapped the back of my hand. That was her most potent weapon against me—to pretend I didn't mean it.

"I mean it," I said, and embraced her.

We kissed, but then she pushed me away and said, "Oh, you're just being silly. Come on, we'll be late for the movie."

So we went to the movie. And on Wednesday I went to Miami, where Joe Singleton met me at the airport. "It's really exciting, Jay," he said. "Watching this tiny band of men prepare for its rendezvous with history, it's really thrilling to see."

"When do they leave?"

"Tomorrow night. It's really thrilling, Jay."

We went out to the motel first, for me to unload my luggage and change into more casual wear. Joe paced the room while I changed, talking about how thrilling it was, and I kept thinking how more thrilling it would be if Linda were in the next unit right now. But she wasn't, was she? I put on Hush Puppies, and we left.

Base Camp One looked a lot different when we got to it. Several of the least-broken-down buildings had been fixed up with new planks and sheets of plywood, with big canvas tarpaulins stretched across the roofs. A big tent had been put up, where the meals were cooked and eaten, and out the far side of the cluster of buildings a rifle range had been constructed; we could hear the flat sounds of firing, and we could see the paper targets—black silhouettes of men in threatening positions on white backgrounds.

And there was Arnold. I hadn't seen him for quite a while, and I welcomed him like an old friend. He was always so completely himself; cigarettes rolled in T-shirt sleeve, one lit cigarette stuck to his lower lip, dead white complexion that sometimes became an unhealthy pink after exposure to sunlight but never tanned, and that slightly bitter inward expression as though he were listening to his body crumble from the inside out.

"Hello, Arnold," I said.

"Lo," he said.

"Long time no see," I said.

"Uh huh," he said.

That was a big conversation, for Arnold.

Bob Grantham and Phil Bifrat were in the mess tent, sitting at a table strewn with papers, drinking beer. It looked like a meeting between Civil War generals. Joe and I walked in, we all exchanged greetings, and Joe said, "Well, how's it coming?"

Phil said, "Same old trouble. Bob still wants to put in too much of this anti-Communist shit."

Bob said, "In the first place, you can't have too much anti-Communist shit; it's what the American public wants. And in the second place, that's what our story's *about*."

Phil said to him, "In the first place, Bob, that *isn't* what our story's about, and you know it. And in the second place, you're gonna alienate the youth with all this anti-Communist shit."

Joe said, "Well, we'll want *some*."

"Sure, some," Phil said. "We don't want to alienate the old folks either. But let's try to get us a balanced program."

"Something for everybody," Joe said.

"That's right," Phil said.

Bob said, "Phil, let me ask you something."

"Go ahead," Phil said.

"Phil," Bob said, "don't you have any *conviction* about anticommunism? Where do you stand, Phil?"

"Firmly behind management," Phil told him. "If management wants anticommunism, that's what I'll give them. But what management wants right now is balance, with an emphasis on the youth market, which is the eighteen to forty-nine age bracket, and from me that's what they're gonna get."

"That's quite a bracket," I said.

Everybody ignored me and went on talking, so I went out of the mess tent and wandered around a little. I watched the rifle practice for a while, noticed that the recruits all looked young and tough and stupid and seemed totally incapable of hitting the targets, and then I wandered some more and ran into Rudy, who looked to left and right and then said, "That crate's here again."

"The one with the dent in it? Did you tell Joe?"

"Sure I told Joe."

"What did he say?"

"Don't make waves."

"Did you tell Mr. Clarebridge when he was here?"

"I didn't make waves."

"Oh." I looked around, squinting inside my sunglasses. It was even hotter and muggier than the last time. I said, "How are things doing down here?"

"Put your money on Mungu," he said.

"That bad, huh?"

"This crowd," he said, "couldn't take the Chicago police."

Remembering what Linda had asked me, I grinned at him and said, "You want to go along and film the invasion?"

"Naturally," he said, and we heard shouts and screaming from the rifle range. "For Christ's sake," Rudy yelled, "where's my camera?" He dashed away, and I headed for the rifle range.

What had happened, one of the guns had malfunctioned and blown up in a trainee's hands and removed most of his right ear. There was blood all over the place, the trainee was sitting on the ground looking astonished, and half a dozen other trainees were off in the swamp throwing up from the sight of blood. Oh, they were going to make a great invasion force.

As an eyewitness, and I might even say a trained eyewitness, let me say right now that the allegations that the Network, or individuals connected with the Network, refused to permit medical assistance to be given the trainee until footage could be shot of him sitting there bleeding are malicious lies. It's true that Rudy Patelli knocked over the camp medic and broke most of the contents of his medical bag, but that was pure accident, the result of Rudy's haste to get to the wounded man with his camera. After that, Rudy and I and everybody else from the Network stayed strictly out of the way, merely observing as the wounded man was seen to by the medic and his fellow trainees, who staunched the blood by wrapping rags around his head.

Now, it is true that the wounded man, Ernesto Rivera, a Cuban, twenty-seven years of age, was driven to the hospital in Miami in an automobile rented by the Network, but I don't see how anybody can make inferences about anything from that. It was common humanitarianism, that's all. The car was faster than the truck, which was the only vehicle the invasion force had available at the camp, and it would also give a smoother ride than the truck, and because it was air-conditioned it would give Rivera a much more comfortable trip than the truck would.

About Rivera, I have the feeling he's just been caught in the clutches of a greedy lawyer, and that's the whole explanation right there. I mean, even with the loss of his right ear and the impairment to his hearing, it seems to me he's behaving very badly right now. An ear, after all, isn't that important. Look at Van Gogh.

Anyway, when the excitement was over, it was decided I would start doing my interviews. I don't see any point in including any of them; they were mostly very dull and contributed nothing to the world's knowledge. They were also very short. Phil and Bob gave me a few suggested questions, told me not to go over three minutes with any trainee, and Rudy and the rest of the crew set up so we'd have the rifle range in the background. A group of trainees were sent over to talk to me, and they stood on line just out of camera range, as though they were here to get their shots. One at a time they would come out and hunker down with me in front of the camera, and I'd ask three or four questions, and they'd mumble answers that came out of propaganda speeches they'd heard on television or from their various leaders. What it was most like was the personality part of the Miss America contest: "What do *you* think is the role of the woman in the modern world?"

There were forty or fifty trainees all told, and I interviewed about ten of them that afternoon. Then the day's work was done, and we all went back to Miami, and I rode in the same car with Richard Conford. You remember Conford, he's the man from the local Network affiliate, the liaison man who was along ostensibly to assure cooperation between the Network men from New York and the affiliate men from Miami but who was actually along to make sure the Network men didn't harm, tamper with, or take away any affiliate-owned property. I have promised that Conford will have a vital role to play—I don't know which of these details are new to you, there in the elevator, and whether you know about Conford or not, so I'll assume you don't—and he will, but not yet. Now he simply rode back to Miami in the same car with me.

We did talk, though. Him first: "What do you think is going to happen?"

"I think they'll get killed," I said.

"The Bay of Pigs," he said.

"Oh, much worse than that," I said. "Say what you like about Castro, he's civilized. The Bay of Pigs people were sent back to us, traded for tractors. Mungu doesn't want tractors."

"He'll kill them?"

I thought of the autopsy table. "Eventually," I said.

"Shouldn't we tell them? Shouldn't we stop them?"

"They already know it," I said. "They're taking a chance, they're hoping they'll make it."

"But how can we just . . . let them go?"

"It isn't up to us," I said.

"But if we know they're going to get killed—"

"We *don't* know it. Not till it happens."

He looked fretfully out the side window. "It doesn't seem right," he said.

"We're just television people," I said. "We're just here to watch and record. What if television people started taking part? What then?"

"I know," he said. He still sounded fretful. "I know."

Back at the motel we all changed again, and then Phil and Bob and Joe and I had dinner. I'd preferred it the last time, when we'd stayed at one of the beach hotels and could eat dinner right in the same hotel, but this time we'd been switched to the motel for some reason and had to drive someplace else for dinner.

In a way, it was like being in the bar with Harvey Osgood again, back on Abulia, except that this time Bob was with us and Harvey was not. And we had the addition of Phil. But the subject was the same as before—the gut issues of our time.

It all grew out of the hassle between Bob and Phil about the quantity of anticommunism in the special, with Joe chiming in to speak for the New Morality. Phil kept talking about "alienating" different groups of potential viewers, but he wasn't exactly dealing with alienation the way Harvey had meant the word, so this time I took Harvey's place, expressing what I thought Harvey's viewpoint would be, until finally Joe turned on me, exasperated because he wasn't getting anywhere with the others, and said, "Will you for Christ's sake forget Harvey Osgood for a minute? Think for yourself."

"Well, I don't have an opinion," I said. "And Harvey isn't here, so I thought I'd—"

Phil said to me, "You don't have an opinion? You don't believe in alienation yourself?"

"Well," I said, "I don't believe or disbelieve. It's a point of view, that's all, and the guy isn't here that expresses it, so I'm—"

"But what about *your* point of view?"

"I don't have one," I said. "I don't have to have one. You people hand me the questions, and I read them, and the interviewee makes up his own answers. I just do what I'm told."

Well, then it got kind of sticky. The three of them had realized by now they were never going to convert one another, since each of them already was full to the brim with his own convictions. But me, now, they figured old Jay Fisher doesn't have any convictions at all, he's empty, so it became a contest among them as to which one could fill me up.

Which was pointless, as I tried to tell them. "I agree with you all," I said. "I see the cogency of all your arguments. You don't have to try to convince me, I'm convinced."

You'd think that would please them, but it didn't, and the meal ended with a certain general irritation all around, with most of it directed at me. And I was the only one who hadn't argued! But that's the way people are.

Back at the motel, Bob went off somewhere with Arnold, Phil decided to sit in the crews' poker game awhile, Joe disappeared somewhere by himself, and I went to my room to call Linda. She'd asked me to call every evening while I was away, and I'd been happy to promise I would. We talked, and I told her what was happening, speaking in veiled hints because you never knew when a phone was being tapped, and then I spent the rest of the evening watching television. The Network stuff was fine, naturally, but I must say I didn't think much of the stuff generated by the local affiliate. But that's just my opinion.

At around one-thirty I was getting ready to sack in for the night when the phone rang, and it was Joe. I braced myself for a drunken half-hour of salesmanship on behalf of the New Morality, but it turned out not to be that at all. It turned out to be much worse.

"Get the boys," Joe said. His voice was so hushed and awed he sounded as though he was calling from an echo chamber.

"It's one-thirty in the morning, Joe."

"Get the boys," he said. "Meet me in Opa-locka."

Do other people have crazy things said to them all the time, or is it just me? "Meet me in Opa-locka." What kind of statement is that to get over the telephone at one-thirty in the morning? It sounds like a song in a failed musical: "Meet me in Opa-locka,/ 'Neath the hocka-wocka moon."

All right, I can't sing. But I can remember, which is more important. And I remember I said to Joe, "Why? What's the problem?"

"Problem?" From the sound of his voice, he was in total awe of himself. He said, "No problem, Jay, no problem at all. You just come to Opa-locka, with the boys, ready for a filmed interview."

"What's in Opa-locka, Joe?"

"Not much," he said, with heavy irony. "Just the Pulitzer Prize, that's all."

"More welfare hoors, Joe?"

Stung, he said, "Forget all that crap, Jay, this is the real thing! You just come down here with a crew, and you'll thank me the rest of your life."

"Joe, maybe in the morning—"

"In the morning could be too late! Goddam it, Jay, do I have to call Walter Clarebridge and have *him* tell you to come over here?"

"You mean call him tonight? Now?"

"You're goddam right! What I've got here is *dynamite!*"

I considered. If Joe's dynamite was in all truth another welfare hoor, and if he called Mr. Clarebridge at home at one-thirty in the morning to tell him about it, tomorrow morning it would all turn out to have been my fault, and Joe would hate me forever and would probably jap me with Mr. Clarebridge. On the other hand, if Joe's latest welfare hoor turned out to be dynamite and I'd refused to bring a crew to Opa-locka and watch it blow up, tomorrow morning would be equally heavy weather and I would have japped *myself* with Mr. Clarebridge. All in all, it looked as though if I wanted to sleep easily tomorrow, I'd have to give up some sleep tonight. So finally I sighed and said, "Okay, Joe. I'll bring a crew."

"I knew I could count on you, Jay," he said. Which isn't, of course, what he says about me these days, but we'll let it pass. Anyway, he said, "Meet me by City Hall, on Sharazad Boulevard."

"Sharazad Boulevard?" Another song from the same show, obviously.

"Get here as quick as you can," he said.

"Sure, Joe," I said, and hung up, and put on my shoes and left my motel unit and walked down the muggy bower to break up the poker game.

Which was in no mood to be broken up. Sound-man Hank Tashwell seemed to sum up the general opinion when he said, "You call Joe back and tell him to get eat by an alligator."

"I can't call him back," I said. "He's waiting outside the Opa-locka City Hall."

"A good place for him," Hank said.

Rudy Patelli said, "Jay, sit in for me, I gotta take a leak."

"Listen," I said.

Rudy was already on his feet, dancing a little. "Come on, be a good guy, will you? I got a great hand here."

"More bullshit," Hank said.

"Just sit in for me," Rudy said, backing away toward the john. "Don't make me fold such a great hand." And he disappeared behind a closed door.

Irv Berg, who with Hank had been the sound crew on the Ilha-

Pombo Island trip, and who was currently dealer, looked expressionlessly around the table and said, "Do we fold him, or does somebody take his hand?"

They were playing seven-card stud, of which four cards had already been dealt, two down and two up. Rudy's up cards were the ten and king of hearts. From halfway across the room I looked at those two cards, and the two face-down cards beside them kept sending me telepathic messages: *"We are the jack and queen. We are the jack and queen."*

"Oh, all right," I said, walking around to take Rudy's chair. "But just this hand. Then we have to go to Opa-locka."

"Sure," Irv said, soothing me, and said, "Pair of sevens bets."

The pair of sevens was a local affiliate man, another technician, named Leroy Something. I don't mean his last name was Something; I mean I don't know his last name.

Anyway, Leroy bet five dollars, and I said, "What's the limit?"

Hank merely snorted, but Irv said, "Pot limit. Dealer antes a dollar."

"Good God," I said. With pot limit—I don't know if legal department people play poker, but I suspect you play bridge—you can never bet any more than the amount already in the pot. On the first round of betting, that limit is a dollar. Assuming there are no raises, the most you can bet on the second round is seven dollars, being the dealer's ante and everybody's dollar bet from the first time. Third round—still without raises—the most you can bet is forty-nine dollars. In seven-card stud, there are five rounds of betting.

(click)

There's probably a click on the tape there; I just stopped it for a second to figure something out. I see I'm getting near the end of the tape again, but I want to make this point, so I stopped to figure out some math here about pot-limit poker.

Now, what I'm about to describe doesn't ever happen, let me make that clear, but it is a *potential* of the game. Okay? Okay. Now, let us assume a game with six players, pot limit, dealer antes a dollar, seven-card stud. Let us assume, in other words, the game these guys were playing. Now, let us further assume a hand in which nobody folds and in which every bet is a full-limit bet—two things which almost never happen. And let us further assume that there is only one raise each round, that it too is a full pot-matching bet, and that it comes from the player to the original bettor's right. Do you know how much money will be in the pot at the end of the hand?

Seventy-two million, two hundred twenty-three thousand, four hundred eighty-eight dollars. Which is a hell of a distance from that dollar the dealer put in back at the beginning.

Of course, in real life the pots are usually no more than one or two hundred dollars, but you do see, I hope, the potential for chaos in the game these guys have chosen to make their life's work, interrupted though it may be by occasional chores for the Network. The point I'm trying to make is that, while they weren't crazy enough to want to rush out and collect Joe Singleton's Pulitzer Prize, on the other hand they aren't sane. That's the point I'm trying to make, and the reason I'm trying to make it is that you people in the legal department might be tempted to talk to some of the crew members about the Ilha Pombo Affair, and if you do, you should bear in mind that you are talking to men whose view of reality has been developed by pot-limit poker. That's just something to think about.

This tape is running out fast, and I haven't even gotten to Opa-locka yet. I want to explain what happened to me in that poker game before I get to Opa-locka and it's beginning to look as though that's going to have to wait for tape five, which means after lunch.

Did you hear that ring sound in the background? The doorbell; it rings a lot these days, and I never answer it, because it's never anybody I want to see. I answer the phone because I keep hoping it will turn out to be the Network calling, saying come-home-all-is-forgiven, and because when it isn't the Network I can always hang up. And do.

Now there *is* tape left. Christ, you never know. All right, that guy Leroy made his five-dollar bet, and it was called around to me, and I looked at Rudy's ten and king of hearts, and picked up his down cards to see if they'd telepathed truthfully or not, and they had lied. One of them was a jack, but it was the jack of clubs, and the other was the seven of spades. "Fine," I said, trying to sound really pleased, and tossed five of Rudy's dollars into the pot, and Irv dealt out cards to me and Hank and Leroy, the only hands left in, and what I got was the jack of hearts.

Hank, who had a potential low straight showing, looked at the ten and jack and king of hearts showing in front of me, and said, "And that's more bull

TAPE FIVE, SIDE ONE

THAT SIZZLING SOUND is Alka-Seltzer; please excuse it. I am not peptic, I am not at all peptic.

All right. I had this poker hand; on top, it looked like a beautiful royal flush building, but underneath, in the world of truth, I had a pair of jacks. If it had been my own money I would have folded, but it was Rudy's crumpled bills I was tossing in, and he'd strongly stated he didn't want the hand folded, and I kept thinking he'd come back from the john—how long can one man leak?—so I stayed until the very end, at which time the pair of jacks won. I pulled in the money, while Hank said disparaging things—he'd finished with a busted straight and a queen high—and then a local man named Archie Something—no relation to Leroy Something—started dealing a new hand, and Rudy wasn't back yet.

"Hey," I said. "We've gotta go to Opa-locka."

"Rudy's still in the john," Irv said, and Archie said, "Ace bets."

I had the ace. "Oh," I said, distracted, trying to play poker and stop the game at the same time. "Uh, a dollar."

"Now he's bulling the game," Hank said. "That's sweet."

So I won that hand, too—three nines—and then it was Rudy's deal, and he still wasn't back, and I said, "Look, guys, we've really got to go to Opa-locka."

Hank said, "Shut up and deal."

"But—"

"Wait till Rudy comes back," Irv said.

"Don't forget to ante," Leroy said.

So I put a dollar of Rudy's money in the pot, and dealt. I gave myself a pair of queens down and a ten up, stayed for Irv's dollar bet on his king, and was dealing the next round when Rudy finally returned and pulled up a chair to sit beside me on my left. "How we doing?" he said.

"Won two hands," I said. "Here, it's your deal."

"No, you finish the hand."

So I finished the hand, and won with two pair—queens over threes. Irv said, "That's three hands in a row," and Hank made a comment of his own.

"Now," I said, firmly, "about Joe—"

"I tell you what," Rudy said. "You're so hot, just give me my money over here, and you take that pot for yourself, to stake you."

"That's a great idea," everybody said, and while I sat there trying to talk about Joe Singleton and Opa-locka, they all shuffled money this way and that, and said a lot of words to me, and the first thing I knew Rudy was dealing, and he was dealing seven hands, and I was the seventh.

"Hey," I said. "Stop that. We've got to go to—"

"If there's one thing I hate," Hank said, "it's a guy comes in, wins a couple quick hands, and tries to walk away with everybody's money."

Irv said, reasonably, "Jay, you've got to give us a chance to win it back, that's only right."

"But Joe, Opa-locka, we have to—"

"Eight bets," Rudy said.

I looked and the eight wasn't me; I had a four of spades. The eight was Leroy, who said, "Check." Everybody else also said, "Check." When it was my turn, I said, "Now, look, Rudy's back and—"

Hank said, "Do you bet or do you check?"

"I check, but—"

"Check," Rudy said, and so on around, and Rudy dealt another card to everybody, and this time Hank was high with a pair of fives, and he bet a dollar, and I had a miserable collection of cards, which I folded. "Now," I said.

"Don't talk while the hand's in progress," Leroy said. He was irritable because he couldn't decide whether he should try to bluff against Hank or not.

Well, it went on like that, with my struggles growing weaker and weaker, like a fish in a bucket or a fly in a spider's web, and finally I stopped struggling entirely, and settled in to play poker, and when Joe Singleton burst into the room about an hour and a half later I was about a hundred forty dollars ahead.

This is why I've dealt with that poker game at such detail, because of course these days when Joe Singleton talks about how I was in league with the technical people against him, if he isn't talking about the desk clerk on Abulia he's talking about that poker game in Miami. And I want you to really understand just how that poker game came about, and how it wasn't at all my fault, and the same thing could have happened to anybody.

So we went to Opa-locka. Joe just wanted Rudy and Hank and Irv and me, but the three local men came along too; Leroy and Archie and the third one, whose name I forget entirely. Started with M. Morris? Manfred? Merwin? Malcolm?

It doesn't matter. They came along for the ride, in Leroy's car, while the rest of us transported ourselves and the equipment in two of the cars the Network had on rental.

What is there to say about Opa-locka? The streets are called Harem, Arabia, Sultan, Ahmad, Kalandar, Aladdin, Caliph, Salih, and Alibaba avenues, not to mention Cairo Lane, Alexandria Drive, and Port Said Road. I was only there at night, and I have detected in myself no craving to go back there in the daytime.

At any rate, our destination was a small pink bungalow off Dundad Avenue. I had carefully arranged things so that I shared a car with Rudy, leaving Hank and Irv to ride with Joe, so that he was over his mad by the time we all stopped at the curving curb in front of the bungalow. We got out of the cars, and Joe came back to me and said, "You're going to thank me, Jay. You're going to thank me."

"Thank you," I said.

He didn't hear me. He looked around to be sure his army was present and in contact with its equipment, and then led us up the walk to the narrow porch. The bungalow was in total darkness and gave every impression of having been abandoned along about the Coolidge Administration, but Joe confidently mounted the porch and rapped his knuckles against the front door.

Immediately, a dim pinkish light went on somewhere inside, reaching feebly to the chintz curtains over the front window. We stood and waited, and nothing else happened, and finally Joe rapped his knuckles on the door again, and a crotchety voice from behind us said, "Hands up."

We all turned, astonished, and an ancient man, skinny as a sapling, was pointing a Sears Roebuck shotgun at us. "Hands up, I said," he said, and we all put our hands up.

All except Joe, that is. He left his hands at his sides and said, "Mr. Rommel, it's me, Joe Singleton. I said I'd be back, remember?"

"You know these people?" He was hard to see, crouched over his shotgun down there on the walk like a belligerent rabbit, but his voice was acid with distrust.

"They're my crew," Joe said. "Remember, Mr. Rommel, I said I was going to get my crew?"

"What's that stuff they got?"

"Their equipment, Mr. Rommel."

"You ain't going to do anything to *my* head."

"Television equipment, Mr. Rommel. For the interview."

"I'm not sure I want to be interviewed." The shotgun was sagging somewhat and by now threatened the stoop more than any of us, and Mr. Rommel's voice had gotten somewhat whiny and surly. "It's too damn late at night," he said.

"Mr. Rommel, think of Israel," Joe said.

The shotgun snapped up again—not to threaten us, merely to stand at attention—and Mr. Rommel said, "That's right, by God. All right, you and your troops remain deployed on the porch. I'll be right with you." And he backed away and ducked suddenly behind a hibiscus. We watched him as, scurrying from cover to cover, he made his way around the side of the house and out of sight.

Rudy said, "It's a welfare hoor. It's another welfare hoor."

"Just wait," Joe said. "He's an old man, he's a little—"

"Oh, really?" Rudy said. "I thought he was a young girl."

"You'll all thank me," Joe promised. "You wait and see."

The pink light went out.

"Why do I have this feeling," Irv said quietly, "that I am about to get a hotfoot?"

The porch light went on; amber, in a wall fixture beside the door, shaped like a minaret.

Leroy said, "Does anybody's navy still shanghai people?"

"Only ours," Rudy said. "It's called the draft."

The door opened, and Mr. Rommel was there, sans shotgun. "Come in," he snapped. "Don't hang around out there."

"Thanks, Mr. Rommel," Joe said, and we all entered a small square living room that looked to have been furnished from motel bankruptcy sales. "The way I see it, Mr. Rommel," Joe said, "we'll set up in here, you and Jay can talk a while, and then you bring up the model, and Jay can ask to see it, and the two of you go on through to the back. Don't worry about the equipment; we can follow you, it's all highly mobile stuff."

I heard Hank muttering in the background, something to do with where Joe could put his highly mobile stuff, but Joe either failed to hear it or chose to ignore it. Whatever the case, he went on talking, saying, "Now, Mr. Rommel, this is Jay Fisher; he'll interview you, you'll be in good hands, he's a professional."

"I only deal with professionals," Mr. Rommel snapped. He was a dried-out raisin of a man, of average height but seeming shorter, and his expression was constantly shifting between belligerent and sullen. He had perfect little white false teeth, the plates differentiated into thousands of narrow little teeth, but they didn't shine. It was as though they'd been painted with flat white wall-paint; they didn't reflect the light or anything. Very strange.

But stranger was to come. Joe was still doing introductions, and now he turned to me and said, "Jay, I want you to meet Field Marshal Erwin Rommel."

"How do you do," I said, and stuck out my hand, and he took it in his bony claw and said, "I do fine." And *then* what Joe had said finally sunk into my head and I said, "*Erwin* Rommel?"

"That's right," Joe said, smirking at me, while Field Marshal Erwin Rommel untaloned my hand and said, "Well, let's get on with it," and went over to sit on the Danish ancient sofa.

I looked at Joe, begging him with my eyes not to mean what he was saying, and I said, "The Desert Fox? World War II?"

"He'll tell you all about it," Joe said, and turned briskly to say to the crew, "Okay, let's set up."

They set up. They don't give a damn, the crew never gives a damn, they're all union men, they have blue-collar immunity. I was seated on the sofa beside Rommel, who glared suspiciously at the crew all the while they set up, and I kept looking at his profile, hoping to find in it some slight trace of humor. Far better a practical joker than a nut. But Rommel was about as humorous as your telephone company representative.

"Okay, Jay," Joe finally said, from behind the camera and lights and sound equipment. "Let her roll."

I have since then seen the footage we shot that night, and it's a mark of my mental state at the time that not only was I silent for the first thirty seconds of filming, and not only did I sit there with my mouth open while I stared cloudily to the left of the camera (at Joe Singleton) instead of looking at the crab apple I was supposed to be interviewing, but during that time I was holding the microphone *in my lap*. Now, I'm a professional, just as Joe told Mr. Rommel, and I do know better than to hold a microphone in my lap; it looks absolutely obscene.

In the film—screen it for yourself, if you want, though it adds nothing to the world's knowledge of the Ilha Pombo Affair—I am seen to gather myself laboriously into one piece, slowly lift the microphone from my lap, rustily turn my head to face the interviewee, and in a very dazed fashion say, "So you're General Rommel."

"Field Marshal Rommel," he snapped.

I said, "The Desert Fox. You commanded the German troops in Africa in the Second World War, is that right?"

"Libyan commander," he said impatiently. He was peeved that I knew so little about him. "Later commander of Army Group B in France, under Von Rundstedt. A pompous ass."

Hesitantly I said, "Weren't you killed by Adolf Hitler toward the end of the war?"

He offered a sort of smile—an Arctic winter in Florida—and said, "He thought so. The idea was, I would take poison."

"Didn't you?"

He couldn't believe how stupid I was. "Do I look it?"

He did, as a matter of fact. He looked as though he lived exclusively on poison, and always had. I didn't say that, though. What I said was, "How did you manage to get away?"

Well, he told me. If you're interested, screen the film, it's all there. Double identities, triple agents, quadruple crosses; the story circled back on itself more than the Boston shuttle over Kennedy Airport. It seemed to me I recognized a lot of early Eric Ambler and middle Alfred Hitchcock in the tale—in fact, that might have been Hitchcock himself waiting for a bus on a Mannheim street corner in the background of one incident—but I knew better than to raise any awkward questions. When all hope is gone—and all hope was gone—the mark of the professional interviewer is that he does nothing but nod. I nodded so much I looked like a judge at the pogo-stick championships.

Well, the story of his escape from Nazidom took slightly longer than a dental appointment, and when it was finished I made a game attempt to wrap it up: "Well, sir, Mr. Rommel, that certainly was fascinating, and I'm certainly glad I had this opportunity to—"

"Come take a look at my campaigns," he said.

I did *not* look toward Joe Singleton. I kept smiling glassily at the interviewee and I said, "Hah?"

"In here," he said, and got to his feet and started walking.

Joe yelled, "Hey! Hey!"

I put my hand over the mike, tried to look at the half of the room behind our lights, and said, "What's going on?"

"Just a minute," Joe said. "Just a minute."

I said, "Joe? What's going on?"

What was going on was the poker game, out on the front porch. Rudy had put his camera on a chair, pointing toward Mr. Rommel and me, and had walked away from it. Hank and Irv had started their tape running and had left *their* machinery. The three of them had joined the three local men out on the porch, and they were back into the game again.

Joe, of course, had been so absorbed in the fascinating story of Field Marshal Rommel's escape from Adolf Hitler's vengeance that he hadn't even noticed his crew abandon ship, and now he was terribly upset about it. He carried on at some length, while I continued to sit on the sofa with one hand over the mike. Mr. Rommel stood in the middle of the room with his hands on his hips, looking as though he was prepared at a moment's notice to demonstrate Teutonic discipline, but Joe all by himself finally got the crew back together again with their machinery, ready to roll. He then asked Mr. Rommel to sit down on the sofa and give me the invitation once more, and said to me, "Jay, this time try to sound a little more enthusiastic when he makes the offer."

"I'm an announcer," I told him, "not an actor. But I'll try." Which was absolutely the only remark I made in the interviewee's presence, as you can see for yourself if you run the film. When Joe

Singleton starts talking these days about how Jay Fisher was always undermining his authority, just bear in mind that I uncomplainingly sat down and *interviewed* the welfare hoor and Field Marshal Erwin Rommel.

Anyway, Rommel testily sat down once more, waited for the okay from Joe, and then asked me the question all over again: "You want to see my campaigns?"

"I certainly would, Mr. Rommel," I said.

"Come take a look," he said, and got to his feet, and I followed him into the next room. And following *me* were Rudy and Hank and Irv and Joe and Leroy and Archie and M———, all carrying the lights and the camera and the sound equipment. And nobody dropped anything.

Except me. I dropped my jaw, and very nearly the microphone, when I saw the layout that guy had in his dining room. Four-foot by eight-foot sheets of plywood had been placed on sawhorses, to make a tabletop surface that ran around three walls and practically filled the whole room. Real sand, fake palm trees, and little model buildings were distributed over this tabletop, like a model-train set without the trains. An army of toy soldiers was deployed over the field; several armies, in fact, in different color uniforms.

"Now," Rommel said, "this is Libya."

Well, the next half-hour was both weird and fascinating. That guy might not have been the original Erwin Rommel, but he made one hell of a good substitute. He knew the North African campaign down to the last detail, and he spared us nothing. World War II seesawed back and forth over his sanded plywood, and before he was finished I was rooting for his team to win. It was really a fascinating performance, and I'm only sorry Rudy ran out of film partway through and decided not to mention the fact to anybody. (I can understand Rudy; he knew as well as I did that none of this stuff was ever going to be used anywhere, so why sweat it? Particularly when the alternative would have involved Joe Singleton mounting a 3 A.M. scavenger hunt through the Greater Miami area for film stock.)

Anyway, Rommel was so interesting in this phase of the interview that when I inadvertently brought out the fact that he didn't understand German I felt much more embarrassed than he did—he didn't notice any discrepancy in that at all—and I even did my best to cover it up again. There was no need to, though, as I later discovered; Rudy had already run out of film by then. Though the tape hadn't broken yet.

As a matter of fact, the tape broke just before the most interesting part of all, when I asked Rommel how come he'd decided to reveal his true identity a full quarter-century after he'd disappeared from view. I started that by saying, after the African campaign had been brought to its unhappy conclusion, "You must be terribly old by now, Mr. Rommel."

"November 15, 1971, is my eightieth birthday," he said. He sounded very proud to have made it so long.

"Then why," I said, "have you decided this late in your life to reveal your true identity?"

"Israel," he said.

I remembered then that Joe had said something to Rommel about Israel while the old man was still holding the shotgun on us. I said, "Israel? I don't understand."

"I never felt right about the Jewish situation," he said. "You know what I mean—in Germany."

"Yes, I know what you mean."

"Well, I'm a desert warfare man," he said. "And I know those Ay-rabs. Now, that Dayan fellow's pretty good, but he's no Rommel. What I mean to do, I mean to offer my services to Israel. You follow me?"

"I think so," I said.

"I'll run their army for them," he said. "Look here." And he turned to a section of plywood table we hadn't looked at before. "This is Israel," he said. "Here's the Suez Canal. Over here's Jordan."

And we were off again. I'm kind of sorry we don't have film of that part, or even just tape, because it was really something to see. The six-day war was nothing to what Rommel had in mind; before you knew it, Israel was controlling everything between Tunisia and Afghanistan.

"That's really fascinating," I said, when he was finally finished. "And when do you intend to go to Israel and start this campaign?"

"I'm in communication with them now," he said. "I'm simply waiting for air fare."

We were interrupted then by a crash. Irv, dozing over the broken tape, had fallen off his chair and directly into the lights we'd set up, and now the lights came careening toward the Field

Marshal and me like tiny flying saucers, and the first thing anybody knew the tabletop Israel had been blitzkrieged by klieg lights. "Gonefs!" cried Rommel. "*Now* look what you done!"

Well, he was not to be soothed. Joe tried, and I even tried a little, but Mr. Rommel was having none of it. He drove us out of the house the way, thirty years before, he had driven the British out of Libya, and as we stumbled off his porch and headed for the cars he was loudly seeking his shotgun back in the house.

So the whole thing ended in confusion and chaos and recrimination, with Joe recriminating all of us for not being sufficiently enthusiastic about the scoop of the century, and everybody else bitching about alleged damage to the equipment, and me simply trying to keep my head down and be neither complained at nor shotgunned.

And so it was that Rommel routed one more army in one more desert; we enemy soldiers hastily packed our gear and our wounded in our vehicles and proceeded apace for friendly territory.

I personally was so confused and routed that I even permitted me to wind up in the same car with Joe. I was driving, Joe groused beside me, and Rudy lovingly stroked his camera in the back seat. Joe kept saying things like, "I expect that kind of reaction from lowbrows like the crew, but when a man like you, who's supposed to be educated and middle class, won't even give me the cooperation to do something that's going to make the names of every last one of us—" And so on.

What surprised me, above everything else, was the fact that he didn't really sound drunk. Insane, yes; drunk, no. And it had been the same in Oklahoma, for the welfare hoor. And it had been the same on Abulia, when he'd had me interview myself after the Mungu playroom incident. These fits came over him, apparently, with little or no assistance from alcohol. There's just something inside Joe that craves an apocalyptic vision that he can turn into the Pulitzer Prize, and in the last analysis the dividing line between apocalyptic visions and screwballism is a very fine one indeed.

But the point is, and the reason I've gone into this business of the Field Marshal is, that when Joe these days talks about me being against him and trying to undercut him and embarrass him and keep him from accomplishing things, what he's talking about is his moments of monomania, and what he's complaining about is that I'd never let it turn into *folie á deux.*

Though I had my own personal folly frequently enough, God knows; including being in the same car with Joe during the retreat from Opa-locka. Joe beefed on and on, and I took it as long as I could, and finally I said, "Goddam it, Joe, if that was really Erwin Rommel, how come he can't speak German?"

"Well," he said, and now he was *really* outraged, "you'll try *anything*, won't you?"

Try to argue with somebody like that. Try to drive, in fact, with somebody like that in the car, and you too will wind up going the wrong way on Opa-locka Boulevard, a one-way street, at three-thirty in the morning, which is how I happened to bump into Arnold and the stoles.

When I say "bump into," I mean "bump into." I hadn't realized the other two cars, containing Hank and Irv and Leroy and Archie and M——— and the cards, were no longer with us until the instant I looked at the headlights coming toward me through the windshield and realized I was about to become involved in a head-on collision.

We both hit our brakes and our horns at the last minute, of course—or just after the last minute, as it turned out—and then we hit each other. Both vehicles were traveling at less than ten miles an hour at the instant of impact, and none of us human beings inside were hurt at all, but the cars were practically demolished. They must make automobiles out of Reynolds Wrap these days; the front ends of both Arnold's red Mustang and my yellow Dart looked like used paper towels. Headlights broken, bumpers bent, radiators cracked, hoods dented; the cars looked as though a roving band of ecologists had set at them with sledge hammers.

One thing I must say for Joe, he is instantly adaptable to new situations. Glass was still tinkling onto the pavement when he cried, "Take film, Rudy! That son of a bitch was in our lane!"

Rudy's answer seemed unnecessarily calm. "It's a one-way street," he said.

"Even more so!" cried Joe. "Take film!"

"His is the one way," Rudy said, and at the same instant Arnold stepped from the Mustang like a ferret from a chicken coop, shut and locked the door, didn't look in our direction at all, and turned around and quietly started to walk away.

"My God!" Joe said. "It's Kuklyn! Honk at him, Jay!"

I was so rattled I misunderstood his meaning, and said, "It's too late, he already hit us."

Joe was already scrambling from the car, shouting, "Kuklyn! Kuklyn!" And Arnold just continued to amble briskly away.

Getting out of the car did seem like a good idea, so I did it, too. Joe was still shouting, Arnold was still leaving, and finally I raised my own voice, which has been trained in projection, and I said, "*Arnold!*"

Sorry. Hope that didn't hurt your equipment there in the elevator. I just get carried away sometimes, reenacting all this.

Anyway, my shout got him. He stopped, he turned around, he frowned in our direction, and then very slowly he walked back again. And in the meantime Rudy had gotten out and was looking at the cars and saying, "Very colorful."

It was, too. Green radiator coolant was leaking from the yellow Dart, and blue radiator coolant was leaking from the red Mustang, the two swirling together on the pavement in a marbleized effect, with silvery chrome and sparkling glass shards over all.

As Arnold approached us, Joe called to him, "Where the hell were you going?"

"Just for a drive," he said. He unrolled his cigarettes from his T-shirt sleeve.

"No no, I mean just now. You were walking away."

"Calling help," Arnold said. He stuck a crumpled cigarette in the corner of his mouth. His shifting eyes met mine, and he gave me a small nod, which I returned.

"Oh," said Joe. "Well, I don't think we need an ambulance or anything. Everybody's all right here, aren't we?"

Everybody was all right. Rudy said, "Here comes somebody."

Arnold, in the process of lighting his cigarette, froze. It was a hot, humid, airless night, and he was holding the match in cupped hands as though a gale were blowing, and his shoulders and head were hunched over the little flame, and I saw him tense and for half a minute move nothing but his eyes, which kept shifting back and forth.

"This is luck," Joe said happily. "It's the police."

Motionless, Arnold blew out the match. He hadn't lighted his cigarette.

"No, it isn't," Rudy said. "It's a cab."

"So it is," Joe said. "Flag him down, Rudy."

Arnold straightened and flipped away the used match. There was no expression on his face at all. He lit another match, lit his cigarette, glanced my way with no message in his eyes, stuck the cigarette back in the corner of his mouth, and turned as we all did as Rudy flagged the cab to a stop.

The driver was a transplanted New York cabby, without the cap but with the cigar. He stuck his head out his window and shouted, "This is a one-way street, you know."

"We know," Rudy said.

"You could have an accident."

"We know," Rudy said.

A little discussion followed, about where we wanted the cab to take us, and what we wanted to do about the two cars, and it was finally decided the cab would take us back to the motel, from which we would call the car rental agency's nighttime emergency number and tell them where they could pick up their two cars.

By the way, do you notice how simple and unmelodramatic all this stuff is when you know the facts? The wild theories and rumors I have heard about the story of the two wrecked rental cars in Florida are absolutely incredible. They were *not* used by trainees in simulated tank attacks. They did *not* smash through police barricades in desperate attempts to get the invasion force out of the country. Arnold Kuklyn and I bumped into each other on a one-way street in Opa-locka, and that's absolutely all there is to it.

So. Once the decision about the cab was made, Arnold volunteered to wait with the cars until the rental agency sent its wreckers around, and we all agreed. But then it turned out that once Rudy and all his equipment—from which he would not be separated—were settled in the cab, there was only room for one more passenger. Joe and I looked at each other, and I said, "I'll wait with Arnold."

"Fine," said Joe. Arnold didn't say anything, but from the tight-lipped way he was puffing on his cigarette I had the feeling he thought the arrangement something less than fine.

Joe got into the cab beside the driver—Rudy and his equipment monopolized the back seat—and at last the cab drove away, and Arnold and I were alone. Arnold gave me a look that said I was a grim fact of life he was adapting himself to, and aloud he said, "I'll be right back."

I watched him leave, frowning after him, wondering what he

was up to. He disappeared, and I was standing there alone. Deserted Opa-locka Boulevard stretched away in both directions, with not a single person in sight. It was too late for drunks and too early for fishermen, and I had the world to myself.

Would Arnold come back? Why was he so twitchy? I went over to the Mustang, curious about it, but he'd locked the doors and I couldn't get in. But I could *see* in, and on the back seat I saw what at first looked to be a hibernating bear but which I peeringly realized was a fur coat. A lot of fur coats. No, a lot of fur stoles.

"Hmmmm," I said, aloud, and straightened, and looked around, and Arnold was coming back. The cigarette glowed and subsided in his mouth, glowed and subsided. He came up to me and I said, "What the heck are all the fur coats for?"

"A friend."

"She must either be very cold or very beautiful," I said.

"It's a guy," Arnold said. His eyes shifted back and forth. "He's picking them up."

"You just called him?"

"Yeah."

Arnold never had much to say for himself, and I never had much to say to Arnold, so for the next five minutes or so there was very little conversation between us. We leaned on crumpled fenders, folded our arms, and waited for whatever would happen next.

What happened next, a gray Volkswagen squareback with flower decals all over it came around a corner and drove over to us and stopped, and out struggled a short and very fat man wearing a Hawaiian shirt, Bermuda shorts, argyle socks, and oxfords. And a presumably Jamaican cigar, which smelled like Carbondale, Pennsylvania. He gave Arnold a disapproving look and said, "Ah juss doan know." Making him about the only person I'd met in Florida with a southern accent.

Not that I met him. In lieu of introductions, Arnold said, "It happens."

I said, "It was all my fault. See, my car's the one going the wrong way."

The fat man swiveled his eyes, but not his head, and gave me a quick hard look. Then he switched back to Arnold and said, "Whass this?"

"A friend of mine—from television," Arnold said.

"Tee Vee?" The fat man was suddenly looking in every direction at once, his expression startled and angry.

"Not Candid Camera," I said, laughing as though I thought it was a joke.

Arnold said, "Come on, let's load."

It was all done very briskly. Arnold unlocked the passenger door of the Mustang, while the fat man struggled back into the Volkswagen and positioned it so the rear was right next to the open door of the Mustang. Then, grunting and puffing, he popped himself out onto the pavement again and trotted around to open the back of the Volkswagen.

"Let me help," I said. I admit that this whole scene, and Arnold's manner ever since I'd bumped into him, was definitely suspicious, but on the other hand it was very late at night, so that my perceptions weren't possibly at their keenest, and also I was primarily feeling responsible for having complicated Arnold's life, so that I was more aware of my own guilt feelings than any guiltiness that might have been demonstrated by him.

So I helped. Arnold, who had crawled into the Mustang, handed the stoles out one at a time to me, and I turned around and handed them to the fat man, who put them in the Volkswagen, having first pulled a length of canvas out and dropped it on the pavement.

We were still doing it when the wreckers arrived from the rental agency. Two trucks, driven by identical chunky, middle-aged black men, with graying mustaches. The drivers got out and started asking questions about the accident, which I answered while continuing to help in the transfer of the stoles, and which one of the drivers wrote down on a long form on a clipboard. The questions and the stoles ran out simultaneously, and the fat man at once spread the piece of canvas over the furs, shut the rear gate, and without a word squeezed himself back behind the wheel and drove away.

Arnold backed out of the Mustang, didn't turn to look at or say hello to the drivers, and quietly said to me, "I'll call a cab." Before I could say anthing in response, he'd sidled away.

So it was that I handled all the paperwork and questions concerning the accident, both for the wreckers and for the police, who showed up a minute after Arnold left. Since I was from out of state and therefore mentally retarded, and since the driver of the other car wasn't present, and since both cars were owned by the same corporation and had been rented by another same corporation, and since nobody was going to be pressing charges against anybody or accusing anybody of anything in court, the police did no more than express their contempt for me, fill in their forms, watch the wreckers depart with the two cars, and then go away themselves, leaving me alone with the radiator coolant and the glass shards, which one of the cops had assured me the Sanitation Department would be getting to within half an hour.

Well, at least I wasn't there that long. No sooner had the police disappeared when Arnold returned, in a cab. He picked me up, and the two of us went back to the motel, and that at last was the end of the evening's adventuring.

The next morning, Joe arranged for some more cars from the rental people, and we all rode out again to Base Camp One. Richard Conford traveled in a different car, and I saw him from time to time in the course of the day, but not to talk to.

I did most of my talking to trainees. The idea was to get every one of them down on film, since even in the unlikely event that the invasion should be a success and they took over the Ilha Pombo government, *some* of them would wind up dead, and we definitely wanted to be sure we had some filmed conversation ahead of time with any casualties.

The only exception was Colonel Enhuelco. On and off all day just about everybody tried to persuade him to be interviewed, but he wouldn't do it. We offered to show him the questions ahead of time and ask only those of which he approved, and he said no. We offered to let him write the questions himself, and he said no. We offered to write his answers for him, and he said no. He was even offered more money—I heard Bob Grantham ask him directly if he would do it for some extra money—and he still said no. "I am a soldier," he said, "not a baseball player. No interview."

Frankly, I think he had mike fright. But that wasn't something you could say to a man with the kind of eyes Colonel Enhuelco had, and if you can't discuss the problem you can't very well solve the problem. So he didn't get interviewed. Rudy got some footage of him when he wasn't looking, but none of us managed to get the sound of his voice on tape.

There were plenty of them to be talked to as it was, even without Colonel Enhuelco. Every ten minutes or so I had to stand up and stretch my legs and walk around a little bit—you just can't hunker forever—and about once an hour I would go sit in an air-conditioned car for five minutes and try to breathe. Then it would be back outside, hunker down, and talk to the next trainee. In the background, the trainees not training were swigging beer from bottles, and between takes I did some swigging myself. I felt a long way from The Three Mafiosi.

With all of these anonymous people giving the same dumb answers to the same dumb questions all day long, it was a real pleasure to run into Ramon and Luis again, the two Cubans I'd interviewed back in February, during the first gunrunning film session. Not that their answers to the dumb questions were any less dumb than anybody else's answers; it was just that their faces, having been seen before, were spuriously familiar; it was as though, during those two interviews, I was talking with old friends.

Ramon apparently felt the same way. He greeted me with big smiles and a big handshake, and it was tough to get him to look solemn and high-minded for the filming, though he finally did get into the swing of things after we'd been hunkering for a while and his legs had started to hurt. But his spirits returned when we were done with the interview, and he left with a cheery wave and smile, saying, "See you around, buddy."

"See you around, Ramon," I said. It's odd how human sentiment enters in at the most unexpected moments. I found myself hoping that somehow Ramon would survive the coming invasion.

As to Luis, he was as charming as ever, and approached me as though he hoped I'd drop a crate so he could punch *me* in the nose. I think his own nose was out of joint now that Colonel Enhuelco was around and Luis was no longer undisputed boss, and his personality hadn't been all that amiable to begin with. We squatted together, and I asked my list of questions, and he rumbled the usual rote answers while looking at me with eyes that challenged me to fight him to the death bare-handed in a circle in the dust, and neither of us offered to see the other around when he swaggered away.

In the afternoon, word spread through the camp that Ernesto Rivera, the earless one, was doing well in a Miami hospital and was in no danger of dying. Everybody seemed relieved by that, as though it were a good omen.

All the training I ever saw, by the way, at that training camp, was people shooting at those FBI-type silhouette targets, and usually not hitting them. Nobody seemed to be instructing anybody in how to shoot better than that; the trainees just took turns shooting and not hitting things. Nor did I see anybody train anybody to do anything else warlike, like follow the platoon leader, advance across broken terrain, respond to sniper fire, how to approach a fortified position, or anything at all of that nature. Rudy told me that some training did take place the two days the trainees practiced coming ashore from the boat that either was or was not rented by the Network for the purpose of their coming ashore from it under Rudy's camera, but according to him the training was mostly inadvertent training in the art of artificial respiration, since three of the trainees wandered into water that was over their heads and nearly drowned because of all the stuff they were carrying in the packs on their backs. Two rifles were lost that way, and Rudy said everybody was upset about that and said somebody was going to have to pay for those rifles. Rudy said he was under the impression that Joe at one point quietly took a roll of bills from his pocket and reeled some off and gave them to Colonel Enhuelco, and that there was no more yelling about the lost rifles after that, but Rudy also said he wasn't absolutely sure he saw any such thing and would certainly not testify that he saw it or even be willing to mention it in any kind of official or semiofficial investigation. So I don't mention it as a possible danger to the Network, or possible use to the Network, but simply to give the flavor.

Anyway, the day ended with me exhausted, with cricks in both knees from all that hunkering down. But at least I was going back to the motel and not to Ilha Pombo. The trainees climbed up into the back of two old stake-sided open-topped trucks that had black paint smeared over old company names on the cab doors, and off they jounced toward their rendezvous with history, as Joe described it, or their rendezvous with destiny, as Bob described it. Though I think I'd prefer to let Ramon describe it.

Ramon, of course, did survive the expedition, and at our next meeting I asked him to describe the series of events that followed after those two trucks jounced away from Base Camp One, and he did, and I have it all on tape. It wasn't a filmed interview, but I do have it all on tape, and I'll include it, and you ought to listen to it after you finish listening to this side. Before you go on to the rest of what I have to say, I mean. Because I think what Ramon says—and I believe he can be believed—casts a lot of light on what I have left to say. So listen to that before you go to the rest of what I have to tell you.

I see I have a little tape left. Don't forget about listening to the Ramon tape; it's clearly marked on the outside of the box. In the meantime, while I have some tape left here, I'll go on with the story.

We Network people—and the affiliate people helping us out, Richard Conford among them—all drove back to Miami and went our separate ways. In the morning the New York contingent would be taking a charter flight home. In the morning we should be hearing the first reports about what was happening on Ilha Pombo Island.

It was like an election night, the same atmosphere of suppressed impatience, the same waiting for the first returns.

Anyway, Bob and Joe and Phil and I had dinner together again and managed this time not to discuss gut issues, and afterward Bob inveigled me to come with him to his room, where he had a girl named Dodo, whose brain was extinct, and he and Dodo spent an hour or so trying to find a girl for me via telephone, and after I felt the humiliation had gone on long enough I excused myself and went back to my own room to call Linda, and when I opened the door Linda herself was in there, sitting on the bed.

"Linda!" I

APPENDIX FIVE

Jay Fisher Interview with Ramon, Last Name Unknown, at Flamingo Follies Motel, Miami Beach, Florida, August, Current Year

Q: Ramon, would you, in your own words, describe what happened to the Ilha Pombo Island Expeditionary Force from the time it vacated Base Camp One to initiate Operation Torch of Liberty?

A: Sure. What happened was— Thanks for the beer.

Q: It's okay.

A: Well, what happened was, first we drove all over the damn place. We was in two trucks, packed in tight so you couldn't hardly sit down noplace, and if you *did* sit down you got your ass all bumped by the bottom of the truck, all hard metal, goin over them bumpy roads; I'm lucky I didn't get piles. So we drove and we drove, and we Cubans did some singin because it reminded us of goin home from the cane after a hard day, and sometimes in the truck you'd feel like singin at the end of the day. Cause the bullshit was over for another day, you dig?

Q: Yes.

A: So we rode and rode in the back of the two trucks all over all those damn lousy roads they have through the swamps down there, and the sun started to go down, and we kept ridin, and sometimes we'd sit and sometimes we'd stand, and after a while we didn't feel like singin anymore, and then a couple fights broke out.

Q: In the trucks?

A: That's where we was. The trouble was, you'd rear back to hit somebody, your elbow'd hit somebody else. So we got a couple good brawls goin in the back of the trucks. I was in the first truck, and I could see they were havin the same sort of thing in the second truck. But they had all the rifles and ammunition back there in the second truck, so they might have had somethin real bad after a while, but they didn't.

Q: That's lucky.

A: Sure. So we knew the whole outfit was lost for a long time, but the driver there in the first truck wouldn't admit it. Because he had Colonel Enhuelco in the cab there with him, see, and he was afraid of the colonel—shit, we were all afraid of the colonel; even Luis was afraid of the colonel—so he just kept drivin around and drivin around, and it gradually got down toward nighttime, and he kept drivin around hopin to find somethin he knew.

Q: Did he?

A: What?

Q: Did he find something he knew?

A: Shit, no. He finally stopped the truck, and the other truck damn near run into us, and the two drivers got out and yelled at each other, and then Colonel Enhuelco got out with his club and hit the driver over the head and knocked him out. The driver of the first truck. Then he asked if anybody knew where we were, and one fellow in our truck said he knew exactly where we were, and the colonel told him come on and get down and drive the truck, and the fellow said he didn't know how to drive, but he did know where we were. So then the colonel said who knows how to drive the truck, and a lot of fellows said they knew how to drive the truck, so he picked one of them to drive the truck and told the other fellow that said he knew exactly where we were to get down and get in the cab between him and the driver and tell the driver how to get out of here. So these two fellows got down off the back of the truck, and the colonel had them pick up the driver and put him up in the back with us, and then they got around and got in the cab with him. Both of them scared, because the one fellow wasn't all that sure exactly where we were and the other fellow wasn't all that sure he knew how to drive the truck. And in the meantime two or three fellows got down off the back of the truck and run off into the swamp.

Q: You mean they deserted?

A: I mean they run off into the swamp.

Q: But they weren't coming back.

A: Hell, no. They probably still runnin.

Q: All right. What happened next?

A: Well, we drove around some more, and the driver that got knocked out woke up and was real sore and said as soon as he got his rifle and his bullets he was gonna put a bullet in the head of the colonel, but everybody knew he was a bullshitter. But meantime we were all sick and tired ridin in the truck, and nobody even wanted to fight anymore with each other. So we just stood there or sat there, and the trucks went on and on, and then we got to a road with a sign on it, and we found where we were, and we headed for the boat.

Q: What boat was this? Was it the same boat as the one you practiced with?

A: No, this was a boat Colonel Enhuelco got from Fort Lauderdale, from some Cubans there that owned it.

Q: Okay. Go on.

A: Yeah. So then we drove to the boat, and when we got there it wasn't there, because we were so late. So we took everything off the trucks and ourselves off too, and we stood around, and the colonel and the other regular driver went off in one of the trucks to make a phone call. Now, this place where we were supposed to meet the boat that we were late for used to be some kind of marina that went broke or something years ago, and now it's all fallin apart. But one boat can still get in to the dock at a time, if it isn't too big. But there isn't any buildings there or anyplace around that you can go inside or sit down or anything. So we just stood out there on the dock with the rifles and the ammunition, and we waited. And we got eat to death by mosquitoes out there; you know how they are down here in the summertime, they're really murder.

Q: Yes, I know.

A: So we just stood around there for a couple hours, and some of the fellows said the colonel had walked out on us, and some of the fellows said it was all a big joke anyway and no invasion or nothing, and some more of the fellows walked off back down the road we come in.

Q: Deserted.
A: Walked off down the road.
Q: Okay.
A: But then the colonel come back and gathered all us together, and had a headcount and said we was eleven men short and wanted to know what the hell happened to the eleven men, and nobody told him. Then he said it was gonna be tough on those eleven men later on, but everybody knew that was bullshit because nobody even had a list of anybody's name, so how's it gonna be tough on eleven men that aren't there and you don't know who they are? But nobody said anything to the colonel, because we *were* there and he could make it tough on us if he wanted. And we were surprised anyway that he knew how many we were supposed to be. You know, to come right out and say you're eleven men short, we all of a sudden knew this colonel was an army man and it was like bein in the army. But anyway, he finished about the eleven men, and then he said he called Fort Lauderdale on the phone and the boat wasn't back there yet but he left a message and when the boat got back to Fort Lauderdale they'd get the message and then they'd come back and pick us up and we'd go ahead and do the invasion like we planned. Then he told us again about how there wasn't any army on Ilha Pombo, just a palace guard armed with swords, and that we could—
Q: He told you there wasn't any army on Ilha Pombo?
A: That's right. Just a palace guard armed with swords. Why, that's bullshit?
Q: You've got a way with words, Ramon.
A: You mean it's bullshit.
Q: I mean it's bullshit.
A: Yeah, well, a lot of us figured it was bullshit. But what the hell, the colonel was comin along with us, so even if it was bullshit it couldn't be too *much* bullshit, because an army man like the colonel don't ever go anyplace he could get killed.
Q: He was going to this time.
A: Yeah, well, maybe. Only if he was, he didn't know it.
Q: I'll go along with that. I'm sorry, I interrupted you. What happened next?
A: Well, the colonel told us we were gonna have a couple hour wait until the boat got back, and then he said he wanted a dollar from each man to go get food, because the delay meant

an extra meal we hadn't counted on. A lot of the fellows got upset about that, but he had Luis and a couple other real tough types on his side, and they were the ones come around to get the dollars, so we all gave them a dollar for food. Except three fellows didn't have any money, and they got beat up a little and searched, and when it was proved they didn't have any money the colonel said that was okay, we could share with them. Because we was all for one and one for all. So then the colonel and Luis and a couple others took off in one of the trucks again, and now a lot of fellows said that was it, it was all over, we'd been brought way out here to get taken for a dollar each and now we'd never see the colonel again. But a lot of us said the colonel was too big a man to go through all that for a dollar each from a bunch of dishwashers like us, and we were sure the colonel would come back. But a couple of fellows went over and knocked down the driver of the other truck that was still there and took the key off him and drove away in the truck. Three of them. Then the driver that they knocked down and took the key off of said the colonel will kill me when he comes back and the truck is gone, and *he* left.

Q: That's fifteen now. How many still there?

A: I don't know, maybe thirty-five, forty.

Q: Did the colonel notice when he got back?

A: I don't know. He didn't say nothin. He didn't have any more head counts or nothin, but he might of known. All he did was, he come back with the truck and he looked around and he said where's the other truck? And nobody said nothin; everybody just scratched their bites and looked at each other. So the colonel said some things under his breath and said we would eat now. The only light we had was the truck headlights, so we set up the rifle crates in front of the truck to make a like a kind of a table, and we brought the food around from the back of the truck. Then we all ate and—

Q: What was the food?

A: It was loaves of bread and coldcuts and bottles of beer. We had sandwiches and beer, and then we all went off into the swamp to take a leak and like that, and I think maybe a couple fellows didn't come back from takin a leak. Only I'm not sure. It was real dark by now, nighttime, gettin close to midnight, and we picked that night because it was the night when there isn't any moon at all, so it was real good and dark. Except we kept the truck headlights on, so we could have one place where we could see somethin.

Q: It was midnight then? What time did the boat show up?

A: Around three-thirty in the mornin. We'd all been bit to death by then, and the colonel was asleep on the seat of the truck, and the rest of us were walkin around and wondering what the hell we were gonna do now and then damn if the boat didn't show up after all. It come in and docked, and the captain got off it and wanted to know where the hell the colonel was, and we said he was asleep in the truck, so the captain went over and banged on the truck door with his fist, and the colonel woke up and got out of the truck and was pissed off at the captain for the way he woke him up. And the captain was pissed off because he come all the way down from Fort Lauderdale and went all the way back again when we didn't show up and then had to come all the way back down again, and what the hell did the colonel think he was gonna do now? And the colonel said he thought he was gonna go take over Ilha Pombo if the captain could get the lead out of his ass, and the captain said it would take eight hours in his boat to get to Ilha Pombo and that was why they were gonna leave at seven in the evening, to get there at three in the morning when it would be dark and everybody would be asleep. But now it was already three-thirty in the morning, and it would be noon before we got to Ilha Pombo, and even in Ilha Pombo people were awake at noon, and the colonel punched him in the mouth and told him not to insult Ilha Pombo. Only it was a piss-poor punch, and the captain didn't even pay any attention to it; he just said first things first, where's the money? And the colonel handed him a check, and the captain said you got to be kiddin me, you think I'm some kind of jerk? So they argued, and then the colonel gave him some cash money, and the captain said it was supposed to be more, and the colonel said that was all he had, and the captain said he could go fuck himself, and the colonel said that was all he had, take it or leave it, and the captain said he'd leave it, he didn't want to go down to Ilha Pombo anyway. So the colonel said hold on, maybe I can get some more money, and he sent Luis and the other tough boys around to shake us all down and take all the money we had, and the colonel counted it out and gave it to the captain and said now that's *all* we got, and the captain grumbled and then he said oh what the fuck. So then we loaded all the rifles and ammunition on board the boat, and we all got on ourselves, and just when we were gonna head out to sea a big searchlight from out in the water turned on and a voice on a bullhorn said, *Halt, you are under arrest.*

Q: What happened then?

A: We got arrested.

Q: Yes, I know, but tell me about it.

A: What tell? We got arrested.

Q: Ramon, who arrested you?

A: Customs.

Q: Customs?

A: Yeah. What happened, it was a Coast Guard boat out there in the water, and we couldn't get past it. So we were thinkin about it, and everybody was talkin it over, and the colonel wanted the captain to bust through the Coast Guard or anyway give him his money back, and then these headlights came along up behind the truck that we left there, and these Customs men came out and told us to get ashore. So we got ashore. So then they told us to get back on board and unload all the rifles and ammunition and put them back in our truck, so we did that. Then they told us get up in the truck, so we did that. But it was very crowded, even with all the fellows that had run off. And they made the colonel get in back with us, and he was really sore and told them he was supposed to ride up front in the cab because he was the colonel, and they told him to shut his mouth. Then one of the Customs men got in the truck and tried to start it, and it wouldn't start because the battery got run down by havin the headlights on for six, seven hours, I don't know how long. As long as we was there. So they made us stay in the truck, and nothin happened for about an hour and a half, and everybody was tired and mad and kind of scared, and then the Customs men showed up with a big truck they borrowed from the post office that said US MAIL all over it, and they made us get down from our truck and carry the rifles and the ammunition over to the post office truck and then get up in the post office truck ourselves, and then they shut the doors and we took off. You know, it was a different kind of truck, with sides and a top, and we couldn't see nothin. We just knew we were movin.

Some fellows said they was gonna drive us into the ocean and drown us, but nobody much believed they'd use up a whole post office truck on a bunch of dishwashers like us, so we didn't panic or nothin. But we was scared and worried, and we didn't know what was gonna happen.

Q: Let me get this straight. They put you people *and* the guns *and* the ammunition all in the same truck?

A: Yeah.

Q: Were there armed guards in there with you?

A: There wasn't nobody in there but us. And no light to see by or nothin.

Q: Didn't they realize you people could have loaded the ammunition into the guns and fought your way out of there?

A: Are you kiddin?

Q: Well, you could have.

A: You must be out of your mind.

Q: Well, didn't anybody suggest it?

A: Course not.

Q: Not even the colonel?

A: The colonel was tryin to get his money back from the captain. We had the captain and the other two guys from the boat in with us. The captain kept tellin him to go to hell, and the colonel kept sayin men, search that man. But nobody wanted to do any of that bullshit.

Q: So then what happened?

A: They took us to the compound.

Q: What compound?

A: How do I know? The truck stopped and they opened the doors in the back and said get out, and we got out and went through a gate in a big metal fence and it was all blacktop inside. You know what I mean? All blacktop, and surrounded by the big metal fence on three sides and this building on the fourth side. Brick. And it was kind of morning by then, but there were these big lights shinin down all over the compound. And there were a bunch of cops there with billyclubs. And they told us to lay down—

Q: What happened to the guns and ammunition?

A: What?

Q: The guns and ammunition in the truck. Did you unload it there?

A: Naw, we didn't unload it at all. They unloaded *us,* and the truck went away.
Q: With the guns.
A: Yeah, sure. They were still in there.
Q: All right, I'm sorry. They told you to lie down?
A: Yeah. They told us to lay down on the blacktop, face down, with our arms up over our heads and our feet apart and don't move. Then they took us in one at a time to ask us questions, and everybody else had to stay where they were on the compound and not move. There were these cops walkin up and down and up and down, and if you moved and they caught you they'd come over and hit you on the bottom of the foot with their billyclub. And if you had to take a leak or somethin you had to do it right there, in your pants.
Q: How long were you there?
A: About four hours.
Q: Four hours? Lying facedown on blacktop?
A: Except for when they questioned you.
Q: Tell me about the questioning.
A: Well, they'd come along and hit you on the bottom of the foot with their billyclub and say on your feet. Then you'd get up, and they'd make you walk to the brick building, and you'd go inside, and you'd go into this room where these people were, and they'd make you empty your pockets on the desk, and then you'd sit down and they'd ask you questions like what's your name and what the fuck you think you're up to and like that, and there was this guy that looked like a fag with this little machine like a typewriter only smaller, and he was takin down every word you said. Then they'd let you put all your stuff back in your pockets and go outside and lay on the blacktop again. And then after a while they'd come hit you on the bottom of the foot again and tell you on your feet, and they'd make you go back into the building again to a different room and sit you down at a table where they had this typed-out paper, and it would be everything you said and everything they said the last time, only without the swear words, and they'd say read it and sign it. So you'd read it and sign it and ask to go to the bathroom and they'd say no, and you'd go back out and lay down on the blacktop again.
Q: All right. This went on for four hours. Then what?

A: Then they put us into some police vans and they took us to a court and they charged us with some stuff and set bail at sixty thousand dollars a man, and then they took us off to jail.

Q: Just a second. They charged you with some stuff? *What* stuff?

A: I ain't a lawyer, man, how the hell do I know?

Q: But you were the one being charged. What did the judge say?

A: A lotta bullshit, man. I know it wasn't Spanish, and it sure as hell didn't sound like no English. One fellow said it was Latin. Anyway, they charged us and took us off to jail.

Q: And you were there until this morning?

A: Fuckin A well told.

Q: Did they question you some more?

A: Shit, yeah, all the time. They asked a lotta questions about you people, you know.

Q: They did? You mean the Network?

A: I mean you people. You people in a shitpot of trouble, man.

Q: We are?

A: Oh, yeah. A shitpot of trouble. I don't envy you, man.

Q: You want another beer?

A: Thanks, man. You're okay. You know what you oughta do?

Q: What?

A: Skip the country. Thanks for the beer.

Q: You're welcome. I don't think it's that bad, you know.

A: Yeah, okay.

Q: There'll be some questions asked of the Network, but after all, we're simply a news-gathering media, we simply observe.

A: You're gonna like that blacktop, man. You're gonna love it.

Q: Shut up and drink your beer.

TAPE FIVE, SIDE TWO

ALL RIGHT. Assuming this chaos of cassettes hasn't gotten out of sequence somewhere along the line, you have just listened to Ramon's story of what happened to the Ilha Pombo Island Expeditionary Force after we Network people left them. If you haven't listened to that tape, find it and listen to it and come back, and then I'll tell you what happened to us *Network* people that night, and primarily what happened to me.

After spending an hour or so with Bob and Dodo while they failed to get me a girl for the evening, I went back to my motel room and found Linda sitting on the bed. "Linda!" I said.

She got to her feet.

"You came down after all," I said.

"You're under arrest," she said.

I said, "What?"

She flashed an identification card, with her picture on it. "You're under arrest. Don't make trouble for me, come along quietly."

"But Linda—!"

"Not Linda," she said. "Linda McMahon was my cover name. I am Mary Marie Conroy, and you are under arrest."

"Mary Marie—" I'd heard that name somewhere before. "My God!" I shouted, "the St. Louis Thirty-seven!"

"That's the case I'm proudest of," she said.

"Damn those Japanese watercolorists!" I cried. "Let somebody take a *picture* in the court, let me *recognize* you!"

"That's just what we didn't want," she said. Her smile was atrociously smug.

I said, "The Women's Liberation Movement. Are you under cover there too?"

"Barely," she said, and suddenly blushed.

"An agent provocateur," I said. "Trying to get them to break the law."

"All part of my job," she said.

"And everything we meant to each other," I said. "Was that all lies, too?"

For the first time, she looked uncertain. "I have my job to do," she said.

"And none of it meant anything to you," I said.

Her eyes swiveled from mine. "I can't say that."

"But here you are," I said. "To arrest me."

She looked back at me, her expression tense but somehow sainted. "You angel," she said. "Well if you get a good break you'll be out of San Quentin in twenty years and you can come back to me then."

"Twenty *years!*"

"I'm going to send you over," she said, and her eyes glistened as though from tears. "I'll wait for you."

"Wait a minute," I said. "What the hell are you talking about?"

"You're taking the fall," she said.

"I'm doing the *what?*"

Were those tears glistening in her eyes, or madness? "I'm not Thursby," she said. "I'm not Jacobi. I won't play the sap for you."

And then I got it. "You're doing *The Maltese Falcon!* You're doing Spade's lines from the finish!"

Her eyes glittered. "Making speeches is no damn good now," she said. "I don't care who loves who. I'm not going to play the sap for you."

I screamed, *"I'm not Brigid O'Shaughnessy!"*

She blinked. The glitter faded from her eyes. In a more businesslike way, she said, "What?"

"I'm not Brigid O'Shaughnessy," I said, more quietly.

"Well, of course not," she said. "You're Jay Fisher, and I'm arresting you on a charge of aiding and abetting a military expedition formed within the boundaries of the United States for the purpose of attacking Ilha Pombo Island, a sovereign nation with which the United States is and has been at peace."

"You were doing Sam Spade from *The Maltese Falcon,*" I said.

She frowned at me. "What on earth are you talking about?"

"You don't remember doing it?"

"It's a little late to try an insanity plea," she said. "Come along. I won't have to handcuff you, will I? Or call for assistance?"

No. She didn't have to handcuff me, or call for assistance. We left the motel room, and a gray Ford with DC plates was out front. We got in, Linda—or, that is, Mary Marie—driving, and headed away from the motel.

I said, "No wonder I could never get you into bed."

"Some sacrifices my government doesn't ask of me," she said primly.

"I'm sorry to think you'd consider it a sacrifice," I said.

She made no reply, and we were both silent for a while. A traffic light stopped us, and I thought about our conversation in the car so far, and her use of the word *sacrifice,* and I looked at her and said, "Good Lord."

She gave me a calm look. "What's the matter?"

"You're a virgin!"

She faced front, her face etched in thin-lipped lines of disapproval. The light turned green. The car moved forward.

"A virgin," I said. "I knew federal agents were *clean,* but my God—"

"That will be enough of that," she said tightly. Her hands were clenched on the steering wheel; she was facing forward. "My own personal business is my own personal business."

"It sure is," I said. "I only wish mine were."

"I'm not ashamed of being pure. What's good enough for the Director," she said, still staring forward, "is good enough for me."

"Oh, now, wait a minute," I said. "Are you suggesting that Hoover—?"

She rounded on me. "Don't you talk filthy about the Director!"

"I wasn't going to! Watch the road, will you?"

She watched the road. "He's never been married," she said.

"Well, that doesn't mean—"

"I said don't talk filthy!"

So I didn't say anything at all. What I did instead, I thought about the episode in the phone booth, the only time I'd ever come really close to sexual intercourse with this girl, and I found myself grateful for that unfortunate woman on the phone who kept insisting I was the delicatessen. If she hadn't called and called again, I might have completed my filthy plans *in re* Mary Marie Conroy, and I shuddered to think what her vengeance would have been once she'd returned to her right mind. Or, that is to say, her usual mind.

Did she herself remember the phone booth episode? I looked closely at her grim profile—a piece of beautifully sculptured granite—and decided she didn't remember it, any more than she remembered her brief dip into Sam Spade. Would that she would never remember.

I was taken to an office building in downtown Miami and turned over to some men in gray wash-and-wear suits who locked me in a barren office and went away. Gradually the office filled with Network men—Bob first, then Rudy and the rest of the poker players, then Joe, then Phil, and finally even Arnold, who came in snarling and yanking his elbow out of his escort's grip—and then we just stood around for a while and tried to figure out what was going on.

I think we'd all known vaguely that what the Ilha Pombo Island Expeditionary Force was up to was illegal, that it was against United States law for them to train and arm themselves on American soil and then depart for military reasons from that same American soil, but I don't think any of us for a second thought that the Network could eventually find itself tarred by the same brush.

Certainly Richard Conford didn't think so, and now at last he will step forward and take his proper place in this chronicle. Way back on that first day of filming in Florida, back in February, Richard Conford had seen those truckloads of guns arrive at the flamingo rustlers' camp and he'd decided that officials somewhere along the line ought to be told what was going on. Not Network officials; oh, no, that wasn't Richard Conford's style. To talk to Network officials would mean talking to *New Yorkers,* and Richard Conford talks to New Yorkers only when he has a complaint.

No, what Richard Conford did, that day in February, was go talk to the FBI. The instant we all got back from the flamingo rustlers' camp Conford went to the FBI office in Miami and told them what he'd seen and asked them what he should do about it. They apparently questioned him at some length and then sent him to the Customs people, since the laws that were being broken came under the jurisdiction of Customs and not of the FBI.

But the very next day, if you'll notice, Mary Marie Conroy made my acquaintance in the hotel pool. I won't say anything about the morality of a virgin who behaves the way she behaved that day; it could have been no accident that her top was on the bottom. I'll let that incident speak for itself.

As to my own behavior, I admit I was wrong not to tell Joe the truth about Linda right away. I mean, Mary Marie Conroy. No, I don't, dammit, I mean Linda. That's the name I always knew her under, and that's the way I think of her now—Linda McMahon. If you use this report for anything legal in the future, just bear in mind that every time I say *Linda,* I am actually speaking about Mary Marie Conroy. Okay?

Anyway, it is true that when Joe and Phil and Bob and all the others were brought in and stuffed into the barren office with me, and were all saying such things as, "What happened?" and, "What the hell's going on?" I did not volunteer the information that I had been dating an undercover FBI agent for the last six months, and I completely admit I was wrong to keep silent about that. Though in the long run I don't see what difference it would have made. I mean, the damage was done by then; we'd all been arrested, the invasion was being nipped in the bud, the fit had already hit the shan.

Still, I should have told them, I don't argue the point. But in keeping silent I was *not* covering guilt, as some individuals have allegedly alleged; I mean, what guilt? I was covering embarrassment, that's what I was covering, and if you were to discover you'd just spent half a year trying to get into the pants of an FBI agent you'd be embarrassed, too. I don't care how phlegmatic you lawyers are, you'd be embarrassed, and you too would have a strong reluctance to talk about it.

So I didn't talk about it. Not until way later, back in the motel, when I told Bob privately. Though it didn't turn out quite as private as I had in mind.

Well, that's rushing ahead. At this point, we're still in the barren office, a dozen of us, and it's getting later at night, and none of us knows exactly what's going to happen next, but nobody is really worried. This isn't, after all, Ilha Pombo Island. This is a civilized nation, and so far as we were all concerned none of us had done anything wrong and therefore this could only be in the nature of a temporary inconvenience.

I understand that Joe Singleton and Phil Bifrat have both had a lot to say about how I in particular spent that night, and that's why I want to make it clear that *nobody* was sitting around being tense and worried, and I mean Joe wasn't and Phil wasn't. Nobody was.

Bob Grantham, as a matter of fact, pretty well summed up the general feeling in the room when he said, "Now, right here is the difference between a free democracy and Godless Communism. If we were in a Communist-enslaved land right now, we'd all be in trouble, serious trouble, but we're not. We're in the good old USA, and we are free citizens who have committed no crime, and so we're *safe.* And the proof is, they haven't given us our rights. If we were in any kind of real trouble and they were going to arrest us or charge us with anything, the *first* thing they'd do is give us our rights. Let us make a phone call, for instance, or warn us that anything we said could be used against us, or have a lawyer here to represent us, or like that. Those are our *rights*, given us by the Constitution, that no man can take away from us. And the fact that they haven't given us our rights, that they're holding us here incommunicado and haven't charged us with anything or let us make any phone calls, that's a proof to me right there that we aren't in any serious danger at all."

Well, that made darn good sense to the rest of us, and as it turned out Bob was pretty well right, since ultimately we were all released and none of us was charged with anything. But the point I want to make is that what he said there was the general feeling in the room, and in that light, and given the fact that I still had a hundred forty dollars of the crew's money that I'd won the night before, you can see how it was that when a poker game started up I couldn't very well refuse to sit in.

We were the same seven as the night before; Rudy, Hank, Irv, Leroy, Archie, M———, and me. There was a desk in the room, but not enough chairs so we seven sat on the floor to play. Hank, naturally, had come equipped with a couple decks of cards.

As to the other five, they early on separated into two groups.

Group One consisted of Joe Singleton, Phil Bifrat, Bob Grantham, and Richard Conford; they all sat around the desk and discussed the situation and its probable effect on the special. At that point, we were all still unworried enough to believe that "To Free an Island" was still a live project, and in fact Bob and Phil roughed out an approach to the finish of the program that would have involved the circumstances of our general arrest. That was how far we all were at that point from understanding the real depths of the mess we were in.

Richard Conford, by the way, didn't mention his finking to the Feds that night, any more than I mentioned anything about Linda, but in his case I don't think it was exactly embarrassment that kept him silent. I understand the Network has kept him on, and I've heard it alleged that he wasn't fired because everybody was afraid the FBI wouldn't like it, and I'd just like to point out the inequity in that. Conford blatantly betrayed the Network, and I have never tried to do anything but what was best for the Network, and look at where he is and look at where I am. It just isn't fair.

Oh, I forgot about Group Two, a minute ago. Group Two was Arnold. He hunkered in a corner all night, talked to no one unless he was directly spoken to, puffed away at crumpled cigarettes, and practiced his Humphrey Bogart facial twitches.

The authorities already knew quite a bit about us, and about the Ilha Pombo people, but in the course of that long night they questioned every last one of us at length, and toward morning they even took our pictures and fingerprints, which I think was more to be snotty than for any other reason. Anyway, their technique that night was to take us one at a time to another room and ask us a lot of questions about Operation Torch of Liberty, and I suppose we all told the truth. I know I did, I saw no reason not to. I still see no reason not to. The Network has done nothing wrong, though I don't question that various individuals within the Network have made mistakes, some of them more serious than others.

Anyway, I suppose all the interrogations went approximately as mine did. I was the fourth or fifth one called, and when the two neat young men in gray suits came and called my name I was sitting there with a bad hand I knew I should fold on, but I hadn't folded on it yet, and so it was with a big grin on my face that I turned my cards over and scooped up my money and got to my feet and said, "Coming!" I suppose Joe Singleton is making something out of that smile these days, but I take my vow it had to do exclusively with poker.

The two neat young men—they made me think most of ushers at a wedding—walked me down a hall to an elevator, and up in the elevator to a different floor, and down what looked like the same hall to a room almost as full of men as the one I'd just left, except that nobody was playing poker. They brought me in, they faded unobtrusively into the background and leaned against the wall near the door, and an older man—but just as neat—said, "Sit down, Mr. Fisher."

He was sitting at a desk, and there was a chair facing it; leatherette back and seat, wooden arms. I sat down, and I was more or less surrounded by people looking at me, either sitting in other chairs along both side walls or standing beside other pieces of furniture, such as filing cabinets and hat racks. The venetian blinds behind the neat man at the desk—he had neat gray hair and a freshly shaved jaw—were angled so as to show me that it was still night in downtown Miami.

The man at the desk said, "I am Agent Kylety, Miami District Office, Federal Bureau of Investigation. I am not necessarily in charge of this case."

I contemplated a remark on my own feelings of uncertainty at the moment and decided he probably wasn't looking for comments just yet, so I let it go.

And I was right. He went on, with only the slightest of pauses, saying, "Because this affair concerns so many different bureaus, divisions, departments, and offices of federal, state, county, and municipal government, no one at the moment is fully in control here. The FBI is only one of several bodies interested in your answers to several questions."

"I'll cooperate as best I can," I said.

"You'd be advised to cooperate," he said, and then frowned at me; he was thrown slightly out of phase just for a second.

I realized I'd gone too fast for him. "Sorry," I said. And then, to get us back in alignment again, I repeated, "I'll cooperate as best I can."

The frown cleared, though traces remained, and Agent Kylety remained just a bit distant and vague throughout the rest of my time in the room there. "I'm glad to hear that," he said, sounding somewhat puzzled, and then he went on to introduce all the other people in the room, absolutely none of whom I remember. At the federal level they represented Customs, the State Department, the Coast Guard, the Interstate Commerce Commission, the Immigration & Naturalization Service, the National Park Service, the Secret Service, and a few more I don't remember. And by the time Agent Kylety got to the state level, much less county and city, I wasn't even listening to the introductions anymore, I was just automatically smiling and nodding at each face in turn; again, like a wedding.

An underrehearsed wedding, unfortunately. As Agent Kylety had said, nobody was fully in control there. Everybody in the room wanted the chance to ask a question, and there just weren't that many relevant questions to go around, so the result was more like a press conference after an ax murder than like a police interrogation; half a dozen people asked questions at once, they interrupted each other, they asked questions that had already been asked except that they phrased them somewhat differently, and a number of them—particularly city and county people—got very irritable. In fact, they'd been irritable before I got there, and as I say I was the fourth or fifth one questioned, so they'd already had some time to start building their enmities toward one another. Rudy was the next to the last one they called, along toward morning, and when he came back I asked him how it had gone and he said, "Fine, until one of them punched another one in the mouth." Apparently it got pretty close to a donnybrook in there by the time they were finished with us, and if there'd been twenty of us to interrogate rather than twelve I don't believe they would have made it.

However, they did. With all the questions they insisted on asking, they pretty well got from me just about every fact I knew in connection with the Ilha Pombo Affair, and if they hadn't kept interrupting my answers with new questions they would have gotten even more. As I say, I saw then and I see now no reason to lie to the authorities. The Network is not a criminal. The Network is a neutral observer of the passing scene.

Anyway, they finally finished with me and Agent Kylety said, "I'll make a note in your dossier that you cooperated with us fully."

"Thank you," I said. "And I'll stay in Miami as long as you might need me for anything else."

"You'd better stay in Miami for the time being," he said. "In case we need to talk to you again." Then he got that sort of vague, glazed look in his eyes again, and I realized I'd done it once more.

"Yes, sir," I said. "I'll stay in town."

His line then was, of course, *you can go now,* but he didn't say it. He just sat there, hunched slightly, head thrust forward, gazing at me in a baffled, brooding way, and his lips were moving. But he didn't say anything.

I finally had to prompt him. I mean, the people all around us were beginning to get uncomfortable, shuffle their feet, clear their throats. So I said, "Can I go now?"

That got him back on the track. His eyes cleared somewhat, and he said, "You can go now."

"Thank you, sir," I said. I got to my feet, and the two neat young ushers who'd ushered me here took their places at my sides, and I left the room. My last sight of Agent Kylety was of him frowning toward where I'd been sitting; his lips seemed to be moving again.

At any rate, I was escorted back to the room where we were all being kept, and I took my place in the game again, and about fifteen minutes later they came back and took Leroy away. There was always that long pause between interrogations; they never took one man at the same time they were bringing another back. I don't know why they did it that way, but it helped to prolong things considerably, which had to be at least as hard on them as it was on us.

Well, the last interrogation ended about five or a little after, and then nothing happened for almost an hour. We were all getting tired, of course, and a couple of the boys napped for a while on the floor, but the poker game went on and on. I was around three hundred dollars ahead by then, and Hank and Rudy and one or two others were determined to keep the game going until they got their money back from me, which as it turned out they never did.

At six, uniformed police came in and started being tough, grabbing elbows and pushing shoulders and saying things like, "Move along." We were all too tired to complain as much as we might have—though I did see Hank come very close to letting one of them have it at one point—and we just obediently went with them as they herded us out of the room and down a corridor and down in an elevator and through an underground garage and into a Black Maria, which was painted pale blue. The pale blue Black Maria took us across part of downtown Miami and into an old brick police station building, where we were taken out of the vehicle again and run through a processing that consisted of having our photographs and fingerprints taken.

And might I say, on that subject, that these days when I see the FBI's ten most-wanted fugitives on television just before the sign-off, I view those pictures differently from the way I used to. Those are all mean-looking guys in those pictures, but maybe they aren't really as mean as they look. Maybe it's just that those pictures were taken at six-thirty in the morning after they'd been kept up all night the night before. I haven't ever seen the picture they took of me that morning, but I'd be willing to bet you could scare Marines with it. I was tired, I was irritable, my fingertips were covered with black ink, and the uniformed police kept going out of their way to be unpleasant. "Move along," they kept saying, and I didn't see them once say it to somebody who was standing still. "Move along" was said exclusively to people who *were* moving along.

Someday I've got to ask Bob Grantham about the police in countries that have been enslaved by Godless Communism.

I confess that I did try to start a minirevolution of my own in that building, though definitely a nonviolent one. What happened, I heard one of the cops say to the fingerprint man, "Hurry it up, Abner. If we don't get these birds out by seven o'clock, we got to feed them breakfast." So I quick tried to talk all the others into moving along as slowly as possible, to make it last past seven o'clock. But nobody would go along with me, and on sober reflection I realize they were right. In the first place, it would be cutting off our nose to spite our face to hang around with those cops one second longer than necessary. And in the second place, can you imagine the breakfast they would have given us?

So at ten to seven we were on the street, and by seven-thirty we were all back in the motel. All except the local men, naturally, who went on home. At the motel, Joe Singleton tried to place a call to Mr. Clarebridge, but Mr. Clarebridge was in transit between his home and the office, so we white-collar workers had to stay up another hour and a half until Joe could report to Mr. Clarebridge. The crew, still disgruntled about me winning the three hundred dollars, had gone off to sleep, but Joe and Bob and

Phil Bifrat and I sat in Joe's motel room, rubbing our eyes and yawning, and waited for Mr. Clarebridge to return Joe's urgent call.

Arnold was probably leaving town just about that time, and I've heard those who've blamed Joe Singleton for not keeping an eye on Arnold, and I want to say something about that. I think you must realize by now that Joe isn't one of my favorite people these days, but fair is fair, and how could Joe Singleton possibly keep an eye on Arnold Kuklyn that morning, after the night we'd all gone through? I think Joe did all that could reasonably be expected of him, or of anybody, and besides that, we still had no idea how serious the whole thing was, though the interrogations and mug shots and fingerprinting had certainly given us all food for thought.

As did Mr. Clarebridge, when he called Joe a little after nine. Joe started to tell him what had happened, and Mr. Clarebridge's first instruction was, "Say nothing. Our lawyers will be down on the first plane."

"It's too late to say nothing," Joe said. "They've been interrogating us all night."

"Our lawyers will be down on the first plane," Mr. Clarebridge said, more loudly than before. (I was listening on an extension.)

"All right," Joe said.

"Sit tight. Talk to no one. Don't go anywhere."

"Yes, sir," Joe said.

Mr. Clarebridge said some more, but it was repetition, and at the end of the conversation I went back to my own room and went to sleep, and a knocking at the door woke me around two, and it was Ramon. I let him in and washed my face and ordered me breakfast and him a beer, and then I taped the interview I hope you listened to. Then Ramon borrowed twenty dollars from me—I didn't charge the Network, it was part of my poker winnings—and he left, and I finished my breakfast and went back to sleep, and the police woke me around five in the afternoon to arrest me and take me downtown.

All the way downtown I kept saying, "Why just me? Why me? What about the rest of them?" But police don't talk to you unless they want to talk to you, and these two didn't want to talk to me.

Downtown, I was turned over to plainclothes police, who also didn't want to talk to me, and who took me into an absolutely empty room with two-tone green walls and told me to stand over there. I said, "Will you please tell me what's going on?" and they said, "Stand over there." So I stood over there, which was next to the wall opposite the door.

On the basis of my by-this-point extensive experience with the police, I figured I was good for a minimum of half an hour alone in that room before anything else happened, but I was wrong. It was barely a minute before the door opened again and five men came in, all shrugging into jackets and adjusting ties and shooting cuffs, like a news team taking their places just before air time. They didn't talk to one another, but they all seemed to know what they were doing together, and they came over and ranged themselves along the same wall where I was standing, two of them to my left and three to my right. One of them—the one on my right—said to me, "Just stand easy and face the door. Don't move around or anything when they come in."

"When who comes in?" All I could think of, stupidly enough, was the Valentine's Day Massacre; in my mind's monitor I saw half a dozen hoods with machine guns come through that door over there and mow us all down.

My friend on my right said, "Just take it easy, Mr. Fisher. Nothing to worry about."

"But I don't know what's going *on,*" I said, and the door across the way opened and four men stepped across the threshold and stood looking at us. I looked back at them, and the two in the middle looked vaguely familiar, though I couldn't tell from where. They were both black, middle-aged, wearing sports shirts and slacks—everybody else in the room, including me, wore jacket and tie—and they had identical graying mustaches.

I recognized them just as they recognized me. Both of them nodded and simultaneously pointed at me, and I started to lift my hand to wave. "That's him," one of them said, and the other one said, "He's the one." I let the wave die before it lived, and just stood there with my hand in this odd position in front of me while the two black men—they'd driven the wreckers that had towed away the rental cars night before last—turned to the other two men with them and said some more that I was the one, it surely was me, that was me right over there. "Okay," one of the other men said, and the room emptied as though a bell had rung. Not only the wrecker drivers and the two men with them, but also the five men who lined up along the wall with me; everybody methodically and unhurriedly walked out of the room, and I was alone again.

But not for long. I had barely time enough to realize that I had just taken part in a lineup—in the movies, it's always a brightly lighted stage, with a white wall behind it crossed with height markers, and I hadn't recognized it in its real-life form until after the event—when in walked a uniformed policeman who said, "This way," and led me off down a corridor that smelled for some reason of shrimp.

This way led to a neat but small office where a neat but small man in a neat suit and small bow tie ushered me into a wooden chair beside his desk and then said, in fatherly/comradely fashion, "You want to tell me about it?"

I said, "I was driving the wrong way. Is that what this is all about? Good Lord, I know it's against the law to drive the wrong way on a one-way street, but a *lineup?*"

"What the Opa-locka authorities may wish to do in connection with you and any of their local ordinances," the neat, small man said, "is up to the Opa-locka authorities. I was hoping you'd like to talk to me about the other matter."

"What the heck have those two wrecker drivers to do with Ilha Pombo?" I asked.

He frowned at me. He was about to become less comradely and more fatherly. He said, "Let's not kid each other, Fisher. You know what we're here for."

I said, "It isn't Ilha Pombo?"

He was getting irritated. He said, "What the hell is Ilha Pombo?"

"An island in the Caribbean."

"Fisher," he said, being grim to show he was keeping his annoyance under restraint, "Fisher, I'm not here to fool around with you. I'm here to talk to you about those stolen stoles."

I just looked at him. The phrase made no sense at all. I said, "Sir?"

"The stoles! The stolen stoles!"

Then I remembered, and I was so startled I jumped to my feet. "Those stoles were *stolen?*"

"You can't run, Fisher," he said, more grimly than ever. "That door is guarded."

"*I* don't know anything about stolen stoles!"

"Fisher," he said, "it will go a lot easier on you if you cooperate. You're already in a great deal of trouble, I understand, with the federal authorities. The mug shot those drivers identified was taken this very morning, right here in this building."

I said, "I didn't have anything to—"

"Sit down, Fisher."

I sat down. "I didn't have anything to do with those stoles," I said.

"They were in your car."

"They were not. They were in the car I hit."

He squinted. "You're the one the drivers identified. You were unloading the stoles from your car and putting them into another vehicle—"

"A gray Volkswagen squareback."

"Exactly. Another vehicle which—"

"With flower decals."

A two-second hesitation, then: "What?"

"The Volkswagen," I explained, "had flower—"

"We know all that, Fisher! What we want to know is where that Volkswagen *went* with those stolen stoles."

"I have no idea."

"You unloaded them."

"I *helped* unload them."

He shook his head, irritated with me for wasting time with foolishness. Scrabbling among papers on his neat desk, he said, "The police report on the accident says you were alone on the scene. Here it is here."

"By the time they got there, I was. Arnold had—"

"Who's Arnold?"

"He was driving the car with the stoles in it."

"The stolen stoles."

"I guess so."

"You guess so. This accomplice of yours, Arnold, is he the one—"

"He wasn't my accomplice. Honest, I don't have anything to do with stolen stoles. I'm a television announcer, I don't steal stoles."

"The drivers identified you. The police report says you were alone on the scene."

"For heaven's sake," I said, "I didn't drive both cars!"

He frowned at me. "What's that?"

I said, "I said I didn't drive both cars. I was driving the yellow Dodge Dart that was going the wrong way, and the stoles—I beg your pardon, the *stolen* stoles—were in the red Mustang that I hit. There were two passengers in the car with me; ask *them* what happened."

"Who were these passengers?"

I told him.

"You mentioned someone named Arnold. Was he driving the Volkswagen?"

"No, he was—"

"Who drove the Volkswagen?"

"A short, fat man. I never saw him before."

"Then who is this mysterious Arnold?" He absolutely sneered the name.

"The driver of the other car."

"The Volkswagen!"

"No, the Mustang! The car I hit! The car with the stoles in it!"

"*Now* we're getting somewhere! Arnold was driving the car with the stoles in it!"

"The stolen stoles," I said.

"I know what stoles they are. And Arnold had them in his possession."

"That's right."

"And you just *happened* to know this Arnold."

"No. I've known him about six months."

"Tell me about it."

"It'll take a while," I said.

"I have all the time in the world," he said.

He didn't, really. He kept interrupting me and wanting to know what the hell I was talking about, and it finally took a good half-hour before I gave him a capsule version of the Ilha Pombo Affair and Arnold's part in it and my part in it, and when I was finished he was looking baffled and worried, because he was beginning to suspect there were a few holes in the wall of evidence he'd constructed around me and maybe I wasn't the one who stole the stoles after all. He considered the situation, made notes, asked a few last questions, and buzzed to have me taken away. "I'll speak to you again," he said threateningly, and I was led out.

But he didn't. I've never seen him since. I spent an hour waiting alone in a room, and then somebody came and told me I could leave. I said, "Aren't you going to drive me back?"

He said, "You sure do meet a lot of jerks in this profession," and walked away.

So I took a cab back to the motel, where it turned out I had missed, as a result of Arnold Kuklyn and the stolen stoles, the whole first round of discussions between the Network people in Miami for the special and the planeload of lawyers and executives who'd come down to find out what was happening. Naturally, being the one who wasn't there to defend himself, I was the one who'd gotten the buck passed to him a lot, and by the time I got to the motel my Network reputation had zoomed to just about zero. Mr. Clarebridge was there, and so was Mr. Frank Dorn, and I understand they were both in pretty constant telephone contact that night with Mr. Theodore Pshaw. The lawyers were off having discussions with all sorts of police and regulatory agencies, and the "To Free an Island" technical crew had already been put on a plane and sent back to New York.

I did my best to mend my fences right then and there, but the damage had been done, and to this day I haven't been able to catch up. And of course it didn't help much that I'd been away because I'd been arrested again by the police on a totally unrelated charge, no matter how innocent I'd turned out to be.

And Arnold was gone. The Miami police searched the motel backwards and forwards for him, interrupted high-level Network conferences, came very close to accusing Mr Clarebridge and Mr. Dorn of shielding Arnold from arrest, and all in all simply helped to make matters worse. Particularly for me, since somehow the idea gained currency that in effect I'd brought the police back with me.

So everything turned out to be my fault. The whole Ilha Pombo Affair was my fault, and the police interruptions were my fault, and Arnold's being a thief was my fault, and just about everything you could think of was my fault. And I suppose I did finally get a little irritable with Mr. Clarebridge, when he wouldn't listen to me, but I honestly doubt I said half the things to him that he claims these days that I said. Less than half. And it's perfectly true that I disobeyed a direct order from Mr. Clarebridge to go back to New York on the next plane, because I wanted to settle the problem right then and there, knowing full well that if I went away with people thinking it was all my fault nothing would ever change their minds in the future, but I believe anybody would have disobeyed an order like that. And anyway, this is a network, not an army. It's a business, and in a business it's more important to get at the facts than to maintain discipline. Discipline doesn't do a damn thing for the balance sheet.

Of course, staying in Miami didn't do very much good either, particularly when the lawyers came back from one of their conferences and told Mr. Clarebridge and Mr. Dorn about Mary Marie Conroy. Their faces when they looked at me told me all I needed to know; they'd just had confirmation that I was, after all, the very seat and essence of all their troubles.

I'm not, you know. The Network's problem is not Arnold Kuklyn and the Miami police and the stolen stoles. The Network's problem is not Richard Conford's finking to the Feds or me being infiltrated by an agent provocateur. The Network's problem is not even the simple matter of failing to report an ongoing federal offense; the media have some leniency, some elbow room, in that regard, as for instance when magazines stage pot parties. No, the Network's problem is much more serious than that, and it is this: Did the Network, in fact, *create* news rather than merely observe it?

Here's the question. The Network paid out certain sums of money, nobody knows exactly how much, nobody knows exactly to whom. There is some doubt as to whether those early shipments of guns we filmed ever actually did go to Ilha Pombo, an island that appears to have no indigenous rebels after all, but Colonel Enhuelco's Expeditionary Force definitely *was* going to Ilha Pombo. If the early stuff was fake and the later stuff was real, what can it possibly mean?

Well. The government seems to be saying that it can possibly mean that Colonel Enhuelco and some other people—notably Jaekel Grahame, who wanted to sell arms for money, not promises—staged that early stuff in order to get enough money from the *Network* to finance the invasion. In other words, the Network was inadvertently financing the invasion of a nation friendly to the United States. In still other words, the Network was all unknowingly at war with Ilha Pombo.

Of course, there's always the CIA somewhere in this thing. Way back when I passed on Rudy's discovery about the dented crate, the answer I got was that the CIA didn't want anything to happen to the completion of the special. Was I being lied to? Or was the CIA actually involved? And if so, how? Was the CIA really funneling funds—there's that phrase again—through the Network to the rebels? If so, I think for the Network's sake it's high time somebody came right out and said so.

And what kind of mess do we have if the CIA was financing the invasion at the same time that the FBI and Customs were plotting to keep it from happening? As Bob Grantham says, that isn't the way they run things under Godless Communism.

Anyway, the point is, what is really at issue in all this mess is the disbursement of funds, and I do not disburse funds. I can't say how much Network—or CIA—money got into the hands of Colonel Enhuelco and Jaekel Grahame, nor can I say whether Bob Grantham was a conscious part of the conspiracy from the beginning, nor Arnold the same, but I suspect that Bob was innocent and Arnold guilty. Or maybe Bob was half-innocent and Arnold half-guilty. I just don't know.

What I *do* know is, I'm winding up the scapegoat in this thing, and it isn't right. I never spent a penny of Network money for the purpose of overthrowing the government of Ilha Pombo Island. Can Walter J. Clarebridge say that? Can Frank Dorn say that? Can Joe Singleton say that?

So here I am, in limbo. I've been back from Miami for two months, I get my salary in the mail every week, and I'm told to just sit here and wait. I phone The Hub all the time, and I never get anywhere. Mr. Clarebridge won't talk to me, Mr. Dorn won't talk to me. Joe Singleton was transferred to Los Angeles and won't talk to me, and Caryl Ten Broeck is doing the Townley Loomis lunchtime interviews.

And the doorbell keeps ringing, and the phone keeps ringing, and it's never the Network. It's the police, looking for Arnold. Or it's girls, looking for Bob. Or it's girls Bob failed to get me months ago who are suddenly free. Or it's slight acquaintances from other networks wanting the inside scoop on the rumors going around town. Or it's magazine writers wanting to write about the Ilha Pombo Affair in their magazines. Or it's alleged members of the Ilha Pombo Expeditionary Force, mostly wanting a handout.

Or it's Linda.

Which is maybe the worst part of the whole thing, and the part that will eventually drive me crazy. It started about a week and a half after I got back from Miami; the phone rang one afternoon and it was her, and she said, "Hi, this is Linda."

I said, very coldly, "You mean Mary Marie Conroy, don't you?"

"Oh, I like Linda much better," she said. "How come you don't call me anymore? We used to date a lot."

I said, "What?"

"I know the girl isn't supposed to call, but—"

"Are you crazy? After what you did to me, you think I'll call you up and ask you for a *date?*"

"I was just working," she said, "the same as you. Just doing my job. I don't see why you have to take it personally."

"I guess I'm just grouchy," I said, and hung up.

And she called back a couple days later. "Didn't we have fun together?"

"Leave me alone," I said.

"You used to like to take me out."

"Not anymore."

"Look, Jay," she said. "We'll keep you under surveillance anyway, why not have some fun while we're doing it?"

That time, I hung up without saying anything at all.

But nothing stops her, you know. I go out to the A&P, she comes up to me on the street and demands to see identification. She taps my phone, and when one of Bob's girls calls me, I can count on Linda calling two or three minutes later and saying something like, "I just thought you ought to know about that girl, she's a bad security risk." I get up in the morning and go to the bedroom window and she's on the roof across the way, filming me with a zoom lens. Once she tried to come in disguised as a repairman from Con Edison: "Having trouble with your electricity," she said, in a fake deep voice. I take a cab anywhere, I can count on her being in another cab a block back. My mail comes half an hour later than everybody else's in the building, because Linda takes it all and reads it and puts it back.

I shudder to think what she'll do at Marlene and Wilbur Bricker's wedding next week, if I decide to go. But what the heck, I can't stay away, you can't stay away when your wife gets married.

You know what I think it is? I think she's in love with me and she doesn't know any other way to attract my attention. So she's harassing me to death.

I feel I could handle all these problems, even the problem of Linda, if I just knew what my situation was going to be at the Network. I very much want to get back into the regular swing of things at the Network, and I hope you people in the legal department can do something to help. I see I'm running out of tape again, and I want to call the messenger service to carry this right over to you, but I just want to point out

MEMO

CHIEF,

Intercepted the enclosed package of tapes. Ran them through. Seem full of security leaks. Recommend we put the lid on.

Sincerely,
MARY MARIE CONROY